Infinity Series

Dream Seer

Laura Livingston Snyder

ISBN: 978-1-7351913-0-0

Photography: Anatoli Photograffi
Jewelry: Marcia Whitworth
Publisher: Laura Livingston Snyder
Publisher email: applesnyder6@gmail.com
Cover design: Laura Livingston Snyder

For my parents, my husband, and my children,
for making me, making me who I am now,
and making me who I want to be

And for everyone who helped:

My editors Judy Cass, Rob Santucci,
Kevin Butterfield, and Reid Sullivan

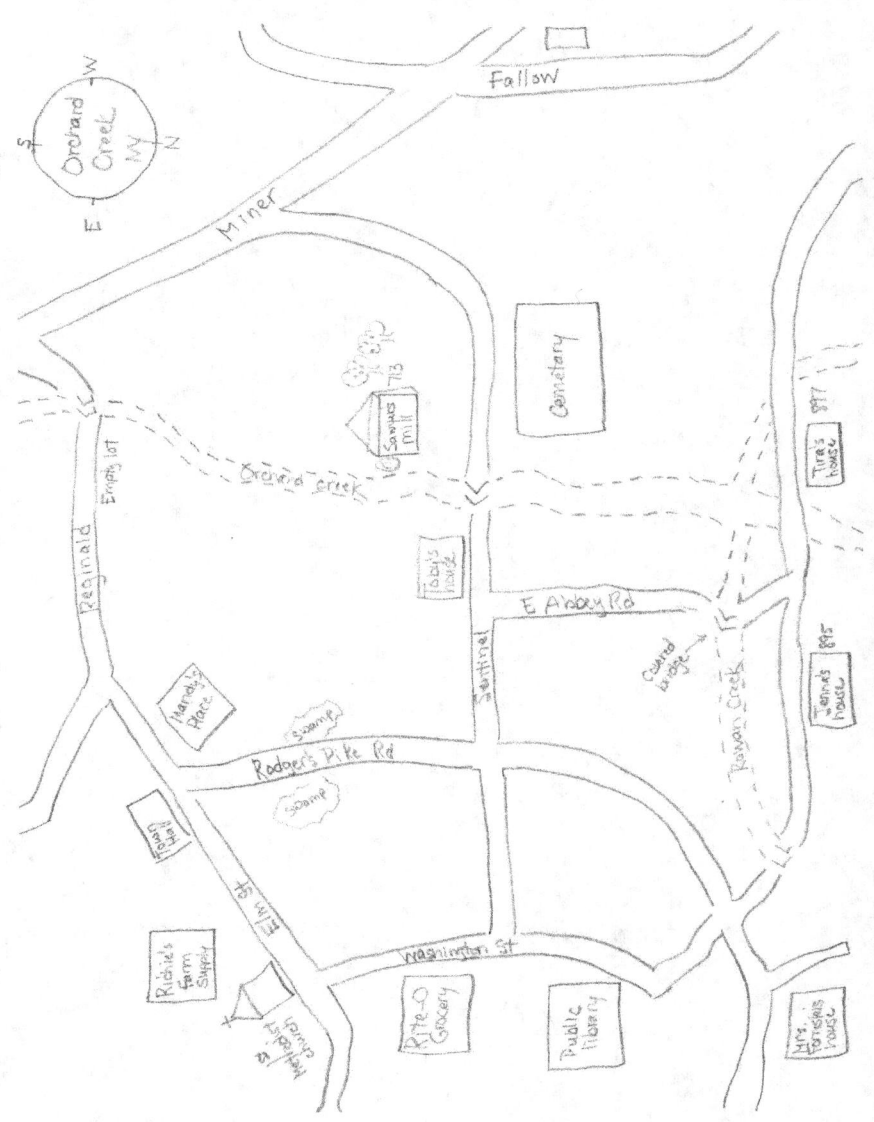

Orchard Creek

Fallow

Miner

Empty lot

Orchard Creek

Sawyer's Mill

713

Cemetery

Tira's House 877

Reginald

Toby's House

E Abbey Rd

Mandy's Place

Sentinel

Covered Bridge

Rodman Creek

Jenna's House 815

swamp

Rodger's Pike Rd

swamp

Town Hall

Richie's Farm Supply

Elm St

Methodist Church

Washington St

Pop-O Grocery

Public Library

Mrs. Tomkins's House

One

*H*OME.

THE EXCITEMENT on Jenna's face fizzled into confusion as the thought drifted through her mind. The ache to get inside that building was just as strong as the shock she felt in feeling it. Weird. It was like remembering a craving she never knew she had. Or maybe waking up and realizing her reality was only a dream. It was overwhelming, even for her otherwise hungry twelve-year-old mind, and she was up on her knees in an instant. For a few seconds, she could do nothing but follow the angles of the building as it slowly passed through the car's side windows. The seat's buckle bit into her knee, but it hardly registered.

"Stupid turkeys," her dad muttered, drumming his fingers on the steering wheel. They came to a stop as the large beasts strutted across the road.

"Relax. Moving is fraught with hiccups, Jack. Besides, nothing screams country more than animals who claim New York roads as territory," her mom answered, rolling the window down, hoping for a stray breeze. Other than the hum of the engine and the occasional sounds of birds, it was quiet.

"I guess I thought I'd be done with rush hour traffic," he joked as his eyes focused on the rear-view mirror. He tilted his head in amusement before his expression shifted to annoyance. "Jenna Stevens, what are you doing? Turn around and sit down. And buckle up!"

Jenna didn't realize she had taken her seat belt off, or that tiny goose bumps had raised the hair on her arms despite the heat. Her brother, Peter, made a poor imitation of a turkey at her, squawking and flapping his arms like wings. He was nine and good at it.

With more pressing thoughts, she ignored him.

The building at 713 Sentinel stood alone on the outskirts of Orchard Creek, nestled on a plot of land between fertile apple trees, unruly and overbearing shrubbery, and the dark creek that wound around and under the water wheel like loose string from an oversized spool. The place had been a solid fixture for many lifetimes, proud and stubborn in its structure as if taunting time to dare its existence. Tragedy was at home there, deep in the quiet stillness, dormant, waiting. Those who passed through the doors would understand, especially those who could connect to the threads that lingered. Heaven help those who had a bit of magic in them.

The building was on a gentle knoll that sloped down sharply to the left to accommodate the creek, exposing courses of foundation partially obscured by a wooden water wheel. To the right, the foundation was barely visible, giving the impression the edifice was stubborn and refused the budge from the earth. It reminded Jenna of her wiggly molars when they weren't quite ready to be pulled.

The throat clearing caught her attention. Jenna twirled

around in her seat and plunked back down, her brown eyes continuing to take in every detail. She fumbled to secure herself in, still mesmerized by the abandoned, dilapidated building. One of the windows was cracked and part of the wooden trim had fallen off. It gaped at Jenna, now like a toothless monster.

"Dad, is that a house?" she asked.

"No, actually, it was a fabric mill in the olden days. You know, way before I was even born. I think the real estate lady said it was built in 1846. So, if it's 1996 now how old is it?"

It took a few seconds and some help from her fingers. "Wow!" Jenna exclaimed. "It's like a hundred and fifty years old!"

"Of course, the first thing you'd focus on here," her mom remarked, "would be your history obsession." She smiled as she glanced back, sighing. "You're right, though. It's an oldie. You'll have to give us some time to settle in, honey, before we go looking for the library. You can check it out then. They should have old newspapers saved on file. We might be able to find a photograph of it in its heyday."

"Wow!" Jenna said again. "Wow" was her word. Her mother said she was going to wear it out someday. She always made that clicking noise with her tongue every time Jenna said it. It made Jenna feel bad, she was really trying to stop; it just popped out of her mouth sometimes.

With the road now clear, the car started moving. With some effort Jenna twisted around once again and stared at the mill until it was only a dot framed by the back window. Strands of her wavy blond hair floated in her field of vision from spinning, tickling her nose. She brushed them aside without making the conscious decision to do so. That gnawing feeling didn't entirely leave. "I'd like that. I love history."

"Yes, we know. You always have, even when you were very

little. I don't understand how anyone could know so much about history in general when you had barely started school yet," her mom admitted. Her face, pensive as she watched the scenery pass, became tight. "You should have been playing with toys and dolls more."

"Not today, Gwen. We know it's irresistible to her. Maybe a fascination in something makes it easier to learn."

"Yeah, Mom. There's a mystery surrounding old stuff. Think about it. It's a physical thing that links the present to the past. We can lay our hands on it and imagine what it was like back then."

"If you say so, honey."

"Well, you can also read about it. I've read everything I could find about old buildings and bridges in Steel City." She could read by the time she was three and insatiable when it came to history. The topic didn't matter. She'd soak up information on artisans and architects, employment and entertainment. She had no interest in playing with the dolls her mother constantly bought her until she was seven and learned needlepoint in a school lesson. From then on, she'd play with them but mostly used the dolls as models for the clothes she made from her outgrown shirts. She progressed from needlepoint to crocheting, sewing, and knitting. When she was ten, she bought a yard or two of soft fleece material with her allowance and made her family mittens for Christmas.

"I don't doubt it," her dad said, his head swiveling at the four-way stop before turning onto East Abbey Road. "Considering it was where you were born and raised, I can see why you'd be interested in it."

Jenna scrunched her nose as if something smelled bad. "All those buildings weren't very interesting, though." Her face brightened. "There are lots of other mid-sized cities in Upstate

New York with better stuff." Peter slouched down with his knees on the back of the seat in front of him, clearly uninterested in the current topic.

"Don't kick, Pete, we're almost there. Economic booms will do that, Jenna."

"Bleh. Renovations and improvement projects just mean they bulldoze down the cool stuff like landmarks for bigger, modern structures. All of it is boring." This wasn't the first time Jenna mentioned this.

"They're all cold and ugly," she had told her history teacher, Mr. Hopkins. He had agreed and told her she had an old soul. For someone born in 1984, she knew her interests were unique. It was just the way she was. From as far back as she could remember, her older relatives always had conversations about her quirky personality at get-togethers. It happened so much it was just a part of family life.

Jack reached over and squeezed his wife's hand. He didn't want her mood soured, and he certainly didn't want her to shut down. This move to Orchard Creek was going to benefit everyone. He knew the things Jenna could do troubled her, especially Jenna's dreams. That was surprising to both of them. What other two-year-old could even remember them? As she was his only child at the time, he always listened and paid close attention to what she said. This prompted her to try to remember more details for him, especially since she told him her Grammy was usually there. She insisted it wasn't Grandma Cates, who visited every Saturday; it was an old woman with long, braided white hair who called herself "Grammy" and had a cane. His mother had, indeed, used a cane but never allowed it to be photographed. With a funny, confused look on his face he agreed it sounded like her Grammy Stevens, who died before she was born.

During these conversations Gwen rarely smiled, her lips

pursed with discomfort. Eventually the day came when she asked Jenna to stop talking about them. Jenna started confiding solely in him. He was intrigued by the dreams as she had a couple every few weeks. In fact, if he had thought to keep track of the number of her strange dreams, he'd have noticed they corresponded with the cycle of the full moon, and occurred in October and May than at any other time of year.

On more than one occasion, Jenna related particulars of these dreams that suggested a special gift. The very first was when she toddled down the hall one Sunday morning when she was almost three years old repeating "mama, cookie, baby, mama, cookie, baby." It was the day after Gwen had bought Chinese for lunch and surprised him, through a fortune cookie, with the news they were expecting again. Jenna was napping soundly upstairs at the time.

On the second of November when she was five, he was promoted. Before he could even get in the door from work that day Jenna asked if he liked his new office with the orange chair. With her father speechless, Jenna told how she dreamed the night before that the man with the drippy nose was going to give him the room the lady with the bright dresses used. Jenna had never been to his office and certainly had never met Dan and Barb. They were the company's CEO and operations manager. Up until later that day he hadn't been in Barb's office to see the orange chair.

Rational thoughts could account for most of Jenna's nighttime imagination. She had of course seen pictures of the people she dreamed about and the rest could be coincidence. But when she asked him one winter morning why Gramp Stevens visited her while she was sleeping, Jack Stevens began to get goose bumps. Jenna related that he waved at her and disappeared through the wall with Grammy who had the cane. Later that morning, the call came telling them that Gramp Stevens had passed away during the night. A closer relationship grew between him and Jenna, and he never doubted the sporadic glimmers of talent she had. Never disturbed by them, Jenna just shrugged them off as something that seemed normal to her.

"A covered bridge? Wow! Orchard Creek is a complete opposite of Steel City," Jenna observed.

"Rural and old, kiddo. And the cemetery we just passed, the one across from that old mill, dates back to the 1720's. Even though the place looks like nothing but farm country, it has a strong community. You'll see when we take a trip into town. This bridge brings us over Rowan Creek, which snakes everywhere. That's the small one. The other covered bridge separates the east and west sides where Orchard Creek actually runs. The common park still holds the annual strawberry social, Fourth of July picnics and the apple festival. They have scarecrow contests."

"Now you're talkin', Dad," Peter chimed in, sitting up. Jenna smiled, it sounded like the ideal place to live.

"What's in town?"

"There aren't any traffic lights or fast food dives…,"

Peter frowned. "Whatsa 'fast food dive', Dad?"

"Like a Mickey D's."

"Aw, no way."

"Don't worry, there's a mall in the next town over. We have a Rite-O grocery, Health Line drug store, and Richie's Farm Supplies. This part of the country supplies much of the East Coast with apples, potatoes and corn, you know."

Jenna had been eager to move. She had fallen in love with the whole atmosphere the day her father came home with a picture of their new house. "Where's the library? Can we go tomorrow?" Jenna asked excitedly.

Peter made a whiny, grumbling sound. "No, not a library! I want to go fishing. Dad promised we would."

"How about we take out books about Halloween?" Jenna coaxed, trying to get her way and appease her brother. "We could decide on costumes."

"Oh, for heaven's sake, Jenna, it's August twenty-fourth!" her mother exclaimed, her hands up and outward towards the sky. "Let's not start that so early this year."

"But it's coming up and it's my favorite holiday!"

"I know. I know you both can't wait to get out and about. We'll see tomorrow," she replied. "Let's start with making this house our home. Your dad and I will be busy unpacking today. It's a good thing we already moved over all the furniture without you two under foot. I can see this isn't going to be easy with both of you itching to go places."

"I liked sleeping on the floor in a sleeping bag, Mom," Peter announced. He was breathing on the window and using his fingers to draw in the condensation.

"It's not so much fun when you get older, dude," his father said as he turned his blinker on to make a right. "Be happy your rooms are almost done and you'll be able to sleep in your own bed tonight. I know I will."

Jack had also wanted a change. Life in the city was rushed and impersonal. With some research, he was able to make a lateral change in his job with Firsten Enterprises in order to spend more time with his family. Earning a higher salary due to his city experience in credit, he was easily able to become an analyst for companies with earth-moving machinery. With country living expenses, he no longer needed the thirteen-hour days and weekend hours.

"I'm with Jenna on this," Gwen announced. "I can't wait to get back to nature. I've passed places like this on my drug rep route. It brings back memories of my childhood. City life can't replace simple pleasures of solitude and birdsong. And taking walks. Believe it or not I even miss planting flowers and pruning shrubs. I used to have to do that when I was a teen and swore I'd never do it again."

Taking his hand off the steering wheel, Jack reached for her hand. "At one time, you liked the city."

She thought it over. "Sure. It was exciting at first, something different. But after a while I realized the people in my social circle were self-absorbed and overachievers. Anyway, Jenna's gonna love it here, and Peter can finally run and play outside among the trees and grass. I've felt guilty about denying these two those experiences."

The car pulled into the driveway. Their new home was a two-story farmhouse next to a free-standing garage. It was rustic, warm and inviting with over two acres of land, shaded in places by mature weeping willows, maples, and poplar trees. It had country charm, having been built back when everything was made with pride. The only modern touches were the appliances, plumbing and heating.

Jenna squealed with delight when she walked in her new room. It was so different with familiar furniture in a completely new place. It was everything she had ever dreamed of, bright and airy with high ceilings and a bay window that overlooked a tall birch tree in the backyard. There was even a window seat for all her hidden treasures.

The heavy oak bed and armoire set that had been passed down from her great grandma seemed smaller in this vast space. Jenna and her dad had restored them together, stripping, sanding, and re-staining over winter break one year. She took a huge breath around a smile and sighed. Her dad had even made sure her favorite picture, a reproduction of Renoir's "Two Girls at a Piano", had made it onto the wall already. The room was modestly decorated for some but simply perfect for her. Two years ago, she had insisted on the soft white eyelet curtains and bedspread that made her room complete. Her world did not include the pink frilly stuff her friends had, and she absolutely refused "The Little Mermaid" motif her mother had suggested.

She ventured to Peter's room next door. It was done in boy-friendly blues and reds. Peter was the typical younger brother, interested only in cars, karate and pirates. He mostly ignored Jenna, but on occasion teased just to get a rise out of her. As soon as he came into view she stopped to watch. His short, mousey brown hair, compliments of their mother, stuck up on its own accord (that trait was his own) as he darted about, oblivious to her presence in the doorway. His room was smaller than hers but bigger than his old one. He was already in mid-play with two Mighty Morphin Power Rangers in his hands, jumping and kicking at the air on his way to the built-in bookcase where the other four were displayed.

"Oh, hey, look Jenna! I can kick in here and not hit my wall!"

"That's great. Did you find any secret compartments? Dad said this house has been around for more than 175 years. Sometimes during the Civil War people hid their money in their house so no one could steal it while they were away. Sometimes they never came back, and that money wouldn't be found unless someone clever like us looked for it."

"Ooh, neat!" Peter said, wide-eyed, as he began pushing on the walls and knocking on the floor. Both Jenna and Peter spent the rest of the morning playing detective. As the initial excitement died down and her brother became more annoying than helpful in their search for lost treasure, Jenna wandered downstairs to where her parents were organizing the kitchen.

She watched her father balance on a chair as he reached up to place an heirloom vase in the soffit. He grunted and wiped his forehead with the back of his arm. His blond hair near his hairline had curled from being sweaty. He usually combed it out straight to get rid of the waves.

"No Jack, not like that. Get down a minute, I'll show you," her mom said, setting down a stack of dinner plates and putting her fist on her hip. Jenna realized she was really pretty, with an hourglass shape she accentuated by wearing nicely fitted clothes.

"This is the way you told me, dear."

"Can I help?" Jenna asked. Her mother turned to her voice and banged her head on the open cupboard door, muffling her words as she rubbed her temple and tightened her ponytail.

"Not right now, sweetie. If you want to go outside and explore that's fine." She turned and tried to shoo her husband down from the chair. "She'll be safe by herself, right?"

Her father didn't budge. "I'll put it up there by myself, just tell me how." Then he answered, "Yes, she'll be safe, as long as she's mindful of strangers and doesn't get near the creeks. They're everywhere around here. Don't go too far, Jenna."

"Just don't go too far from home until you know your way around better."

"Are you sure?" she asked.

"Yes!" they answered in unison.

"Be home by five for dinner," her mom added.

"I will. Thanks."

Jenna strode out of the front door feeling a bit odd. She had never been allowed to go anywhere in her old neighborhood by herself. Now she had a whole world to discover on her own terms. A mischievous grin filled her face. In two seconds, she was running to the left, where her bike was leaning against the side of the garage. She pushed it to the edge of the driveway and stopped. All she could hear was a low buzz from crickets or grasshoppers in the surrounding fields. Cupping her hand just under her bangs and over her eyes she looked around. A breeze chose then to move in, causing her thick hair to blow off her shoulders where the relaxed curls at the end bounced at her bottom. Trees, trees, and more trees as far as the eye could see except for a house or two down the road. The leaves were still green as they swayed together, but the color was a little off, mixed with yellows and the occasional orange. Fall wasn't far away. But today it was warm and sunny.

With no particular destination in mind, she pushed off and started to ride, liking the sound of rubber on the tiny rocks at the edge of the road. It was so quiet! She never thought about what a bike tire sounded like. She could never hear things like that in Steel City. She rode alone in silence, only two cars passing her as she made her way towards the first house. As she neared it and the house became larger, a harsh and mournful cry grew louder.

Two

A GRAY HOUSE CAME into view. Jenna could see a girl about her age standing on its front porch. The girl held an object in her arms while intently looking at a thin metal stand. With a few more pedals, she could see as well as hear what was going on. The girl was playing a violin. Attempting to play was more like it. The sound stopped as Jenna neared a silver mailbox that had "897 Levy" on its side. The girl dropped her arms as she watched her come closer. They were still too far away to say anything to each other, so Jenna smiled and waved, receiving a smile and wave in return almost immediately. The girl set the instrument down and came down the stairs. She was a tiny thing, thin in the extreme, unlike Jenna who had the start of some curves.

"Hi." Jenna broke the awkward silence first. Before the girl could say anything, the wind picked up again and blew the papers from the metal stand behind her. "Oh no, your papers!"

The girl turned around, her fine, black hair following her

like a wave across her shoulders as she dashed to the porch. "My music!"

Jenna dropped her bike and ran into the yard where two pages went skittering across the grass. She grabbed them, zigzagging with the girl who was doing the same, and watched as another took off nearly past the driveway. Jenna followed and bent to pick it up. Another gust took it a foot more, and Jenna, not coordinating her feet with her reach went down on both knees in the driveway. "Oof, I got it!" she exclaimed, trying not to grimace. When she looked up, the girl skipped the rest of the way towards her, the excitement on her face falling as she saw Jenna's skinned knees.

"Thanks. I'm sorry about that." She was also out of breath, tucking a stray hair behind her ear that escaped her plastic butterfly barrettes. The china blue clips matched her eyes. "It seems like Mother Nature doesn't want me to practice either. That's why I was banished outside. My mom said she couldn't take it anymore."

Jenna giggled and handed her the pages of sheet music while brushing off the tiny stones imbedded in her knees. Luckily, other than the stinging, she wasn't banged up too badly. "It's okay. I guess I've officially been broken in to country living."

The girl giggled back at her as she tried to organize her papers. "My name is Tina Levy. Maybe you should come inside so my mom can help clean up your legs."

"'Kay. I'm Jenna Stevens. It's nice to meet you. I just moved here from Steel City."

"For real? That's cool. I've never lived in a big city," Tina said as she led her towards her house. "Actually, I've never lived anywhere but here. It gets kinda lonely in the summer. I'm too far away from my friends."

"Oh," Jenna said. She never really thought about that.

"Well, it sure is quieter than all the taxis honking and subway noise."

Tina's eyes got wide. "You've been on a taxi and subway?"

"Yup, lotsa times. It's actually what I hear as I fall asleep each night. I mean, I used to."

"Out here," said Tina as she jerked a thumb at the field across from her house, "you'll find it's a lot different. I mean, sometimes the peepers, you know, frogs, will be loud and annoying, but I think I could fall asleep to that much quicker than a honking car. Hey, are you thirsty? Do you want some lemonade?"

Jenna nodded and followed her new friend into the house, helping with the music stand and violin case while Tina carried the violin and her sheet music. She was introduced to Tina's mother, who was happy to wash and bandage her knees and set the girls up with lemonade and a snack. As Tina put her things away, Jenna looked around the house. It was neat and tidy and kind of basic. A simple gold cross on the wall of the living room was the only decoration. She noticed Tina was dressed simply as well, wearing solid navy shorts and a plain, baby blue tank top. It was the style of clothing Jenna, too, preferred.

As the girls sipped their drinks, they got to know each other. Jenna looked around the house. "It's quiet in here, too. Do you have sisters or brothers?"

"Neither." Tina rolled her eyes. "I'm an only. A one-and-done deal is what my dad says when he thinks I'm not listening."

"I have a pain in the butt younger brother. Be lucky you don't have one of those," Jenna confided. Tina snorted a little laugh around her pretzel, which made Jenna giggle again.

"I have two younger boy cousins who follow me around at every birthday party. They do it on purpose to drive me crazy. Does that count?"

"It sure does. Oh brother, that must stink." Jenna took another sip.

"Stink like a brother?" Tina asked in a timid voice, watching her closely over the rim of her glass. Jenna choked on her lemonade and had to wave off her new friend while she caught her breath.

"Exactly like a brother. He does stink," she managed to say before they both erupted in a fit of laughter. "So, what do you like to do?"

"I ride my bike and read a lot."

"Wow! Me too! I love to read."

Tina stared at her for a moment as she swung her feet back and forth in the space under her seat. "Was it hard leaving your best friend behind?"

Jenna shook her head, chewing her pretzel. "I had lots of girlfriends but no real best friend. I hope I have better luck— that is, if I can get the hang of being in the wilderness here." Her eyes drifted to the two bandages across her knee.

"Me either. I mean, I don't really have a close girlfriend either. It's hard in the summer, too. Not many girls to play with."

Jenna thought about those people who felt it was odd how she spent more time on her hobbies than on having friends. It had never really bothered her before, but for some reason she really wanted to be friends with Tina. She hoped Tina didn't think she was weird. She was just about to mention her interest in the mill when Tina continued.

"My closest friend is Toby Jacobs. He complains I don't like to do the same things as him anymore." She scrunched up her nose and shrugged. "Our dads have been friends since way back, so we've been around each other for as long as I can remember. We were pretty close up until this past school year.

He's still a good friend, but he lives way over by the Ghost House."

Jenna almost choked on her drink again. The same prickly feeling from earlier inched down her neck. "The what? Ghost House?" Her heart began to beat faster.

"It's the old mill. I'm not supposed to tell people there's a ghost. My dad said so." She rolled her eyes again and leaned closer as she lowered her voice. "But everyone at school knows the rumors. The bus goes past it every day. Sometimes we see shadows in there. Toby says he's seen the ghost himself."

"We drove past it today. Something about it is kind of scary. I want to know more."

"Welcome to town, Jenna," Mrs. Levy said as she re-entered the room. "If your family needs anything, please let us know. We're so excited to have new neighbors! Now girls, it's still summer. Finish your snack and go outside." With a basket of clean-smelling wet clothes in her arms, she slipped on her flip flops and disappeared out the door.

Tina looked at Jenna, her eyes lit up with excitement. "All right, let me run upstairs for a sec and then we'll go."

After a minute Tina bounded down from her room. She had a little Hello Kitty purse slung across her shoulder. "We'll be on our bikes, Mom!" she shouted through the window to the back yard.

They rode down the country roads, and Jenna took in all the old houses on the way. Tina kept up a running commentary about each one, describing who lived there and for how long.

"How do you know all this stuff?" Jenna asked, coasting down a small hill next to Tina and enjoying the rush of air against her sweaty face.

"My dad works in the school's superintendent's office, in educational finance," Tina said the last part slowly to get it right. "But when he's not there he's in town at the Historical Association. He's a history buff and so is Toby's dad. His dad runs the place."

"Wow, he does? They were kids together?"

"No. They took a lot of the same classes in college and were in the same fratertinty."

"You mean fraternity?"

"Yeah, fratertinty, I just said that. They lost touch after graduation," she continued. "Dad said a few years after that they bumped into each other in the Rite-O and laughed when they realized they had both moved to Orchard Creek with their wives and babies. That would be me and Toby. Since they both loved history, they got together and started reorganizing the Historical building with the official okie-dokie from the association's president, Mr. Robertson. Dad said the broken-down mill was the perfect place for the new Historical Association's home and wanted to fix it up."

"Why there? It looks like it needs a lot of work."

"Lotsa reasons, I guess. He says an old building has the perfect ambil, no wait, uh, ambee…"

"Ambience?"

"Yeah! It has the perfect ambience for old stuff. And the size is perfect because each area of history can be separated into the different rooms. It's also been empty for years. Anyway, my dad loves the water wheel thing. He said when he was a boy, he lived down the road from an old water mill. He's always loved them."

"That's what your dad says?" Jenna was skeptical. Tina nodded. "How do you remember all that?"

"I have to go to the town meeting with my mom to support my dad. I hear it every year when they try to get the mill renovated. Every single year." Her head bobbed as she emphasized the last three words.

"Were there ghost stories back then?" Jenna asked.

Tina held her hand out in a stopping motion. "He doesn't believe in that stuff. He was raised by his grandparents and they were pretty strict Catholics. That's why I'm not supposed to talk about it."

"What about Toby's father?"

"Well, my parents don't care if he talks about it. He knows the stories. He says if the town helped, the Historical Association could buy it dirt cheap and fix it up."

"Huh." Jenna weaved her tires in an *S* pattern and Tina copied her. "He knows how to do that?"

"Not really, but my dad does. They work good together."

The road leveled off. It ran between never-ending fields that emitted the warm, sweet smells of wildflowers patches and made Jenna happy. Soon green and white road signs came into view on their left, and they both stopped. Birch Drive was nothing more than a very long dirt drive leading to a two-story white farmhouse barely visible through the rows of trees that lined the road. The sign said Dead End.

"Who lives there?"

"I call it 'the widow's house.' It's where Mrs. Forrester lives.

"What's she like?" Jenna asked, balancing on her bike.

"I don't know if she leaves the house much. I've never seen her outside the town meetings," Tina admitted, shielding her eyes with her hands from the bright summer sun. "She's really old, though. Dad says her husband died in World War II and she lives there all alone now."

Jenna's furrowed her brows. "What happened to her family?"

"I don't think she has any left," Tina said, shrugging.

"Wow," Jenna said, brushing the hair from her face. "I wonder what she does in there all day."

"I don't know. We could ask my dad. He knows most people in town."

The girls were quiet a moment.

"Does your dad know a lot about the old mill?" Jenna asked.

"Yeah, but so does Toby's. He says his dad can get the key," Tina added helpfully. "Come on, we're almost there. I can show you."

The girls got on their bikes, the 'widow's house' almost forgotten. The mill wasn't very far away. They talked excitedly as they neared it, pulling off into the grass when a big tour bus went by so they weren't swept away by the airstream.

Jenna stood next to her bike, staring in silence at the remainder of the old mill while Tina fiddled with the barrette that had slipped down her baby-fine hair again during the ride. Rowan Creek babbled away under the dry, rotted water wheel. Off to the right was a mature apple orchard spotted with bright red apples just about ready for picking. The front door was on that side, along with five steps to a modest porch area that wouldn't do more than let people gather there to go in or out. Back from that, nearer the orchard, jutting out from the ground, was a small triangular structure with a door. Jenna was sure it was a storm cellar because Grandma Cates had one. The building itself was almost three stories tall and had intricate trim work around most of the roof. There were windows on every floor except near the top. The lower ones were dark and covered with moss and grime. Its weathered wooden siding looked like it might have been yellow at one point. It wasn't as large as some textile buildings had been, Jenna noted, but it seemed large in a different sense, looming over her.

As hot as the day was in these dog days of summer, a cool breeze was blowing from the back of the building where the trees shaded everything, bringing with it the thick smell of shrubbery. An undercurrent of fear ran through her briefly. Jenna got off her bike and walked closer. She shivered.

"My dad says it was a fabric mill and a lot of women worked there. The richest guy in town at the time, Seth Sawyer, ran it. Dad said something about it being a sweatshop. I didn't know they had sweatshirts back then," Tina said, her forehead wrinkling in confusion.

"Not a sweatshirt shop," Jenna corrected gently, "a sweatshop. That's when people were forced to work long hours at hard work for little pay. It sounds like Mr. Sawyer was greedy. He probably made everyone work really hard and kept all the money for himself."

"He sounds like a dummy," Tina added. "Anyway, rumor has it that this poor girl moved into town with her family and she started working there. Her name was Elizabeth something. The story is she fell in love with his younger brother, Joseph. They couldn't let anyone find out about them. Joseph Sawyer was supposed to marry some rich girl from a neighboring town, but he didn't love her. He was crazy about Elizabeth, and they planned to run away together in secret."

"Huh. Secrets are cool," Jenna commented, leaning her bike against the kickstand.

"Not really," Tina continued. "Elizabeth knew she couldn't tell anyone because she needed the job. She couldn't let her boss know she was in love with his brother. The only way they could see each other was to meet at the mill late at night. From what the stories say, they met there a lot."

The girls walked toward the front of the mill. "Then one night, Halloween actually, Seth went by the mill and saw people inside. He found them. There was a struggle, and somehow, Joseph fell out the window and died. I don't know how he could have fallen out the window. The old stories say that all the doors were closed and the windows were always shut, even in the summer.

"Some people say that once in a while, when the autumn leaves fall, they hear angry voices and a woman's scream in the wind. On Halloween nights there have been sightings of a woman in a cloak standing in that window, crying." Tina pointed to the window on the second story, overlooking the orchard. "They say it's Elizabeth up there, and she's waiting for Joseph to meet her so they can run away together."

Jenna's shivered again, in spite of the summer heat. "What happened to Elizabeth?"

"Some say she couldn't live without Joseph and became sick and died by the creek. Others say she wouldn't believe he died and went around repeating his name, waiting for him. Some people in town say she haunts the mill."

The girls had walked around to the side that was dotted with apple trees, hiking through the wild sweet pea blossoms and Queen Anne's lace. They stared at the creek.

"That's a double wow," Jenna breathed. "What happened to the brother?"

"He moved away and the mill closed. He was so depressed his brother was dead, he couldn't live here anymore. They say he went mad."

"And that's the creek, huh?" Jenna asked.

"Yep. It powered the mill. My dad says it was a lot bigger back then. The creek made this town rich for a while. It's hard to believe," Tina said, practically reciting what she had heard her father say over and over since she was little. The sound of water running over the rocks was the only thing they could hear. They made their way back through the tall grass towards the other side of the mill surrounded by the chirps of crickets and the songs of the summer birds.

"I like to peek in the windows. It's a little scary when I go around to the orchard in the back where most of the apple trees are because it's so dark. Sometimes I bring a flashlight." Tina cupped her hands around her eyes as she bent down to look in the window, her purse scraping against the rough siding. Jenna did the same, at first thinking the window was broken. It wasn't. It was just covered with thin vines and grime. Something changed the instant she touched the wooden frame.

Release.

The thought whispered through her mind. It didn't make sense to her, and yet, at the same time, something felt right, like coming home in a way. Just like earlier she couldn't explain how the feeling had weight to it. She would have thought about it more but became mesmerized as soon as she took in the view in front of her. The basement was fairly large, covered in decades of dirt and cob webs, and empty except for some old papers and broken pieces of wood. It was old, really old, and that surprised her. Of course, it was old. She knew that without a doubt. Why wouldn't it be? For some reason, she had a picture in her head of when it was occupied and cleaner, newer. Odd. It made sense but didn't.

She stood and backed up, jumping to see more on the main level, which was just above her line of vision. It took several jumps to figure out the large room by the front door separated into another room or two just past a grand staircase. She saw nothing else except for a few odds and ends that must have been left from when it was cleaned out.

"Your mom and dad let you come out here?" Jenna asked.

"No way! I tell them I'm picking some berries or apples, whatever's in season, and I always remember to bring some back."

The girls checked all the windows that were within reach. Although it was a sunny day, the dirt and thick coating of grunge on the windows made it nearly impossible to see inside.

"Have you ever seen pictures of it when it was new?" Jenna asked after a while.

"No," Tina replied, puzzled. "How could I have seen it when it was new? I'm only eleven, almost twelve."

"Why don't you go to the library?" Jenna asked.

Tina's face scrunched up and her lower lip pouted out. "It's summer vacation. Why would I?"

"So? My mom took us to the library a lot back home. I loved it there. We were going to go to the library tomorrow." Jenna paused, remembering the difficulties her parents were having in the kitchen. They hadn't made it out of that room all day and there were many more that needed to be set up. "I don't know if we will, though, with all the unpacking," Jenna mused.

Tina thought a minute. "I guess we could bike there, too. That could be fun." She got more excited the more she thought about it. "Come on, I'll show you where it is."

Three

*T*HEY RODE THEIR bikes back down Sentinel, crossing Orchard Creek Bridge before Rowan Bridge and reaching Washington Street, which was perpendicular to it. A small, red brick building was the town's library. The library back in Steel City had been huge and reminded Jenna of a court house with long tables scattered everywhere. This one looked more like a small home with a generous yard surrounding it, but once inside, Jenna changed her mind. It wasn't small, it was just more compact. The narrow entryway immediately opened to the librarian's area and desk on the left. Books lined the walls in the rooms in front and to the sides of them with reference tables in the middle. There were a lot of books, but with less space to sit and read like the libraries near the university. The shelves were made of thick, weathered oak, darkened by time and use. Almost across from the reference section, near the far wall, was a metal spiral staircase that led to a split upper level.

For a small building, it had a lot of natural light. The

light that came from the large windows on the main floor was augmented by artificial strips that seemed out of place. Surprisingly, the upstairs was brighter than the downstairs.

"These are really old," Jenna stated as she studied the shelves. She curled her hair behind her ear. Tina just smiled, watching her new friend. "It gives the place a homey feel, don't you think?"

Tina shrugged. She had never given much thought to it. It was just a library and she had been in here maybe once or twice and that was only so her mom could renew some cookbooks.

Jenna liked the old smell of libraries, especially this one. Maybe it was the comfort of familiarity but Jenna started to feel more at home again, and this library had a recognizable feel to her. She walked around the main room, running her hands over each book in a row as she went. Tina copied her actions at the wall behind her, feeling the bookcases.

"Be careful of the side of that shelf, it's sharp." Jenna was looking at a book on the Olympics when the words came out of her mouth without warning or forethought. She hadn't even turned her head.

"What? Ouch!" Tina said, pulling her hand back with a tiny sliver in her finger. She plucked it out and popped her finger in her mouth. "Haw'd djoo knaw thaht?"

"Dunno, "Jenna said casually as she continued to look around. "It just happens sometimes."

There was even a wrought iron spiral staircase that led upstairs. The lady at the desk smiled when they asked about the old mill.

"Most of our papers, the Orchard Creek Chronicles, have been put on microfiche but a few of the older folks around here kept some of the town's highlights and earmarked a section or two of our cabinets. It has helped other young people like yourselves who were doing research on Orchard Creek for school projects. You might want to try there first. Is this for a late summer school class?" she asked.

"Something like that," Jenna replied. The lady directed them to the bottom three cabinets of the middle section of drawers at the top of the staircase, which they were excited to climb.

"How many stairs do you think there are?" Tina asked.

"Fifteen," Jenna found herself answering without thinking.

"Thirteen, fourteen, fifteen. Wow, good guess, Jenna," Tina replied, impressed.

The balcony opened onto a landing so that the librarian's desk was visible below. It was small but cozy and bright, with a huge picture window in the back that kept the upstairs illuminated and quite warm. A large industrial fan was facing away from them to circulate the stuffy air. There was no air conditioning in this building.

Tina had never been upstairs and discovered this was way more interesting than being here with her mom. They easily found the set of drawers that held copies of the old newspapers. It was made from the same heavy oak but somehow not as old looking. It had tiny brass markers that listed the papers by year. Jenna took a couple to begin with and carefully carried the papers over to one of the few tables and spread them out. Tina climbed into the chair with her knees on the seat to see better, her hair swishing in front of her like a black screen. The yellowed papers were very brittle and the musty smell hit them almost immediately. It made Tina sneeze.

Carefully turning the pages, Jenna's finger skimmed the columns. There was an aerial view of the town from July 1930. Jenna found Orchard Creek and Rowan Creek, the easiest way to orient herself to the town. She followed Rowan Creek to the mill and traced the way back with her finger to her road. There she saw a barn next to a newer version of her own house dwarfed by a huge corn field. Tina located and pointed out other landmarks, too. She found a general store and the town's school, which now housed the elementary classes. The topics of the articles ranged from a barn fire on Montgomery Street to how the efforts to build the Empire State Building were not dampened by the Depression. The girls giggled over the clothing ads and their ridiculously low prices.

"Let's try another one," Jenna suggested, delicately folding the paper. When the rest of the stack yielded nothing special on the mill, she put them away. She purposefully moved around the library with Tina behind her while she collected the fiche. They were plastic squares the size of an overgrown index card that held newspapers from the 1800's. Jenna pulled an extra chair over to a large computer-like microfiche desk for Tina and started flipping through the media.

"I don't know why they call these things micro fish," Tina said, taking out a tube of lip gloss, "they don't look like small fishes at all."

"Not fish, fiche." When Tina's face scrunched up in confusion, Jenna gave up. "Never mind."

"Do you want me to get the librarian so she can show us how to set it up?"

"Nah, I use these all the time back home. This one is older, but it works the same way."

A few minutes passed while Tina watched her new friend hold a few up to the light, squinting. From where she was sitting all she could see was a grid with mostly two columns of what she knew was newsprint.

"It's from 1895." She put it on the small shelf that reminded her of a microscope and images appeared above on the screen.

Tina was just getting dizzy from the speed Jenna was browsing when her friend gasped. "Here it is. Look at that, look Tina!"

"Wow!" Tina replied. Both girls turned to each other and burst into laughter. Tina was already picking up Jenna's bad habit. They put their hands over their mouths to stifle laughs and stood up to see if the librarian could hear them. She looked up at them sternly. Tina waved, the light scent of strawberry diffusing around them, and they quietly sat back down.

"The paper says, 'Businessman Seth Sawyer sees the mill as the focal point of the town's future. The mill will do for Central New York what Rowan Creek is doing for Orchard Creek.' The mill was supposed to make the town rich," Jenna said.

"Here's an ad for employment," Tina read. "It says the mill was once a boarding house. Why would a boarding house need a water wheel?"

Jenna had no idea and shrugged, prompting Tina to continue. "'It has been renovated into a functional mill complete with weaving boards, sewing machines and bolts.' Hey, I didn't know this. Seth Sawyer's parents were both rich but died from influenza when the boys were four and six years old." Tina hesitated before turning to her friend. "The flu? Like feeling yucky and staying home from school for a day or two?" she asked skeptically.

"The same," Jenna replied, leaning in to follow the article with her finger. "It was deadly before we had vaccines, you know. It says the brothers were sent to live with a widowed grandfather out West. All the money was put in a trust for them, not to be touched until they were older."

"Wow, people really died from the flu." Tina paused, taking in the gravity of the fact. "That must have been hard losing both your parents when you're that young," she added soberly.

"Seth and Joseph must have been close. That kinda explains

why he took Joseph's death so hard. That was his only family," Jenna observed, putting the film to the side and shuffling through the rest. A minute later she decided on a new sheet.

"Ah, I have a good feeling about this one. It has a lot of pictures. It's also dated 1895." One small black and white photo showed the sewing rooms and the state-of-the-art machinery. Another was of the front of the mill and was a bit larger. Both girls scanned the screen, their heads together, making it apparent how opposite their features were: black hair against blond. Their fingers traced sentences and pointed at pictures, Jenna's bare nails a contrast to Tina's pink, polished nails. The article described the mill and its employees and claimed profit for the town in a very short span of time.

The two-story building looked stately and solid, easily recognizable as the same building the girls had visited. It appeared white and had intricate, detailed trim around the main door and roof. Three windows on the top floors faced the camera. A slanted storm cellar door protruded from the right side. Half a dozen women were standing in front of the mill dressed in high-collared blouses and long skirts. Each had her hair swept up in a bun. As in many old pictures, none were smiling.

"Why did they even bother growing their hair if they kept it up all the time?" Tina asked, twirling a lock of her own that refused to hold a curl.

"Lots of reasons, actually. Short hair wasn't fashionable at all back then, and long hair was easy to keep away from their faces, too. It was dangerous to be worn down with all the manual labor they did, especially around an open fire or in a mill. They also didn't wash like we do. Saturday night was bath night so they could be fresh for church Sunday morning. After a few days, their hair became heavy from their natural oils and all the lye they used as soap. It was more of a practical thing, really."

"Oh," Tina replied, her mouth a little slack. She didn't know any of that stuff. "That made their hair heavy?"

"Yeah. Soap does. My mom forgot to buy shampoo once a few years ago, and I used soap instead. My hair was so heavy it gave me a headache." She stopped a moment to rub her head and think. "And also, a scalp-ache."

Tina's eyebrow quirked up and she giggled. "Scalp-ache?"

"Scalp-ache," Jenna laughed back. The librarian cleared her throat and they quieted down once again.

"Do you think that's why they never smile in the pictures?"

Jenna shook her head once. "Maybe a little, but those kinds of cameras took forever to take a picture. No one could hold a smile that long."

Tina showed her surprise before turning back to the screen. Near the women were four men who looked dapper in suits and hats. All had handlebar moustaches. There was a horse and wagon on the well-worn dirt road in front of the short path that led to the door. The old apple trees the girls walked through earlier were only seedlings that dotted the dry, barren clearing. A few scattered trees accented the background of the picture with only an isolated building off in the distance. The creek was bigger and bolder. Jenna thought the water looked like it might have been very refreshing to those wearing such burdensome clothes on a hot summer day.

"When was Elizabeth there? Do you know?" Jenna inquired.

"Let's see. Usually I'm not good with history or math but I know Seth closed the mill down in 1898. I remember that because Dad always says it's one number more than our house number, eight ninety-seven. It closed a year after Elizabeth died which was two years after Joseph died," Tina paused and Jenna waited patiently. "She must have been there around 1896." She shrugged and her black hair bent upwards on her shoulders.

Jenna found goose bumps creeping up her arms as her mind worked a bit quicker, her fingers already shuffling through the microfiche cards. "Oh boy, it'll be one hundred years this year!" She shivered before turning her attention to the screen in front of them. After a few moments where neither girl spoke, she came across pictures of two gentlemen. The heading was dated November 1, 1896. Just like going over a sharp hill in the car, Jenna's stomach flipped when her eyes rested on the dark-haired young man on the right. The picture was absolutely new to her yet at the same time there was something recognizable about it.

"Wow, check that out," Tina whispered. Neither girl laughed this time. "That's Seth and Joseph, see?" she pointed. Jenna already knew the man on the right was Joseph. She didn't know how, but she did. He was young, about seventeen or eighteen. He was clean shaven, had dark eyes and short, dark hair that was very neat as if gelled. She decided he looked studious. Perhaps it was the way he held his head. Jenna was drawn to him, taking in every feature.

A pink oval fingernail popped up under the picture. "That one is Joseph," Tina said. "He's really cute," she added a moment later, resting her chin in the palm of her hand.

"Yeah," Jenna agreed. She finally looked across the page at the other picture. Seth was not handsome but was very interesting just the same. It was apparent by the shape of their eyes that they were brothers. Seth had the signature moustache of the times, intense dark eyes and was wearing a top hat. Seth looked stern the way Joseph looked studious. Jenna felt this more than anything. She didn't care much for Seth's picture; it made her cringe. She read the caption below.

"'Joseph Samuel Sawyer, eighteen, was found dead last evening by his brother Seth. It was reported that he accidentally fell out of the second story window of his brother's mill.'" Jenna's gaze drifted from the screen towards the large window. She stared off as if deep in thought.

Tina looked up at her for a moment then back to the article. She wished she were more like Jenna. Jenna seemed to know so much about everything and was so confident. At first Tina had been intimidated, but she quickly realized Jenna was too down-to-earth to be snobby. What show-off admits she is nervous about finding a friend and hoping she'll like country living? Other than the week-long vacation at Cape Cod she took with her parents in July, nothing exciting had happened this summer. She'd only spent one day with Jenna and already found she could have fun doing something as simple as hanging out. It made her see her town in a different light. She found the details of the mill she had known for years actually interesting.

"It was my fault," Jenna whispered, not blinking. Her expression was as blank as her tone.

"What?" Tina put her finger on the screen to keep her place and looked up concerned and confused. "Jenna, are you okay?"

"Huh? Sure." Jenna rubbed her eyes. She frowned and shook her head. "That was weird."

"What was?"

"I don't know. It was like I could see it. It's gone now."

"Oh, wow," Tina said.

"Never mind. I've got to get home or I'll be late for dinner," Jenna grumbled looking at her tiny silver watch.

"Me, too," Tina said, mimicking her friend as she checked her yellow Snoopy watch. She started to reach for the media, then smiled, and pretended to pull and reel a fishing pole. "Hey, if you turn this thing off, I'll grab the fiches. Get it? Like, I'll catch the fishes!"

"Put the pictures by the bay window that overlooks the crab apple tree."

"Put the pictures where? But they're not pictures, they're fiches!" Tina exclaimed, her face becoming animated with her play on words.

"Look. Not bored," Jenna mumbled, staring once again into space, completely ignoring Tina.

"I know! It is funny. Come on and laugh, I just made a..." Tina's pout disappeared and was replaced by concern. "What is it? What are you talking about?"

"I have no idea," Jenna said flatly, shaking her head as if to clear it. "I don't remember thinking those things. Anyway, I know I'm not bored. This is fun. Maybe we can come back and do this tomorrow. The sign on the door said they open at ten. I'd like to look up the obituaries, too."

"Okay by me. It'll be cooler in the morning to bike, anyway."

They put everything away quickly, made plans for the next morning, thanked the librarian, and biked home.

THAT NIGHT AFTER dinner, as the cool breeze started to push down the heat of the day, Jenna grabbed her backpack and biked over to the mill alone. She couldn't get it out of her mind. She laid her bike behind one of the apple trees, not needing to worry about hiding it. Dusk was starting to settle over the abandoned building. The frogs, affectionately called peepers by Tina, started their evening chorus. And the smells! Jenna had never smelled such a combination of heat, sweet berries, dew, and clover.

She dumped her backpack and took out the flashlight,

hesitating. She wasn't sure why she had come back, but the thought of this building pulled at her making it impossible to ignore. Jenna thought she might explore a little, hoping she'd uncover something that would make the draw of the place clear to her. She walked through the weeds, around to the back of the mill, wishing she had put a pair of long pants in her backpack. The mosquitoes were monster-sized here and it was tough to see them. The fading daylight blocked the thick vegetation. Cool breezes from the trees mixed with the remaining warm summer air. The thick fragrance of woods and wildflowers filled her nose as twigs snapped under her feet and the mosquitoes buzzed around her. She clicked on her flashlight and took a deep breath for courage as she leaned into the spider webs and looked inside the nearest window. She was so absorbed in what she was looking at she didn't hear the footsteps that approached her from behind.

Four

"WHAT ARE YOU doing?" a voice asked behind her. Jenna jumped, gasping. She whirled around, and the flashlight started to fall, its beam bouncing off everything. She fumbled as she tried to grab it. It landed on a patch of moss, the light flashing in Jenna's eyes. She stumbled backwards and fell in the soft grass. Frantically, she picked up the flashlight and pointed it in the direction of the voice, her vision temporarily blinded.

"Who are you?" Jenna inched away from the stranger. As her eyes focused in the remaining daylight, she could see the voice belonged to a boy about her own age. Standing with his hands jammed in his pockets, he appeared to be just as spooked as Jenna.

He was blond and thin. Even though he was wiry, he had broad shoulders. He shifted from foot to foot uncomfortably, looking over his shoulder at a nearby house.

"Who wants to know?"

"I'm Jenna, Jenna Stevens. I just moved here."

The boy took a deep breath. "No. I don't think so," he answered hesitantly.

"Yes, I did!"

"Here?" he asked suspiciously, pointing his finger towards the mill.

"No, over on Arbor," she said getting up. "Mine is eight ninety-five, the house after Tina Levy's. Who are you?"

"I'm Toby Jacobs," he answered, "and I live over there." He nodded toward the house just down the road.

"Hi. Nice to meet you. Tina mentioned your name."

Toby relaxed a bit. "Oh, I didn't know you knew Tina." He looked a little embarrassed. "I'm sorry if I scared you. I saw your flashlight when I was taking out the trash. No one comes out here. At least, no one that's up to any good."

"That's okay. I suppose I shouldn't be here to begin with," Jenna said, regaining her composure. "I was just looking around."

Toby followed Jenna as she went to retrieve her bike. "I guess I don't need this out here anymore." She spun the flashlight around, illuminating herself as she struggled with the button to turn it off. Suddenly, Toby stopped so quickly, he almost tripped. He stared at her.

"What's the matter?" Jenna asked, feeling self-conscious. She pulled the bottom of her T-shirt down and brushed the hair out of her eyes.

"For a sec I thought you looked familiar."

"I've never been to Orchard Creek until today." Jenna bent down, keeping her eyes on Toby, and scratched at a mosquito bite on her leg. She could see the faint darkening of his face as he blushed.

"Huh. Sorry." His face crinkled up, perplexed. "Well then, what are you looking for?"

Jenna grabbed the bike by the handle, pushing it towards her backpack, thinking about the question. She couldn't really explain her interest in the mill to Toby any more than she could explain it to herself. She shrugged. "I don't know. I love stuff like this. There's something about this mill, though," she looked over her shoulder, "that makes me want to know more about it." She smirked as she picked up her knapsack and swung it over her back.

Toby returned the smile as Jenna nudged her bike through the weeds to the road. She seemed nice, which was good, because the adrenaline he had been feeling when he first came over was almost gone.

"The ghost part is kinda neat, too. Oh hey, I heard your dad wants to renovate the mill."

"Yeah. He thinks a museum might bring in some tourists."

"That's cool," Jenna replied.

"I guess so. My dad and Tina's dad are working on all the legal stuff."

"That must take a lot of time. Tina told me there are a lot of elderly folks in Orchard Creek. I bet they're really excited to see it happen, huh?"

"No, they're not. Our dads are the only two people who want to do this."

"Really?" Jenna was surprised. "It sounds awesome to me."

"The old people in town say it should be left alone, so the town board hasn't approved it."

Jenna slapped at another bug, confused. "Oh. The structure is unsafe?"

"No."

She waited for more, but there wasn't any. "Too much money?"

"Nope."

"That doesn't make sense." This time she stopped walking and Toby followed suit. He avoided her eyes, kicking at a large stone by his sneaker. "I don't understand, Toby."

He looked up and sighed, studying her. "The seniors don't want it touched because it's full of bad juju. They scare away anyone who's interested in buying it."

Jenna giggled. "*Juju.* Tina told me the story about Joseph and Elizabeth and Seth," she admitted.

"That's what the old timers blame it on. They think if we start messing around, bad things will happen again."

"It sounds like you know a lot about it."

Toby nodded but wasn't sure if she could see it. "It's hard not to, it's the closest building to my house. I grew up listening to stories about this old place. And about how my dad wants to restore it. He's a teacher at Cherry Ridge grade school." What he didn't say was how his dad didn't make enough money to front the renovation with Mr. Levy if it ever got approved. Toby wished he had the money to give to his father. His dad would be so happy, and Toby, for once, could be proud of something special.

A cool breeze blew over them as they continued to walk in the remaining daylight. He watched a bat in the distance swoop into a tree for dinner. Jenna seemed nice. She wasn't bad looking for a girl, even with the Velcro-like burrs stuck in her hair from the bushes. And she wasn't a screamer, or he would have had his hearing damaged from sneaking up on her. He figured she could probably dirt bike like one of the boys, noting the scrapes on her knee and leg and total disregard for the girly things like nails and clothes. She didn't seem to mind getting dirty.

"Not to be rude or anything, but why do you care about an old building?" he asked.

"I really couldn't say, but history intrigues me."

They had arrived at a modest split ranch with warm lights from the windows muted by blinds. "Well, this is my house. Hey, if you want to know more about the mill, you can go to the Historical building," Toby suggested. "My dad could give you more details. He works there a lot during the summer."

"I don't think I saw it when we came into town. Where is it?"

"Well, right now it's in the back offices of the town hall. They're open every weekday."

"That sounds great, thanks. Tina and I are going to get together in the morning. We can stop by then. I'll let her know, if that's okay?"

"Sure."

"It's nice meeting you, Toby. See ya tomorrow. Good night."

"'Night." Toby answered, watching her pedal down the road. His nerves were finally settling. It had taken a lot of courage for him to walk over to the mill by himself. It killed him that his shyness always felt like fear.

The summer didn't allow as many opportunities for him to meet his goal and push himself to be more assertive. It was his own ambition, since he was tired of cowering away from people in school. He was a lot skinnier and smaller than boys his own age, and although he only had one incident because of it, last year, it stuck with him. He had no older brother or sister to protect him. But that was for wussies, he thought, knowing he didn't need anyone to rescue him. Besides, he was only a few weeks away from being a teenager. It was time to man up and take charge. Coming over here when he just meant to bring out the garbage was actually a spur-of-the-moment decision. It was so unlike what he'd normally do. He didn't regret it, but he now realized how crazy it was. Still, he had done it and felt a little better about himself.

"I'm home!" Jenna announced as she came through the side door after putting her bike in the garage. She was sweaty from riding but blanketed in the scent of the outdoors at sunset. It was a wonderful feeling, and it made her smile. Immediately she smelled popcorn and glanced around. It looked like a lived-in kitchen, complete with flour and sugar jars lined up on the counter. Plates and silverware remained on the rack by the sink. It was Peter's chore to dry and put away dishes this week, and he was obviously shirking his responsibility. The island counter held a vase of wildflowers next to the popcorn maker and an empty bowl she assumed was for her. Even the soffit was decorated. It felt settled in. She thought about what she expected to see in her own home and knew it was roughly what she saw. Why wasn't it the same with the old mill?

"Is the garage locked up?" her dad asked, distracting her from her musing.

"Yep, it is. I pushed my bike through the side door so I didn't have to fiddle with the big one in the dark."

"No more, Jenna. It's a bit late to be out biking. I thought you said you'd be back in fifteen minutes."

"Sorry, Dad. I met a friend of Tina's and we got to talking." She grabbed the empty bowl and swiveled one of the bar chairs at the island as she passed by. She walked through the dining room and the shiny, polished table, beyond the staircase to the right and into the living room. It was a generously sized room compared to their old place, and bare except for the chairs and television. Three large cardboard boxes were stacked neatly near one of the windows. It didn't matter there were no curtains up yet, it was pitch black outside, and there were no close neighbors to worry about like back in Steel City.

Her parents were sitting on the couch with Peter, watching television. They all munched noisily, their faces illuminated by the flickers of lights from the set. Jenna scooped out popcorn from the big bowl her dad had on his lap, the one he always used. He smiled at her as he swept his feet at hers, trying to trip her up. She grinned and mock hit his shin before heading to her favorite chair.

"Ow! New scores for Orchard Creek: Jack zero, Jenna one."

"'*Friends*' is on. Take your seat," said her mother, pursing her lips at the two of them.

"Speaking of, what was the last name of your new friend?" her dad asked, settling again to get comfortable.

"Levy. I just, uh, bumped into one of her friends, Toby Jacobs, while I was on my bike." Technically, it wasn't fibbing. She knew parents somehow always had four sets of eyes so it was smarter to be up front about it.

"Jenna's got a boyfriend!" Peter teased, making kissing noises.

"Shut up, shrimp. I'm only twelve."

"Knock it off, you guys. Dad and I are too tired for this tonight," her mom admonished gently. "Oh, and Jenna, you've got to watch your brother tomorrow morning while we go to the bank. They need both our signatures to finalize all the transfers and we can't have him running all over the place."

"Please?" Peter begged his mother. "First of all, Jenna's boring. All she does is read and then I get yelled at for getting into trouble. Second of all, I'd rather go into town and see things than sit at home and do nothing." He frowned and rolled his eyes. Clearly, they had all been talking about this for a while now. "I promise I won't run around, Mom."

"Yeah, after five minutes you probably would, squirt. Dad, can't you both go in the afternoon? I already made plans with Tina and Toby."

"Sorry, seniority rules," her dad said. "You'll need to change your busy social schedule to the afternoon, or take Pete with you to keep him busy. Anyway, you have chores in the morning."

Disappointed, Jenna stared at her bowl. A piece of popcorn landed in Jenna's long curls and she looked up at her dad who had tried to put on an innocent expression. "Big sister duties and chores first. It's just a few hours, and then you can play on your own."

"'Kay, Dad." Jenna tried to smile. She didn't even have any phone numbers to call. Maybe Peter could tag along while she let them know, or he could ride along with them.

THAT NIGHT JENNA dreamed about Toby. They were in school and she was watching him. He had a round face and was much shorter than when she met him. He was cornered in the music wing by four kids much bigger than he was. Some hideously loud and awful sounds of ascending and descending scales were coming from the band room. Jenna assumed it was the tuba player's lesson hour. Toby's eyes were huge as he searched the hallway, looking for help. There were no classrooms he could reach unless he went through the boys. They made baby noises at him, calling him *pee wee* and *runt*. Toby's nostrils were flaring with anger, his hands clenching into fists. But he did nothing. When the biggest kid finally stepped forward and landed the first blow, Jenna shook herself out of the dream.

She fell back to sleep immediately and found herself at the mill. She hadn't understood the recurrence of particular dreams back in Steel City, but a tiny, blurry part of her now recognized there was a connection here in Orchard Creek, very specifically that building. It was like the backdrop for the random things that happen in dreams, even though she had never seen it before. And not only was the outside familiar, so was the interior, something Jenna knew nothing about. Still, she could have come across a picture of it in one of her antiquity books or magazines. The memories of those dreams were too shrouded, and there was little detail she could pull up. But from this night, her dreams of the place started to take shape. And the pull began.

Jenna found herself walking through the place, so much different from the little she had seen through the windows. Her hands caressed the polished banisters of the staircase, the fresh pine a light, unmarred tan. Clouds of dust motes swirled around her in the early morning light, kicked up from the daily restocking of wood logs near the hearth. As always, pockets of warm air fought with the coolness of late autumn. Her boots clicked on each stair as she made her way up, her stomach an odd mixture of anticipation and weariness. What if the secret had stayed safe?

Acrid and metallic smells met her on the landing, familiar as always. She turned left and went through the smaller rooms—avoiding the room to the right until the last possible moment—waiting and searching. Always waiting…

The next morning Jenna ate a quick breakfast and started in with her chores, eager to learn more about the mill. The tasks didn't really seem like chores now that she and her family were in a different place. She thought Peter was crazy to be bored here already. The newness was almost like helping out at a friend's house. She had already started a load of laundry, wiped down the table, and washed the dishes while Peter watched cartoons and finished his cereal. He was such a slowpoke and she was waiting on him. Again. She loved her brother but began to envy Tina being an only child.

"Come on, pokey, I've got places to go and people to see."

"Your new boyfriend?" he said around a mouthful of Cocoa Puffs. Seeing the amount of food he was no doubt going to waste, Jenna started to fold the box tops down, her mind wandering.

"I must go to work." *What? Where did that come from?*

Peter stopped chewing to gawk at her. "No, you don't. You're twelve." Then his face split into a Cheshire Cat grin, which, coupled with his hair sticking straight up, made him look hilarious. "You want to see your new boyfriend."

"No! And you better not say that around my new friends. Let's go."

Peter rolled his eyes and opened his mouth so the cereal poured back out and down his chin. Jenna grimaced as she shook her head. It was going to be a long day.

After the kitchen was straightened up, they got their bikes from the garage and rode over to Tina's. Peter shouted the whole way how great it was to ride out in the open, instead of riding in the tiny park their parents often took them to. He was actually riding circles around Jenna. And even though he made it to Tina's mailbox before her, she made him wait on his bike until she caught up.

"Stay here."

"Okay."

Jenna smiled as she walked to the porch. Sometimes he wasn't so bad. She had barely finished knocking before Tina answered, jumping on one foot as she tried to put on her sandal, her pigtails imitating the action.

"We have a tag-along, so I think the library is out."

"Hmm. Do you want to find the obituaries? I asked my dad and he said the records are in the town hall. We can go, but I can't stay long. I'll have to leave from there. I forgot my parents are having an early cookout with Toby's family."

"Oh yeah, I almost forgot! I met Toby last night and I said we'd go to the Historical Association to get some more details. That would be two birds with one stone. I'm not sure how much we can do with Peter, though." Jenna pursed her lips, much like her mother had the night before, as she looked over at her brother. He had gotten off his bike and was bent over with his hands on his thighs, studying an ant or something on the ground.

"If I do this then you have to promise to come over for our next family birthday and help me with my cousins."

"Deal."

After Tina retrieved her purse from her room and swung it over her shoulder, the three set out for the town. On the trip, Peter periodically rode his bike way out in front or way behind the two girls. Jenna described what it was like living in Steel City, and Tina told her more about the neat things to do in Orchard Creek, like where to go for the biggest ice cream and the best toy store.

The roads were becoming more familiar the more Jenna biked them. They traveled down Arbor Road to East Abbey and biked over the covered bridge, which was scary because of the fast-running water below, but exciting at the same time. Then they took a left onto Sentinel, in the opposite direction of the mill and Toby's house. They crossed over Rodger's Pike Road to Washington. Instead of going left again like they had gone to the library, Tina pointed to the other direction which intersected Elm Street.

"I need to take a break. Are you all right, Peter?" Tina asked as she undid the water bottle from the bike and took a gulp. Jenna and Peter were thirsty too but didn't own a bottle.

"Uh huh. I need a drink, too."

Tina handed Jenna the bottle and she took a few swallows, liking how much Tina already considered her a friend if she was going to share her water. Jenna made a motion to ask if it was okay for Peter to have some, and Tina nodded. After Peter slobbered on it, the girls giggled, knowing neither would have any more until it was washed.

"Brothers," Tina teased under her breath. Jenna caught her eyes and smiled.

"Brothers."

"We're almost there. It's not much farther."

"Is the town hall still by the church?" The words tumbled out of Jenna's mouth without her knowledge. Her eyes widened. She had always had moments like this, but not nearly so many.

"Yep, on the other side of Richie's Farm store, and kitty-corner to Mandy's place where the high schoolers hang out. She has good food." Tina hadn't noticed, since she was putting the bottle back and brushing the stray hairs away from her face. As they rode, some of the buildings nagged at Jenna as if she had seen them before. Maybe it was from one of the pictures her dad had brought home before they moved.

After they dismounted and leaned the bikes against the side of the building (reminding Jenna a lot of the Western movies when they tied up the horses), they went inside through the front door. It squeaked loudly. It also smelled a bit funny, a combination of old office and disinfectant. A short hallway split into three small rooms. The two on the right were for the Tax Assessor and Town Clerk, and the one on the left for Planning and Zoning. In front of them was a short wall. A boy with blond hair was looking over the bulletin board posted with Lost and Found, Wanted notices, and business cards. On either side of that wall were two larger rooms. The boy turned around, and just as soon as it hit Jenna, Tina greeted him.

"Hi Toby. What's up?"

Raised voices distracted them before he could answer. Toby inclined his head towards the argument, his hazel eyes wide. "I was giving them some space."

"Who?" Tina asked, her voice nothing more than a stage whisper. She walked toward the room on the left, motioning for everyone to follow her. Curiosity got the best of them as they all quietly inched into the doorway. It was a big area with a huge mural of the town from a hundred years ago, according to the date over the top of it. It was empty of furniture except for a metal thing on wheels that held a bunch of fold-up chairs. A raised platform in front of them reminded Jenna of a court room. A man and a woman were in the middle of the room, each with the same stance of frustration. Jenna's attention kept going back to the mural.

"No, this is realistic. The budget deadline is in a few weeks, and I don't want this shot down again. And I'll keep doing whatever it takes to continue the renovation process. Honestly, Rose, I don't understand your reservations. This isn't a big deal." The man was facing them and had his arms crossed. He had china blue eyes behind thin glasses and short, wavy black hair. He looked so much like Tina that Jenna didn't even bother asking if it was her dad.

Without waiting for a reply, he turned his back on the older woman and walked into a room off to the side, closing the door firmly behind him. The sound echoed around the emptiness. Tina broke from the others, following through the same door, leaving Jenna, Peter, and Toby standing there.

The older woman turned around and faced them without

making eye contact. She was pale and thin. Her frail frame stood straight and erect with determination. Her face was well cared for, and despite the wrinkles, appeared soft. Her faded blue eyes were intense, and her cheeks were high in color from the confrontation. She adjusted the thin wisps of gray hair under her hat and clutched her pocketbook with both gloved hands as she walked towards the door.

"These children should have been taught respect," she uttered under her breath as she left. No one spoke until they heard the faint sound of a squeaking door.

"Who was that?" Jenna asked quietly.

"Mr. Levy called her Rose. She must be the widow Forrester, because I think her name is Rose too," Toby guessed. "I've never really met the old folks on the town board, they all tend to sit together at meetings."

Jenna craned her neck to see if the woman was still in the hallway. It was empty. When she turned back around, Tina and her dad were coming through the door.

"I'm sorry about that, kids. Hi Toby. Good to see you." Mr. Levy put one hand in his pocket and scratched the back of his neck with the other. He looked at Jenna and cocked his head to one side. "And who is this?" he asked.

"Dad, this is my new friend, Jenna, and her brother, Peter. They just moved here from the city," Tina said. A puzzled look crossed his face as he stared at Jenna.

Five

Mr. Levy shook her hand but kept staring. "I'm sorry, you look familiar."

"That's okay," Jenna said politely, thinking that Toby had said that, too. Her eyes drifted to the painting, finding the mill immediately. It looked remarkably like the pictures in the old newspapers.

"Mr. Levy, we came to look at the stuff you have here on the mill," Toby said.

"Sure, help yourself, but keep it neat. Let me know if you need any help," Mr. Levy replied, ruffling Toby's hair. Toby frowned and blushed at the same time.

"My dad and Toby's dad have kind of taken over the Historical Association like it's their own. What has been donated by residents or found in attics is collected and displayed here," Tina explained as they walked to the back of the room.

Jenna noticed a sign she hadn't seen before over the door.

It was a slab of aged wood with the words "Orchard Creek Historical" burned into it. "Was that Mrs. Forrester?"

"I asked my dad and he said it was."

"He was talking about fixing up the mill?"

"Uh huh. I guess it didn't go so well. Again," Tina said, sighing.

"Come on, Peter. Stay with me and don't touch anything," Jenna warned. They all went through the door while Tina pointed her finger around her. "This room is too small for everything, though, not to mention what I hear is in Old Man Robertson's basement. He's been the president of the Historical Association for eons and has been collecting stuff that won't fit here. This was a project that was started way before we were born. They want more than anything to have the funds to fix up the mill to showcase all the history this town has," Tina explained.

"Not to mention other local stuff like the Erie Canal, the women's rights movement, Herkimer diamond mines, and the fact that this area was part of the Underground Railroad," Toby added, his face becoming pink. "There's some neat stuff here on the wall."

"Wow. There are diamond mines here?"

"Pretty close by. They're like diamonds, but not really real diamonds. I've been to the gift shop there, and they look real to me," Tina tried to explain. "The big ones are worth a lot of money."

"You just go and dig them up?"

"Don't try to kid her, Tina," scolded Toby as he swatted her playfully on the head with a nearby book. "There aren't any big ones left anymore. It's been mined to death."

Jenna had more questions about Mrs. Forrester and the mill but she filed them away to take in the items surrounding her. The room was a spacious one that would have been very pleasant if it hadn't been crammed with objects, pictures, and relics on every available surface. Two walls had rows of shelves to house the smaller knick knacks. A glass display case was shoved into a corner, filled with neatly arranged Indian artifacts and placards describing what they were, and the years they were used. One whole wall was sectioned off, dedicated to the water wheel and the particulars of how the water was converted to power. A large picture frame held a poster board with diagrams and arrows.

When Tina and Toby started to bicker about whose father did the best drawings, Jenna tuned them out. Peter was toying with an old tin lantern, quietly trying to figure it out. Jenna walked away, studying everything. There were old pictures on the walls—everywhere—each framed with a label at the bottom. She had to stand on tiptoe to see some of them. Again, that familiar feeling came back. She knew these places.

"Here's something else," Tina announced, pointing above her to see a large picture of the mill and articles about the Sawyer boys. After exploring a while, it was evident there was nothing on Elizabeth or the ghost sightings. They did find the obituary books, which they balanced on a small table. Joseph's notice was found quickly. It was informative, but not flowery like obituaries found in a newspaper. The specifics said the same thing the newspaper did. While Tina was putting that book away, Jenna came across Elizabeth's notice. It was in the book dated 1897. Her disappointment was evident.

"Oh Tina, here it is, but there's less than Joseph's. It pretty much says she was born April 6, 1880, in Boston, Mass, and died here in Orchard Creek October 31, 1897. 'She is survived by her parents and three younger sisters.'"

"Yeah, that's what my dad said. Only the basics. They wouldn't have too much stuff in it because she was not a—what did he say? —a *woman of means*. Not even the paper would bother with it."

"She died on Halloween, too," Jenna said sadly, closing the log.

"I told you she did. Hey, um, Jenna, your brother…"

Jenna looked up just in time to catch a soft, deflated ball-thing that threatened to whizz past her head. "Peter!" she hissed. Luckily, no one else was in the room, and he didn't break anything.

"The sign says it's a ball."

Jenna skewered her brother with her eyes and set the nasty thing on the nearest table. "Those things were made from the bladder of a pig. You know—the part of the body that holds your pee.

Peter's brown eyes grew big. "*Ew!*"

"Exactly. So, don't touch!"

Jenna would have preferred to stay longer but knew her time was up. Once Peter started to get bored, he got into trouble. Reluctantly, they decided to call it quits. It was time for Tina and Toby to go home anyway, leaving Jenna and Peter by themselves. After saying their goodbyes, Jenna and her brother mounted their bikes and set off for home.

Jenna was proud for finding their way back without any problems. It also couldn't come fast enough as she was serenaded the whole time by Peter's version of the Scooby Doo theme song, complete with made up words. Over and over. It grated on her nerves. She was disappointed when she didn't see her dad's car at all. The other was in the garage, so at least someone could re-claim Peter.

"Hi Mom. Where's Dad?"

Her mom was at the desk "office" in the dining room,

clicking away at the computer. She looked up and smiled. "He went to work for a few hours of orientation. Jenna, thank you so much for keeping an eye on Pete."

"No problem. You can take over. I'd like to give him back."

Her mother shifted in her chair to face her daughter, pulling up the loose spaghetti strap of her yellow tank top. "He was okay for you?"

"As much as he could be, I think, but he's standing on the kitchen counter right now."

"Peter, get off the counter!"

"I want Spaghetti-O's for lunch, Mom. I'm starving."

"You won't find them in that cupboard. Get down and I'll get them. Why does it seem like all I do is yell? It's going to take some time getting used to you two building up an appetite from being outside. Do you want me to fix you something else?" She started to save her material.

"And I want crackers, chocolate milk and a fruity ice pop."

"Naw, I'm okay," Jenna said, smiling. Peter had taken a huge leap off the counter, just missing the island. Luckily, their mother couldn't see it from where she was sitting. And it barely made a sound on the floor. Peter looked pleased with himself, and a mischievous grin filled his face. He had found a way to be naughty without alerting their parents. Jenna rolled her eyes, knowing he'd be doing that a lot more.

Her attention shifted away from her brother when her mom came over. She put her arms on Jenna's shoulders and held her gaze. "Are you sure? It doesn't have to be what a nine-year-old would eat."

Jenna was impatient to get back on her bike. There were places she wanted to go. "I'm sure. I'll get something later." She kissed her mother's cheek, which made them both smile. "Can I go back out?"

"Sure, hon—" Her mother's eyes darted to the kitchen, and she scowled. "Peter, how'd you find the cookies that fast? No more. The healthy food first, dude." Her eyes, full of apology, found Jenna's again. "Just be careful."

It was a little cooler out, only in the mid-seventies. Jenna biked to nowhere in particular at first, unsure of her plans. Eventually she found herself riding down the long drive lined with trees. She stopped halfway down, the "widow house" in front of her. The white house seemed much larger than from the road, where she and Tina had observed it. It had a set of stairs in the front that didn't look used, and another set to a small entryway right off the driveway, a short distance from the garage. The lawn was manicured and tidy. Newly bloomed purple flowers reached out of the variegated hostas on each side of both sets of stairs. Other small shrubbery dotted the sides of the home with pink and white petunias filling in between, and bridal bushes anchoring the corners. Her heart beat loudly in her chest as she entertained thoughts of actually going up and knocking on the door. After a few moments, she was surprised to see her feet pedaling down the rest of the dirt driveway to the side entrance.

Jenna parked her bike and took a deep breath. She walked up the stairs, each one creaking its own complaint of old age. She paused again, and finally knocked on the door. A moment later it was opened by the same woman Jenna had seen earlier.

"Good afternoon. Mrs. Forrester?" Jenna asked timidly.

"Yes," she answered tersely.

"Excuse me for bothering you, ma'am. My name is Jenna Stevens. I saw you in the Historical building today. I don't mean to bother you but I just moved here, and I'm interested in the mill, and was wondering why you don't think it should be renovated. If it's a bad time, I could come back later…"

The look Rose Forrester reserved for solicitors of the latest religion and door-to-door salesmen vanished. There in front of her stood a polite and honest-looking girl with an inquiring mind. Many argued their point and a few pushed their views, but not many people asked why these days. She hesitated a moment, but as Jenna started to apologize for intruding, she made a decision.

"Nonsense. Come in out of the sun. I don't actually receive many visitors. Come in." Mrs. Forrester smiled and opened the door wider. "I don't bite, you know," she teased, seeing the unease in Jenna's face.

Now that the door was opened for her to enter a stranger's house, Jenna wavered. Reminding herself that Mrs. Forester wasn't the one trying to lure her in but that she herself had knocked, she went in quietly. The foyer was very neat and sparsely decorated with a rocker, bench, small table, and broom with an old metal dustpan with tiny flecks of paint left intact. A wide-brimmed hat, trowel and spade sat in a wicker basket next to the door. The house had an old people smell to it that reminded Jenna of her grandmother. She took off her sneakers and tiptoed inside.

"I'm a little out of practice. Come into the parlor and sit down. Would you like some lemonade?"

"That would be great, thank you," Jenna said, putting all her manners to use as she followed the woman. "You have a lovely house." Jenna stared around at the flowered wallpaper.

"How kind you are," Rose said, motioning to a seat before going into the kitchen.

Jenna walked slowly around the living room, hearing ice clinking into glasses. That was the moment her stomach started to growl. Wrapping her arms around her middle, Jenna continued to take everything in. The house looked like it hadn't changed in many, many years. The room was bright despite the deep red, dark green, and yellow color palette. Jenna recognized an old brown RCA Victrola in the corner to the left. She had done a project last year in her old school about the record player, so she knew that's what it was. This one was a large, stout, cabinet-like console with two ornately designed pull out doors. She remembered the record player was hidden inside. Mrs. Forrester's was a dark brown and polished so it was as smooth as marble. She would have bet a month's allowance that it worked, too.

Two claw-footed armchairs with a large flower pattern on the sturdy cushions flanked it. A curvy, fancy couch was against the wall to the left, complete with lace doilies on the armrests. A small coffee table was in front of it with a simple linen doily. It was adorned with a candy dish in the center made of pretty multicolored glass. Long, thick curtains pulled back to let the sun in, hung down to the floor. The curtains accented odd-sized windows that were long so as to look proportional to the tallness of the house and yet not wide enough for the height. The ceiling was high and had a vent that led to the next floor's room. The architecture books Jenna had devoured over the years had explained such vents' purpose: older homes didn't have forced air like there was now. In order for a house to keep warm, there would be a fireplace or two on the ground floor. Vents allowed the heat to rise to upper floors.

In the other corner of the room Jenna noticed an oblong antique table in a dark wood, with more pretty glass. A beautiful fruit bowl in turquoise with grapes and maple leaves molded into the sides stood out among several glass slippers and a hurricane lamp. The hardwood floor had braided rugs here and there. Black and white pictures of a young couple in ancient frames were scattered throughout.

Jenna leaned down to take a closer look at the nearest

photograph. It was one of those staged photos with a cloth backdrop and a wicker chair off to the side. The man was standing proudly, although Jenna thought he looked really young to be wearing such grown-up clothes. He was handsome, clean shaven with a square jaw and jovial eyes that matched his dimple and boyish smile. He wore a dark suit with a striped tie. There was a flower in the lapel, and he looked both distinguished and at ease as he held a bowler hat and gloves in his hands.

The woman next to him was just as young. She had short, light colored hair parted low on the left side and styled into neat waves against her face with a rhinestone headband with fingertip blusher. It all reminded Jenna of the Roaring Twenties. The woman had a fitted, light-colored dress with a satiny finish an fell nearly to the floor. Her right hand was tucked in the crook of the man's arm. In her left arm she cradled a ghastly mass of overflowing flowers. She was smiling anyway as if it were the best day of her life. The photo made Jenna giggle.

Jenna stood and continued around the room. The only modern addition she saw was the floor model television set back against the wall, and that looked at least 20 years old. Everything was in its place, cleaned and polished.

A large dark wooden table and six chairs sat in the center of a formal dining room, with another braided rug underneath. A fireplace took up one wall with many more pictures on the mantle along with several more pieces of glass, some a vivid green, others a gold color, and porcelain bird figurines.

Mrs. Forrester came back into the room through the dining room, carrying a tray with two tall glasses of lemonade and slices of what looked like banana bread. Jenna's stomach growled again. The woman looked at Jenna, the pillowy wrinkles of her face pulling up in a smile. She wasn't a tiny woman but wasn't much taller than Jenna. The hat and gloves she had on earlier were now gone, and a full head of gray hair curled gently around her neck, ending in a bun at her nape. She wore a white sweater and a thin summer dress with tiny flowers on it. Mrs. Forrester placed the tray on the coffee table and sat down, but not back against the seat. Crossing her legs at her ankles, she sighed. Jenna joined her, sitting carefully on the ornate sofa. Mrs. Forrester grinned, her pale blue eyes fixed on her visitor.

"Are you one of the girls who stop to stare at my house?" she asked. "There used to be only one. Yesterday there were two."

Jenna's face reddened, and she bowed her head. "Yes, ma'am."

Mrs. Forrester looked at her a moment. "Drink up, now. Why didn't you come down and knock?"

Jenna had never thought about that and said so. She felt embarrassed that she had been spying. "I'm sorry. We didn't mean any harm by it. We were just curious. I just moved here from Steel City and everything in Orchard Creek is so interesting. I didn't think that we were being rude." Jenna took a sip of her drink. It was very tart. It caught her by surprise at first, but then she smiled. "Mmm."

"So, you like your lemonade made from real lemons instead of those chemicals they now call natural."

"It tastes better," Jenna agreed.

"What brings you here, Miss Jenna?" Mrs. Forrester asked, sitting back in her chair.

"Well, I'd like to think if there's a place I could visit when I get older that would bring me back in time and help me remember the past, I would be for it. Excited, really." She traced the patterns in the rug with her eyes as she talked, looking up at the woman when she was met with silence. Mrs. Forrester's expression gave nothing away and Jenna's face warmed as she thought about her words. Was implying she was old a social no-no? Jenna wasn't sure. "But if I'm wrong, I apologize for assuming."

"No offense taken, dear. Now, I can tell you are someone independent and strong-minded since your concern has you sitting on my davenport all by yourself. I admire that. I am also curious. What can I do for you?"

"*I*'D LIKE TO know more about the history of Orchard Creek, especially the mill," Jenna said. "Pardon me for mentioning what happened in the Town Hall today, but you seem so set against the renovation. I would have thought you would be for it." She shook her head as if clearing the confusion away. "I don't understand why you would feel that way."

Mrs. Forrester nibbled on her slice of banana bread, then abruptly got up and left the room. Jenna thought she had somehow insulted her again. Just as she set her glass down and was about to get up to leave, Mrs. Forrester came back in with two books. One was a large, brown leather-bound book, the other a small, well-worn black book.

"My family, as well as Mr. Forrester's—God rest his soul—have lived here for over a century. I have seen a lot in my eighty-three years on this earth, some good and some bad. This town is mostly good. That mill . . . is bad." She opened the larger book. "My great-grandparents started this scrapbook when my grandmother was little. It has been passed down each generation. I was an only child, and they wanted our heritage to continue. Unfortunately, my husband, Royal, and I, were unable to have a family of our own. After that, I had little to add to the book other than town news. I've been thinking perhaps I'll leave it to the Historical Association when I pass. There is quite a bit in here about the mill."

Jenna looked up, her face full of questions. Before she could ask, the woman motioned to the bread and continued. Jenna settled again and began to eat.

"Orchard Creek was a fairly nice place to live, sustainable on its own. The soil was fertile and malleable, and the growing season versatile for many fruits and vegetables. We didn't need fancy to make us happy. But when someone with a large purse moves into a quiet little town such as this, and turns it on its head, well, it was quite the topic of conversation for some time."

She handed the album to Jenna, smiling while Jenna thanked her for the delicious bread. Jenna put the plate back on the tray, taking care to wipe her fingers on the pretty linen napkin before taking the book. It felt as if her very being was starving and this was a gourmet meal promising to satisfy her hunger. The weight of it took her by surprise; even the cover was heavy. Its condition was pristine, obviously used often, but handled with care. All the pages were thick, yellowed paper. The first had 1878 at the top in black ink and listed the birth of Emily Gertrude Strong, the first Strong to be born in America.

"That was my grandmother."

"Wow," Jenna whispered as she read. The entire entry was about the baby and her family. Mrs. Forrester's—Jenna had to stop to think about it—Mrs. Forrester's great-grandmother liked to write. The ink was neat, with curly-cues and flourishes, and spoke of daily life and their first spring in New York.

She turned the pages a bit faster now, and the handwriting changed. Jenna could almost sense the personalities of the individuals who logged the information. The penmanship now was stiff and formal, the letters written without embellishment. It covered how the town was growing and changing. Each new family to the area was mentioned, as well as who had died and how. Businesses were listed as to whether they were growing or folding. On the page dated 1890, it discussed the cost, and apparent increase, of necessities such as a yard of fabric, flour, and sugar at the general store. She continued to turn each page with care. Within a couple more the handwriting became lighter on the paper and flowed at an angle. A few pages even had newspaper clippings and articles on the mill. None of the information or pictures was new to Jenna because she had seen them the day before. She couldn't help the disappointment that showed on her face.

"Not what you were looking for?" The voice startled Jenna out of her reverie, as she was absorbed in the scrapbook in front of her.

Jenna shook her head and tried to articulate the emotions and feelings that were driving her interest. "No, I saw those articles yesterday in the library. But it's not that, either. That place… there's something more. It's just…more."

"What do you know about the mill?" Mrs. Forrester inquired. Jenna told the old woman all the stories she had heard. Mrs. Forrester listened quietly.

"If you've been trying to find out about the legend and the ghost, you've been looking in the wrong places. The library and the Historical Association won't have that kind of information."

Jenna was let down. "Then where do I look?"

"You don't need to look any further than this. My

grandmother's personal diary," Mrs. Forrester replied, handing her the small book. "Most everything you're looking for is in here."

Jenna became excited again, but she was confused. "I'm sorry. I understand how legends and rumors can find their way into a diary. I want to know about the facts."

Mrs. Forrester tipped her head, impressed that Jenna recognized the difference between stories and proof. "You keep reading, and I'll explain in a moment." Without waiting for a reply, she got up and carried the empty plates to the kitchen.

Jenna ran her hand over the black cover, mouthing the word "wow". The leather was butter soft and broken-in perfectly for recording private thoughts and secrets. She looked through the little-known history that sat in her lap. It contained the same pictures she and Tina saw of the mill and the sewing room machinery. The caption under it read:

Come early summer the biggest opportunity for Orchard Creek will be the fabric mill. Papa wishes for me to have a skill other than rearing children and working the land as he and Mama had. He says the first Strong in this great land will be business-minded and confident.

The next picture was the one of Seth and Joseph she had seen in the library. This, too, had a caption.

I have made it onto payroll along with several girls in town! I shall do Papa proud despite my wretched nerves. To work for the most eligible bachelor, happenstance the most handsome man, ever, will be a terribly wonderful burden. If only I don't faint dead away at the looms. Perhaps I can catch his eye and heart, fully breaking the classes that separate us. What lovely daydreams I have about being on the arm of the richest man Orchard Creek has ever seen.

This made Jenna smile. The next few pages talked about the reality of long hours, backaches, stiff necks, sore fingers, and an angry, impatient boss. Emily scolded herself for ever having her head in the clouds.

I was a silly schoolgirl to think ideas of love about the dreadful Mr. Sawyer, and I am so much wiser now. He is a stern man who never smiles. He orders us about and waves away our cares for leaving the hard chairs to go to the water bucket. He makes his younger brother bring it round instead. At least his brother has a friendly smile and is pleasant when he is away. He does not look down his nose at us. My closest friend Elizabeth fancies him. She is daft if she believes Mr. Sawyer will allow a girl who must work to help support her family will be accepted into his own with welcoming arms.

Up until this entry, Jenna was reading the words like she would any book. This recording had pictures exploding in her mind. People's faces became specific and defined, places were vivid and complete with details. Even smells seemed to fill in her nose. Jenna glanced at the entries as she flipped through the pages, images stopping and starting like a videocassette movie being turned from "pause" to "play". Her heart was racing now as her eyes searched, hoping to see Elizabeth's and Joseph's names again. She found them on page one hundred sixty.

The foolish lass went out to see him again last evening. It's all she'll talk about as we walk to work and back. I cannot believe in three quarters of a year's time he has grown into his own, defying his brother's standards. I have cautioned Elizabeth, but she will not heed my warnings. She will get more than fired for treading beyond accepted behavior. To see Mr. Joseph Sawyer alone, away from the conventions of society is the madness of love and the sin of gossip. How I wish I had her constitution! True love will wait for no one. I have discovered Lucien Flynn has difficulty concentrating on herding his cattle when I walk past his land on my way to town to sell our wares. His shy smile has caused at least one cow to wander away when he's bid me hello. Perhaps he is sweet on me?

He is handsome and kind, and comes from a good Irish family like my own.

Jenna couldn't pull herself away. The next page she stopped on was dated October 20.

It is in confidence that I write this. I am privy to information that makes me have faith in fate and God above that love will conquer all. Joseph, for that is what I consider him now as well, has been courting Elizabeth in private for months. Lately when they meet at the mill in the evening, he has been discussing a more permanent relationship. She is beside herself with joy. I have to lower my eyes when mine meet his at work so he cannot know what I'm sure is written all over me. Elizabeth has been working on her handkerchief for some time now. She will say yes, freeing him from doubt about her feelings for him. How can he not know? She assures me she has been coy in the proper manner when they meet, despite her growing love and infatuation with him. Oh, to have such good luck befall a dear, loving friend who has struggled so much in her young life, helping her family so. I might even be a bridesmaid!

Jenna was completely enthralled. Her imagination was in overdrive, filling in much more than what was printed. She reverently turned the pages to continue, having completely forgotten she was sitting and reading a diary in a stranger's house until the woman standing next to her cleared her throat. Jenna jumped as she came back to reality, squealing in surprise.

"I'm sorry, Miss Jenna. I hadn't realized you didn't hear me call your name." Her tone had changed, becoming stern. "Twice."

"Oh, I apologize, Mrs. Forrester." Jenna's voice was breathless. The woman's forehead wrinkled with concern as she sat down.

"You're not looking well. Your face is flushed."

"Oh no, I'm fine! It's just so interesting to learn about the mill. And about Elizabeth and Joseph."

Mrs. Forrester made a noise of agreement but held her hand out for the book.

No! a part of her mind screamed. Reluctantly, Jenna handed it over, her stomach dropping the way it did when she was reprimanded by her parents. It created a void of emptiness much the same as sitting at a table of food and being told she couldn't eat more to get her fill.

"My grandmother, Emily Flynn, worked at the mill for a time and one of her closest friends was Elizabeth Avery. My grandmother told me the stories herself. My, it's been years since I've thought that far back! It was tragic how Joseph died. He was well liked by all the girls, you know, but had taken an interest in Elizabeth. She had confided in my grandmother that they were secretly courting."

"Yes, I read that."

"Elizabeth didn't take his death well at all, she wouldn't accept it. For some reason, she was forbidden to step foot in the mill, which wasn't an issue. She was unable to work, even though she needed the job. My grandmother told me that she changed, falling into a deep melancholia that never broke. She hardly spoke to anyone afterward and was very distant. A year later, to the day, I believe, she died as well. It's all in the diary."

Jenna wanted to speak. She felt out of sorts, with so many questions her mind was plugged up making nothing come out. More than anything, she wanted that book back in her hands.

"It was around those dreadful years the mill took on some strange characteristics. The sewing machines, which were powered by foot pedals, would suddenly freeze up. Then some of them would work twice as fast, almost sewing the women's fingers together. The women would hear someone crying, but when they looked, they couldn't find anyone.

"Also, they would have cold chills, not just during winter, but well into the next season. Their complaints fell on deaf ears. Elizabeth hadn't been the only one affected; Seth wasn't the same after Joseph died either. He was drinking and he didn't sleep. He yelled a lot, and became paranoid of voices following him. He wouldn't go up to the second floor, even to check on the workers. He said it was always too cold up there. It made him feel as if he was being watched.

"I remember my grandmother's house always had a window ajar, cracked on the coldest days and wide open in the warmest weather. She said she never wanted to feel closed in again after suffering at the mill because Seth, by this time unreasonable, had permanently kept the windows closed and locked."

Mrs. Forrester studied Jenna's expression. The girl was slack-jawed. Without really understanding why, she continued. "My grandmother said she knew it was Elizabeth. Elizabeth was so distraught over the death of Joseph. She never truly believed he died. She was sure he would come for her. Every evening for the next year, after Seth left for the day, Elizabeth would come back to the mill and wait for Joseph. She never admitted this to anyone but my grandmother. It all makes sense. Eventually, Seth was unable to work at all, and he moved out of town. I heard he never got better." Mrs. Forrester was quiet a moment, lost in thought. She smoothed her dress.

"The reason I don't want the mill restored is because it would stir up old spirits, and people will get hurt. I believe it happened before and will happen again."

Jenna looked at her, puzzled.

"There was a restoration project about forty years ago, and strange things started in again. Workers complained of seeing shadows out of the corner of their eyes, of the presence of a tearful young girl. Every time they saw her, she was passing doorways looking for someone, but no one could ever find her when they searched the premises. Then they started to get hurt, and one of the men died. Finally, the project was halted permanently. I can surmise only one reason that makes sense to me. Joseph and Elizabeth were two passionate people who died very unhappily. As soon as they start restoring the place, I believe Elizabeth will try to protect it. She won't understand that time has moved on. It's been almost one hundred years. That's a long time to be waiting for your beau, don't you think?"

Distance from the diary had cleared Jenna's head, although the questions were still there. "I guess you're right. I hadn't thought about it that way." She looked at her watch and frowned as something dawned on her. "If this is the only place I can find what I'm looking for, then how is it that so many people here know about it?" Jenna asked.

"I've done a lot of talking in my time. I'm the only living person left who knows the truth about the mill."

From somewhere in the dining room, a grandfather clock chimed three times. "I've taken up half your day. Thank you for the refreshments and your time." Jenna stood up, brushing her hair away from her face, wondering if it would be wrong to ask to borrow the diary.

Mrs. Forrester nodded with a smile and escorted her to the door. "You are welcome any time. Come back, and I'll tell you more."

"Thank you! That would be great. I'd love to read more of the diary and there are so many questions I have, too. Like, what did it mean by Elizabeth was working on a handkerchief? What about—"

"I can tell you after lunch tomorrow if you'd like."

"I'll be here." Jenna waved as she skipped down the steps. She smiled as she picked up her bike. Although she felt incomplete, she still felt contented with so much new information.

Mrs. Forrester returned to her living room and after a moment, put a record on the Victrola, something she hadn't done in a month of Sundays. After picking up her lemonade, she sat down in the chair that gave the best view of her long drive and watched the small figure that was Jenna as she biked away. The girl was peculiar, but genuine, she was sure. Why she was interested in the history of that building was beyond her reasoning. Even the girl didn't seem to know. It was very strange. Then again, that building had so many memories stored there, strong, powerful memories. She hadn't read her grandmother's diary in decades, but she remembered how much was written about it. The young Emily Flynn was only a few years older than Jenna, she imagined.

Polite or not, Rose had no intention of having someone around the age of thirteen walk away with the diary either. It was too special to her, just like her grandmother was special to her. She was astounded she remembered so much of her conversations with the relative she was closest to. They were such grand and loving times. The music pulled her out of her thoughts and opened a flood of emotions. She let her mind wander back to handkerchiefs and true love.

Rose drifted through her past and settled on her favorite memories, of Royal. She smiled when she thought of the butterflies that fluttered in her when she realized that brisk, spring, Sunday morning in church, that Royal Forrester was sweet on her. She kept catching him looking over at her and lost her place in her hymnal, so much that Father scolded her to pay attention. Closing her eyes, she could almost remember the smell of the lye soap they used on Saturday night to get themselves Sunday-ready.

A few weeks later, tittering and giddy, sixteen-year-old Rose Máire Flynn asked her mother about the handkerchief commitment ceremony. She had never paid much attention to the details before, but suddenly she needed to know what to do next. Remembering how her mother's eyes widened, she knew the exact moment she no longer felt like a little girl.

The handkerchief commitment ceremony was a local courting tradition. Once a couple started courting, it was the young woman's decision if it progressed to marriage. In this part of New York, the time it took until an announcement of marriage depended upon two things: the lady's assuredness of the union, and how long it would take for her to sew and offer a handkerchief. In other areas, it was a commitment ring from the young man to his betrothed, signaling their engagement. Here in Orchard Creek, it was a hand-sewn handkerchief made by the girl and presented to her suitor. Just as a ring would represent the means to care for the bride, the handkerchief signified the ability to care for a husband and family. The handkerchief was usually very detailed, with the enthusiasm of the young woman who wanted to impress her potential husband. Many were embroidered with the initial of the man's last name and had an intricate lace trim. They were sewn in many different fashions, depending on the ability, and attention put into it. The only customary standards for the handkerchief ceremony were to allow the woman to be sure of her decision, finish the gift, and continue with the courting. When the young woman offered the handkerchief to the young man and he agreed to take it, they were officially promised to marry.

Rose knew this is what she wanted more than anything. Having never sewn a handkerchief, but sewing since she could talk, it took only a few months to complete. She remembered sneezing as she used dandelion flowers to dye the fabric a brilliant yellow. She was pleased with her handiwork and beamed when Royal said it was the most beautiful handkerchief he had ever seen.

The August wedding had been perfect. Rose raised her hand to admire the new, shiny, fine band on her third finger and her breath caught in her throat. Instead of a pink, slender hand, it was thin, wrinkled, and age-spotted. She sighed. As much as she missed her husband, the daydream was worth it. Rose had never lost her love for him. They had a short, but wonderful life together.

Seven

*T*HAT NIGHT JENNA lay in bed listening to the crickets singing outside her open window. The light of the moon—so much bigger and brighter here in the pitch-black sky—illuminated the little cat Halloween figurines she had lined up on her dresser. With the air heavy and fragrant, she drifted into a deep sleep.

Her dream was fuzzy. She saw a young, thin woman wearing clothes from a different period writing on a piece of stationery. She looked familiar, but Jenna couldn't place her. Even the living room she was in was recognizable. Sort of. A man's voice called to the woman and she looked up, saying she was on her way. Quickly, she reapplied lipstick and tucked it into the pocket of her apron. She fussed with her blond hair as she walked to the front door. There, outside in the swell of humidity, stood a handsome man taking off his fine hat, gesturing to a Victrola…

The dream changed and Jenna was standing in front of the mill, except it wasn't the mill of today. It was exactly like the black and white picture she had seen with Tina in the library. Only now, it was in color and she wasn't looking at a picture. She was there. The sun was beating down, warming the top of her head. A gentle breeze stirred, brushing her long hair off her shoulders.

It was silent, except for the sound of horses' hooves clopping on the road behind her, and the rhythmic whoosh of the water wheel emptying into Orchard Creek. She stood there just staring at the mill, weighted with sadness until the horses were almost upon her. She then turned from the building with her head down, and walked quickly on the dusty path, her long skirts swirling around her legs, kicking up the dirt.

Deep down she worried she would be seen. Another part answered her concern. He never saw what was around him, unless it got in his way. Or threatened his wallet. When she was far enough away, she stopped and watched the men get out of the carriage. The one dressed in black with the bowler hat stumbled. His companions reached awkwardly for him, but he pushed their hands out of his way. Voices must have questioned him because all Jenna could make out was "right as rain, gentlemen." She knew the voice was Seth's.

A tightness built in her chest, and she moved along faster as adrenaline coursed through her veins. Anger moved her legs and heartache killed off another piece of her broken spirit.

The dream changed again, and Jenna opened her eyes, focusing on the full moon. The crickets were chirping loudly. She felt calm but had a sense of awareness, as if she knew she was dreaming. That happened sometimes, so she went with it, wondering where it would lead. She was standing at a wooden window ledge looking down at a small crab apple tree below her as she fiddled with her handkerchief. There was something wrong with this scene. She felt it, but she couldn't seem to pinpoint what it was. An urgent need tugged at her stomach. It was a longing she felt down to her toes, like a piece of her was missing. Elizabeth's name passed through her mind, as well as Joseph's. Like a whisper on a gentle breeze. It suddenly became harder for her to breathe. She struggled.

"Look-not-bored."

The wind blew on her face, clearing whatever obstruction was in her way, allowing her to breathe easy again. She savored the cool, strong breeze that carried the cinnamon smell of late fall. But it was mid-August. That wasn't right. Her long, white nightgown moved against her ankles. Something was wrong with that, too, Jenna thought. She shivered and wrapped her arms around herself to stay warm, concentrating on waking up, which she did. She felt the separation. In that twilight state of coming around where she knew she was no longer asleep, but too disoriented to know exactly where she was, she reached down to pull the blankets up. Vertigo took control and she practically fell over. Her legs held her at the last minute and the involuntary splaying of her hands found a solid surface to grab. A cold chill made its way down her back as she suddenly realized she wasn't in her bed.

A startled cry escaped Jenna's lips as she became fully awake. She was standing in front of her window, looking at the birch tree. A warm puff of air blew her hair over her shoulders, and she felt warm again in her oversized Mickey Mouse nightshirt. Slowly, Jenna walked across the room and got back into bed. She never knew she was a sleepwalker.

"I must be overtired," she said aloud, but sleep did not come soon. When she finally woke up the next morning, she was unable to remember exactly what she had dreamed about.

Jenna went to Tina's house after breakfast the next morning. Her friend was promptly disappointed that she didn't get to talk to Mrs. Forrester.

"I'm so bummed! She was really nice?" Tina asked.

"Very nice but a little lonely. She knows everything about this town; I learned a lot," Jenna said, relating what she learned. Both girls were swinging on the swing set in Tina's back yard. Tina taught her how to twirl the swing around in circles until it couldn't move anymore, then pick her feet up and spin to unwind. Jenna's hair flew out around her head. "You know what's really spooky, Tina?" Jenna asked. A wild idea had been forming since she woke up.

"What?"

"I think about them all the time. Elizabeth and Joseph. It feels like more, but I can't put my finger on it. Sorta like they're around me, but I haven't been paying attention."

"That's not spooky, it's weird."

"Well, there's something spooky about this mill and something about those people. Their names go through my head. A lot. I've been thinking about it, and I just have this sense, like I know how she feels. I think she'd be happy once she's with Joseph and will finally rest."

Tina faced Jenna, squinting from the glare of the sun. She placed her hands firmly on her slim hips, the sun's golden rays lending a glow to her very purple shorts. "You mean you understand how Elizabeth *felt*. Past tense, right? I learned that in Mrs. Bonney's class a few years ago. Besides, there's no way you'd know that."

"I know. That's why it's spooky."

"And by the way, how would we get them together?"

Without missing a beat Jenna replied, "I need to get into the mill at night." Her answer was full of confidence.

"I think too much unpolluted air is getting to your brain."

"Maybe." Jenna sounded defeated. She closed her eyes and tilted her head up, knowing how that must have sounded. It was almost how she was starting to feel. When she opened them again, she squinted at the sun directly over her. "Did you know back in the way olden days people had sundials to tell time? In the not so olden days farmers used to just look where the sun was in the sky. When it's directly overhead, like it is right now, that means it's noon. So, it's lunch time. Do you want to come with me to see Mrs. Forrester after we eat?"

Tina skidded to a stop, her pigtails bobbing back and forth. "I sure do!"

After Tina got her purse and applied her lip gloss, the girls biked across the bridge to East Abbey and took the left onto Sentinel. Longing grabbed Jenna from the other direction, making her sigh. The roof of the mill was just visible over the knolls.

They invented the Freeze Game when the gray Denim Miles Tour buses went by; holding still in whatever position they were in, letting the wind whip their hair around them. They laughed and goofed around as they made their way to Mrs. Forrester's, stopping along the way so Jenna could pick wildflowers.

Jenna bit her lip as she knocked and waited for the door to be answered. Maybe she should have asked first if Tina could join them. It was too late now. The door was opening.

"Good afternoon Miss Jenna," Mrs. Forrester exclaimed, her pale blue eyes lighting on her guest before wandering behind her. "I see I get to meet my admirer at last."

Tina solemnly walked up a step and held out her hand. "How do you do, ma'am. I'm Tina Levy. I'm sorry for being rude on my bike." The comment took the elder by surprise, and she laughed lightly, her face wrinkling in amusement.

"No harm done, dear. Come in, Miss Tina. I made cookies for a snack today."

"These are for you," Jenna announced proudly, presenting a fist full of ragweed, tiger lilies, and daisies.

"How sweet! Have a seat on the davenport while I get drinks." Mrs. Forrester gestured before walking away, leaving Tina confused. She tugged at her Jenna's shirt, nearly tipping Jenna over as she struggled to get her sneaker off.

"What the heck is that?" she hissed quietly.

"It's the couch. Be nice."

"Okay, but if she turns out to be like the witch in Hansel and Gretel and murders us in an old timey oven, I'll kill you."

Jenna rolled her eyes at her friend. They tip-toed to the flower-patterned couch and sat down on the very edge. Tina's eyes bugged out as she took in her surroundings. Jenna watched her face morph from anxious to curious to uncomfortable.

"It smells funny in here."

"It does not. Do you want to hear her stories or go back home?"

Tina was petulant. "Stay for stories."

"Good, I'm glad," said a voice in the entryway, "because I refreshed my memory by reading through the diary and remember a lot more than is printed there."

After a few cookies, Tina seemed to relax. Although she didn't drink as much of the lemonade as Jenna did, she didn't complain. Jenna almost mentioned the pink goo she left on the rim of her glass but decided to ignore it. Mrs. Forrester was drinking tea in a very delicate teacup, her legs swept to the side under her knee-length peach dress.

"I believe for a time my grandmother lived vicariously through Elizabeth Avery. That means she spent a lot of time writing about her because she wanted to be like her."

"She did?" Tina asked. She was pulling a crumb that fell on her chin back into her mouth.

"Who wouldn't want to be wooed by a handsome young man?" The expression on Tina's face needed no translation. Mrs. Forrester sighed. "Going steady. In a few years, when you start dating, you'll understand better. That was what Elizabeth and Joseph were doing. Even though they came from different backgrounds, they found something they shared in common. Both grew up without having money, although Joseph had his saved away for him. Elizabeth, who was the oldest, had to work to help support her family. Each felt they were stuck in a life they didn't like. Joseph had found out when he came of age that having money was not the answer to any of his problems. He wanted a simpler life. Elizabeth just wanted someone to love her for her.

"She complained to my grandmother that her parents were emotionally distant from her, having to rely on her to make ends meet, and even though Joseph was in a fixed arrangement for a wife, he planned on getting out of it. He did not care for the girl. It seemed she was hunting for a husband with a bank roll. Joseph had said Seth was trying to get tied to a family with a prestigious name." Mrs. Forrester stopped to sip her tea before continuing. "Seth had never noticed the petty goings on of his subordinates. It was beneath him. He—"

"Oh, like a caste system!" Tina suddenly exclaimed. She immediately cupped her hand over her mouth for interrupting. "Sorry, I remembered learning about that," she squeaked.

"Very good, Miss Tina! No, you're right. Back in those days one didn't mingle with people who were not in the same social circle and were different from them. And Seth hadn't realized his brother was in love with a lowly sewing maid. He probably wouldn't have seen it at all since they were very good at keeping it a secret. But as fall approached, the change in temperatures made quite a few of the workers sick. My grandmother knew Elizabeth was running a fever. Her face was flushed, and her hands trembled as she worked. Elizabeth had complained to her she wasn't sure how she was going to walk to work the next day feeling as weak as she was. Joseph must have been keeping an eye on her, as he usually did."

Another crumb fell out of Tina's open mouth, but she didn't notice this time, rapt in concentration. Mrs. Forrester kept going.

"The next morning Elizabeth was not waiting for my grandmother by her front gate to walk into town together, so she walked by herself. She was very surprised a short time later. She hadn't yet made it into the mill when she heard an approaching carriage and turned back toward the road. She smiled and shook her head in disbelief. Joseph had driven out to Elizabeth's house to pick her up for work."

Jenna and Tina sighed thinking about the romantic gesture. Their teen years really weren't that far off, and that appeal was not lost on them. Mrs. Forrester continued a bit more quietly. "Seth was there when they arrived. My grandmother told me she became so scared she dropped her eyes and hung her head to avoid the glare Seth gave Joseph. The atmosphere became very tense after that."

Tina's face was wide in awe, her mouth drawn up in a tiny "oh". Jenna's forehead was furrowed in anger. Mrs. Forrester realized these universal feelings bridged all generational gaps.

"Elizabeth was sorta like Cinderella, and Seth was kinda like the mean step-sisters. You know about Cinderella, right Mrs. Forrester?" Tina asked. Mrs. Forrester nodded.

"How about you help me with these dishes in the kitchen, and we let Jenna have a few minutes to look through the diary." Tina rose hesitantly, being very careful with the tiny china plates they had used for their cookies but didn't move further.

"I promise I won't turn the oven on." The soft smile set in the lines of her face was reassuring and Tina agreed. The hunger came back the moment the woman handed Jenna the black book. Jenna barely heard herself whisper "thank you" before she lost herself in the pages.

Today is Friday, October 3, 1896. We received our wages from Joseph as usual. I never imagined how hard I would work for these few coins. Elizabeth was given a whole dollar more. She's told me it is actually Joseph's own money he is giving her. It is to go to her family for their expenses, for she doesn't plan on staying in Orchard Creek much longer. Heaven have mercy on me if this diary gets into the wrong hands!

When she and Joseph met at the mill in the evenings they used to talk about all sorts of things. What her favorite Christmas hymn is, or her favorite flower. Now they are talking about serious topics of what their future plans are. Elizabeth had nothing specific until she met Joseph. She knows she is expected to help feed her family. Personal happiness like a husband and home are far from her for the time, even though she is at that age. Now I believe she will leave her family behind and run away with Joseph. But not yet. She wants to do this properly. Her handkerchief is not done, she needs more time. After she works twelve hours at Sawyer's Mill, she has hours of chores to go in between watching the baby or helping the girls with their studies. She barely sleeps at all! Disaster would have struck many times if I hadn't nudged her awake at the machines.

She is so focused on her handkerchief. I cannot believe how thick in the head she is if they are talking all but marriage, but she feels she won't know for sure until she presents this gift to him and he accepts. It's the one thing she can give him that will show the depth of her love and devotion to him. She says she dreams about it as well. For now, the best way I can help is to keep her awake while Mr. Sawyer walks through . . .

A rumbling of voices in the distance nagged at Jenna's mind and at first, she ignored them. She knew her eyes were open, and yet she felt as if she was asleep and in her own vivid dream.

"Jenna!" The voice was closer and insistent. Suddenly her head was whipped back and forth, making her teeth chomp down on her tongue. "Say something!"

"Ouch, that hurt! Stop!" Jenna hadn't realized she was staring at Tina, who had her fingers tight around her shoulders, digging into her skin. Jenna even felt like she had been sleeping because she was disoriented and wasn't aware of how much time had passed.

"Are you okay? We've been calling you for a while. You were really zoned out. Mrs. Forrester was using words like *cat tonic* and stuff."

"Oh, thank goodness you're back with us!" Mrs. Forrester exclaimed as she bustled into the room and abruptly stopped. She put a thin, wrinkled hand over her heart. The water in the glass she was holding threatened to spill over the rim.

"Sorry. I'm sorry. I'm fine."

Eight

FIVE MINUTES LATER she and Tina were biking back down the long drive. Tina had apparently given up her reservations about the older woman, and was chatting away about how much Mrs. Forrester knew about the movie *Cinderella*. Jenna was frowning. Her tongue was sore and she was in a sour mood from having been told they needed to put their visits on hold for a few days. Supposedly, there were old-lady chores that needed to be done and Mrs. Forrester couldn't receive visitors. Jenna knew the woman wasn't sure what was going on—she hardly did herself—but she knew she was being cut off from the diary.

They were a little over a week away from school starting and Jenna wanted to know every single word that was written in that book. That intense want she felt was back and worse than ever. There were pieces to this puzzle Jenna needed to find, and she shared her concerns with her Tina. Tina wondered if they should confide in a grown-up. Jenna was hesitant because of how strange it all sounded. For the time being, they decided to try to figure it out on their own.

Jenna and Tina visited Mrs. Forrester more than once over the last week of August, but only briefly, and the diary never came out. That need to know more was always there inside Jenna, wanting to get out. It was a struggle for her to keep that feeling at bay.

They sat on the davenport—as Mrs. Forrester liked to call it—and listened, wide-eyed, to her tales. Mrs. Forrester would bake breads and brownies and tell the girls stories of the town. The more she had the girls over, the more she became fond of them. Not all her anecdotes were so serious. They giggled at her hair-style when they saw pictures of her as a young girl. Tina was surprised that Mrs. Forrester only had a handful of classmates in her whole school.

Mrs. Forrester was amused to her to see Jenna and Tina trying to be polite and respectful to their elder as she had done when she was their age. She even treated them to a record or two on the Victrola. Jenna would smile contentedly while Tina sat with her mouth wide open. Jenna told her she was especially impressed with how many months of extra work Mr. Forrester had to put in at his job to earn enough to give his true love the Victrola for their first wedding anniversary. It was almost like Jenna knew her husband would do that.

For Jenna, the dreams of the mill continued. Every dream started out at a window with her either holding the ledge or holding a handkerchief. The words "look-not-bored" whispered through her mind as well as the names of Elizabeth and Joseph. Sometimes they were going about their business as if Jenna were transported in time just to observe. Sometimes she was at the looms herself or was avoiding Seth. At others, she was pacing the floors upstairs, her stomach fluttering with nervousness. In every dream there was the emptiness of heartache, longing, and a need to fulfill. Each morning the details would fade with the sunlight, no matter how hard Jenna tried to remember them. All she could recall was generalities and the passage of time. Slowly, over time, she began to notice how the longing became stronger. Elizabeth and Joseph were definitely having conversations and moving about, but the particulars were absent. It almost made Jenna feel homesick on the mornings she awoke and realized she hadn't dreamed about the mill at all.

On Monday the fourth of September, after her almost-teenager chores were done, Jenna biked with Tina to see Toby in the Town Hall. She talked about Elizabeth and Joseph almost the whole way there. Tina was beginning to understand this interest wasn't going away. Jenna wasn't going to drop it until they tried to get into the mill. Toby was just the guy to see.

Tom Jacobs closed the heavy book he was working on with a start and stood up. He was muscular and fit, with short blond hair the same color as his son's. It was easy to see what Toby would look like in another fifteen years or so. "No, Toby, that's out of the question."

"But Dad, we just want to look around," Toby explained.

"I said 'no.' If your mother ever found out, she'd skin us both."

Toby walked away dejectedly, his dad following as far as the entryway before leaving for the bathroom. Toby went back to the girls sitting at the far table. Jenna looked up from a book of her own with a smile that quickly fell away.

"Any luck?"

"Dad said 'no,'" Toby said glumly. "Are you sure the ghosts are back? We've never had anything going on like this before you moved here."

"Oh. Tina said you'd seen them. Haven't you?" Jenna asked

in all innocence. Toby's face became a brilliant red before he looked down sheepishly.

"Um, not really, I guess. I can't be sure." He fidgeted uncomfortably. Jenna didn't like to see him like that and tried to move away from the embarrassing topic. "There has to be another way to get in there. Someone else must have a key." She sat there thinking, Toby crossed his arms to pout, and Tina continued to look at the artifacts on the shelf behind her. She leaned forward, then gasped, almost tripping over her feet.

"What's the matter?" Jenna and Toby asked in unison.

"I never saw it before!" Tina said as she moved closer to the wall. Her eyes never left the small picture hanging above the pair of granny boots in the display case.

"I'm beginning to understand why Jenna feels the need to get into the mill. Look at this picture."

All three of them looked closely at a picture from 1896 of the mill workers. There, sitting on the floor closest to the camera, was a young girl—who looked exactly like Jenna.

"Yeah! That's who you reminded me of!" Toby said.

"This is why we never saw it before," Jenna breathed. "The girls' names are listed by first initial, then last name. This says E. Avery."

"That's Elizabeth," Tina finished.

"That's cool," Toby said, smiling at Tina.

Jenna took down the picture and stared at it. She cocked her head to one side as if she were trying to figure something out. It was very disorienting, as if she were looking at someone else inside her face. Voices rushed at her as if she were hearing a year's worth of conversations all at the same time. A lifetime of emotions wrapped around her all packed into mere seconds. She stood there, motionless, for what seemed to be forever, on sensory overload. Tina and Toby were talking away excitedly to each other. All of a sudden, Jenna's trembling hands put the picture down as she started to talk. Tina and Toby looked at each other in confusion. Jenna mumbled but didn't make sense. Tina thought she heard the word "bored" but not much else. Suddenly Jenna shuddered, her eyes rolled back in her head, and she collapsed to the floor. The other two scrambled to help her. Jenna sat up almost immediately, calmer but still dazed, holding her head.

"What happened?" she asked.

"I think you just fainted," Toby said worriedly. "Do you want me to get my dad?" He was shaking his head back and forth, not sure what to do. He looked over at Tina for her input. Tina, dumbfounded, her eyes huge, said nothing.

"No, don't be silly. I feel fine now. Just for a minute, I felt so tired." They helped Jenna get up, and she sat down in the closest chair.

"Are you sure, 'cause that freaked me out. Maybe you should go see a doctor or something," Toby suggested, his hands quivering slightly. He was really concerned.

Mr. Jacobs walked back in the room and looked around quizzically. "What was all that noise?"

"I'm sorry, Mr. Jacobs. I fell out of my chair," Tina answered quickly.

"Please be careful in here." Mr. Jacobs shook his head and walked back out.

"Why did you just say you're 'not bored'? And what does a handkerchief have to do with anything?" Toby asked, puzzled.

All at once, Jenna remembered the people in her dreams. She remembered the window, the tree, the cold wind, and the pale blue handkerchief.

Tina still looked a bit apprehensive. "That's not the first

time you've said you weren't bored, remember? You said it a few days ago."

"I have been dreaming about them! Holy cow, I've been dreaming about them a lot! I say the same thing in my dreams. I wonder if there's any way we could get them back together."

"Are you sure you didn't hit your head?" Tina asked. "We're talking about dead people here."

"I'm serious."

"They're gone. It's fun to explore with you, and listen to Mrs. F's stories, and imagine—especially around trick-or-treating time—but I didn't really think you were seriously serious. You know that's impossible," Tina lectured sternly.

"I'm dead serious." Jenna's answer was firm, but an air of concern and apprehension crept into the words. The two girls faced each other, brown eyes to blue, in a stand-off. Toby watched them, intrigued. His face had finally returned to a more natural color.

"This isn't normal." Tina's confidence was wavering.

"Did I act normal when I was saying 'look, not, bored'?" Jenna asked. Her eyebrows were knitted with worry. "Can you explain how the girl in the picture could be my twin?"

"No," answered Tina, chewing on a fingernail. She could tell Jenna was truly freaked.

"And since I've been here it seems I have some connection. I even look like her! That's why I feel it's me she's trying to contact."

"What's happening?" Tina asked in a sing-song voice. It was the same line Drew Barrymore said in the movie *E.T., the Extra Terrestrial*. "I just had a shiver go down my back."

"What does this mean?" Toby asked.

Tina shook her head as if she couldn't believe what she was

going to say. "Something's been happening with Jenna; I've been watching it grow. I think it means she can help. First, we need to get into the mill. Then we see what happens next."

Toby glanced at the door his dad walked through. "How do we do that? My dad said 'no.' How do we do that when we're just kids and have to start school in nine more days?"

"We need to tell someone. Maybe Mrs. Forrester will believe us. In the meantime, we keep working on it when we can, I guess," Jenna offered, shrugging.

THAT NIGHT, JENNA'S dream started in a familiar place: the town hall's room with the mural. The clock on the far wall looked just like the ones in school. It was 6:45. It must have been a yearly meeting because it was full of people sitting on metal chairs, and some on the raised dais. The predominant hair color of the elevated section, the board members, was gray. Everyone was casually chatting to themselves, a few looking at their watches, one or two fanning themselves with a handout; the meeting apparently hadn't started yet. The mural was in front of Jenna's vision, but conversation distracted her.

"Keep your fingers crossed, Mark. This is the year."

"I'd pray instead, Tom, but it's a practical matter. This renovation makes too much sense to keep getting voted down. I don't understand why we're still here trying to sell it."

Tom Jacobs looked at his friend and how his smile didn't touch his eyes behind his glasses. *I hope his frustration doesn't make him quit. I'm not ready to give up yet.*

Jenna realized the men didn't look much different to her. This was confirmed when she spotted a turquoise and brown poster board on one of bare walls, advertising the Harvest

Festival with proceeds benefitting the Orchard Creek Ospreys marching band. It was dated September 29, 1995.

"Well, you know," Mr. Jacobs replied quietly, stealing a glance at their elderly fellow members sitting behind them, "because the old folks don't have much else to do other than gossip."

Mr. Levy tilted his head from side to side as if weighing the likelihood. "True. They should stick to bingo or sitting around listening to Liszt or Wagner."

"Huh. Wagner." There was a moment of comfortable silence between the two of them. Mr. Jacobs sighed and stared at the black and white picture of the mill on the cover of the handout. "Hey, have I told you that building reminds me of Franz Wagner Wright."

"Who? Oh, that obscure architect guy. Yes, every single year at the walk-through when we pay out of pocket for inspection."

"Hey, it's a good idea to be ready for anything, and we both agreed to do it," Mr. Jacobs reminded him. A few more people joined the dais, calling the meeting to order. "All I'm asking is that you trust this will happen. Just give it a few more years…"

Jenna's dream faded and changed from the town hall to the dirt road in front of the mill. A heavy cloak covered her long skirt. The air was cold and little puffs of condensation formed as she breathed. Her fingers worried the lace trim of the handkerchief from corner to corner, over and over in rhythm to her steps. Something made her nervous despite being excited. She walked faster…

Nine

*V*ERY QUICKLY THE week passed as everyone was busy
getting ready for school. There was no time to visit
Mrs. Forrester. Jenna and Peter had last-minute
glitches with registering for classes they had to straighten out;
they also had to go on tours of their respective schools. They had
to get haircuts, summer pictures, and shop for school clothes
and supplies. Her family also took an extended weekend to
Marine Land in Canada, which was fun. Jenna knew she was
still having dreams of the mill. There was a lot of talking and
moving about, but some of the details were too fuzzy for her
to remember when she woke up. The only thing she knew for
sure was the sense of urgency to do something. It was very
frustrating not being able to do anything about it.

School started late in Orchard Creek, and Jenna, Tina,
and Toby were too busy settling into their new classes and
homework to do anything about the mill for the rest of that
week and the next. Toby had his own issues to worry about.
He felt he hadn't made much progress during the summer to

overcome his shyness, even though he was fine around Jenna. Approaching her at the mill that night had been a challenge for him. He had pushed himself to do it and tried to remember that worked out okay. He had not looked forward to another year of harassment and taking it. It wasn't as obvious as he thought it was, but the snide remarks from his classmates bothered him in a large way, and he wanted to get over it.

Although he had shot up an inch or two over the summer, he still felt like a runt being almost a half-foot shorter than the other boys. "You'll get there," his parents kept telling him. The encouragement didn't make him feel better. His self-esteem took another blow when he still hadn't managed to speak without blushing. It made him feel weak. He had been hoping to have Tina and Jenna in his classes. At least he felt more comfortable around them. Both girls were in a lot of the same classes, but none with him. The only time they were together was the same lunch hour. So, he kept to himself and tried not to be intimidated.

On Monday, the twenty-fifth of September, Jenna again found herself looking out at a yearling crabapple tree, holding onto the window ledge. She felt a harsh wind that chilled her yet wondered why her hair wasn't moving. Her bare shoulders trembled and she thought, foolishly, that maybe the blue handkerchief she was gripping would warm her. Handkerchief? Jenna looked down at the delicate, sky blue handkerchief with white lace trim. Why this was important?

"Please-look. Not-bored," she heard herself repeat. Jenna could feel a need and desperation inside her that stopped her breath. She couldn't seem to breathe. Joseph's name drifted through her thoughts once again. She began to gasp and sat bolt upright, wide awake, in her bed. The coldness and tightness in her throat seemed to peel away from her, and once again she was warm and breathing normally. This time the vision stayed with her, as well as the previous dream at the mill, fresh in every detail. She had a nagging feeling of familiarity with that window. It taunted her, just beyond her reach, as her head swam with the intense feelings surrounding her dreams.

"There's something I need to do. I need to help her. I can feel it," she muttered. She stared at the ceiling for a long while, wide awake. Her thoughts were a jumble of emotions bouncing in her head like captured bees. A common thought kept coming back of Jenna giving something away. It never got clearer than that.

The next day Jenna noticed there was a lot more excitement in school than usual. The first roller skating party of the year was being held in the gym on Wednesday night. There were poster boards everywhere, especially the cafeteria. Jenna counted seven as she ate her lunch. A girl from the student council sat outside the bookstore selling tickets. There was even a line.

"Roller blading?" Jenna asked as she finished her chocolate milk.

"No," Tina giggled, looking over at Toby. He had a smirk on his face as if they shared an inside joke. "Roller-skating. As in, ugly white shoes with four wheels, a DJ, and a disco ball hanging from the ceiling."

"Really?" Jenna didn't have this back in Steel City.

"Welcome to Orchard Creek," Toby announced formally.

"Do you guys go?"

"I don't go," answered Toby, his smirk falling away. Jenna's brows shot up.

"Are you too good for it, or is it you're really bad at it?"

"Uh oh, Tobe. She's on to you, now."

"Do you go, Tina?" Rounding on her friend, Toby tried to hide a grin.

"I've gone once," Tina replied defensively. Toby slapped her on the back.

"At the beginning of seventh grade, maybe. There are four every year, Jenna."

"What's wrong with it? Do only the dweebs go?" she asked in a hushed tone. Both friends shook their heads. "Then we should go! It'd be fun. I've only ice skated at the rink in the city, but I'm sure it's pretty much the same."

Toby blinked, his eyes tight as the realization hit him. "Really?"

"Sure." She noticed a look of nervousness crossing his face. She knew him well enough by now to know how uncomfortable he was around others, and that Tina would follow her if she went. "We're all okay when we're with each other, so we'll stick together. It's tomorrow night so there's no stressing about it. I'll even buy my ticket now." She bent down and pulled the tiny purse that sat atop her books out from under her seat. "I have money from chores. Only the lame don't have fun. Even in Orchard Creek."

"Okay, I'm in," Tina said, taking up the challenge. "I still have birthday money from last month." She fumbled with the tiny clasp on the pink smiling kitty purse that was ever present across her chest.

The hand that Toby had curled around his lunch tray squeezed and released a few times, his face a screen of revolving emotions. One finally won out. "I think it's lame that some people have birthdays so early in the school year no one knows them, so they don't get as many presents." Toby took out the cloth wallet from his jeans pocket and opened it, the Velcro making a ripping sound. He had just enough to cover them both. "I told you I owed you one anyway. Happy belated birthday, Tina."

Jenna made her way around the tables to the line and the two others followed. "I've got your back, Toby," Jenna said, casually. She nudged him with her shoulder, lowering her voice. "Don't forget the power of confidence and having friends."

Toby looked up at her and she held his gaze. She knew. He had dreamed about that day not too long ago, after thinking about the memory. "You heard what happened last year?" Jenna tilted her head to the side as if something didn't quite make sense.

"I guess I did."

"Is this the latest talk in the hallways?" There was an edge to his voice.

Jenna's face cleared as she thought about it. "No. I haven't heard anyone saying anything in between classes."

Toby sighed. With effort, he kept eye contact with her. "I didn't know what to do." His voice was barely audible.

"Well," Jenna lowered her eyes to the floor and kicked at a straw wrapper before bending her knees with her arms out in front, her hands flat in a defensive position, "learn something to protect yourself for when we're not together." He gave her a shy smile and returned the bump. Next in line, she gave the girl five dollars and stuffed the ticket in her front pocket so she wouldn't lose it. She smiled, pleased.

Jenna skipped the length of the driveway after getting off the bus. Her mom was working on the computer. As a drug rep, she was always on the computer when she wasn't on the road visiting doctors.

"Hi Mom! Can I go to the roller skating party tomorrow night at school? 'Cause I already bought my ticket. It's from six to eight-thirty and the teachers will be there to make sure we all behave. Please?"

The apprehension Jenna initially faced turned into happiness. When her mother smiled, she really was beautiful. Jenna knew not liking the traditional things girls liked upset her mom. A pang of guilt crossed her conscience. For the first time in her life she realized how different she was from everyone else. She hadn't been a typical daughter.

"I remember roller skating when I was your age. It sounds like fun, honey. I suppose I can drop you off right after dinner and Dad can pick up."

"If you take me and Tina, I think her mom can bring us home."

"Okay. I'm glad you're finding something suitable for your age."

"Sure, Mom." As much as she felt good about pleasing her mother, she felt she was unfaithful to the place that took up a good portion of her attention.

The next evening at dinner Jenna finished her homemade mac and cheese as her eyes darted to the clock on the wall every few minutes.

"Excited?" her dad asked, clearly amused. His elbows were on the table with his hands holding his milk glass. Her mother had her head resting in the palm of her hand, watching her brother. Peter was busy lining up his elbow macaroni in rows across his plate, his lower lip jutting out as he concentrated. Jenna had a mouthful and could only mumble.

"Mmm hmm." She got up, still chewing, and pushed her chair in. "Dad, can I have some money for a drink at intermission?"

"Intermission for roller skating? Hmph. Let me get my

wallet. I see they thoroughly work the crowds around here, too. Intermission, my Aunt Fanny."

Peter snorted and almost choked. "Ha, ha. Dad said 'fanny.'"

"Eat up, Pete. Be careful, Jenna. We're out in the country now. This place is full of wild and reckless natives just waiting to get you sweaty and thirsty before charging for water." He handed her a few dollars. "Where are you keeping this?"

"In my pocket. Tina said they don't have lockers. People just put their coats and shoes on the floors. I don't want my purse stolen."

"Good idea."

"Come on, Mom. I don't want to be late." Her parents smiled as she tugged on her coat, flipping her braided hair over the top and heading to the car. Her mom was just about to pull out of the driveway when she yelled.

"Ooh, stop! My ticket is in the pants I wore yesterday!"

Her mother backed the car up, the windshield wipers scraping against the glass from the light rain that was falling. "You're lucky I didn't do the wash last night."

"Yeah, that would have been bad."

Jenna and Tina met Toby just inside the school doors. Thick, gray rugs were placed everywhere to keep the floors dry. Not sure what to do, they followed the kids in front of them, moving out of the way when a few boys began roughhousing. Immediately Mrs. Goldberg, the principal, pulled them off to the side to dole out the discipline.

They waited in line with their tickets, got their hands stamped, and advanced to the counter where there were several rows of portable storage units that held all the roller skates. Three men bustled about for the correct sizes and gender, goofing up with the girl named Fay in front of them by giving her a tiny size eleven instead of a seven. Toby had to wait longer than the rest because Oren Delis from Home Economics class budged back in line, needing to exchange for a bigger size. The inside of the gym wasn't visible from their location but random lights flashed out at times and the thumping of music enticed them. It seemed to take forever.

Once they had their skates, they were told to keep anything wet off to the side, by the display case of baseball and football trophies, and follow the black rugs to the gym. They found a spot on the floor for their things and put their skates on.

Tina had difficulty getting up, her arms pin-wheeling as she stood, a goofy grin on her face. Somehow Toby had it mastered after only a few minutes. With a smug smile on his face and his arms crossed, he watched Jenna and Tina as they practiced on the rugs along with several other classmates.

"Suck in your butt, Tina, you look silly."

"Shut up, Toby!" the girls hollered in unison.

"We just need to get the feel for it," Jenna explained as her feet scissored back and forth. "How'd you do it?"

"I figured out where my center of gravity is. Then it's easy," Toby replied.

"How'd you know that?" Tina asked, exasperated. She was bent over and inching along with her bottom still stuck out.

"I dunno."

"Maybe it's a math thing. I'm not very good in math," admitted Jenna, emulating Toby. She stood straighter and began to hold her own.

"This isn't fun, Jenna. It's stressing me out," Tina complained, trying to stand like her friends. She ended up bobbing up and down like a duck as her feet alternately took off on their own by the wheels. Jenna was now able to look around them. There were at least a dozen kids on the rugs with them.

"We're not the only ones, Tina. There are lots of people figuring this out." Very slowly Tina stood up. She didn't move.

"I'm gonna fall down."

"I bet I will, too. What's the worst that can happen?"

"I could break my leg. Or my arm. Then I wouldn't be able to play the vio—" a slow grin filled Tina's face. "Oh, I get it. Ha ha."

"We'll be careful. Come on." Finally, they ventured out onto the gym floor. It was a bit scary leaving the resistance from the rugs, but noting how several others were still struggling, they wouldn't be drawing much attention.

The gymnasium was not transformed as Jenna thought it would be. All the wooden bleachers were pushed back against the wall just like they were for gym class, except for one wall where they were out just a little, creating two rows of seats. Colored lights scattered around replaced the regular lights creating a nightclub atmosphere, complete with the huge disco ball Tina and Toby talked about. It made her giggle. Off in the adjacent corner from the bleachers was a DJ and his set-up. Loud music was already playing, setting the tempo of the evening with the bass drums.

There was a bottleneck of kids standing and falling in the entryway. Mr. VanNifen, the shop teacher, was trying to get them moved to the bleachers. Only a few kids were proficient enough to be skating normally. Cat calls, whistles, and laughter reached their ears, and every second or so someone else would lose their balance and ungracefully land on the floor.

Knowing she was responsible for dragging her friends to this, Jenna plucked up her own courage and motioned for them to follow on the floor. She joined the others fumbling with their balance as they traveled counterclockwise around the gym. By the next hour the music had gotten louder, and the crowd skated faster as most got the hang of it. Even now there were those in the middle of the gym stuck, standing still or shuffling their feet along, barely moving. People like that had already caused several pileups. Miss Tyson was out there like a referee, skating backwards, leading the slower learners away from the others. She was Jenna's and Tina's English teacher, and was a lot of fun. She wore brown stirrup pants under a long tan sweater, her brown ponytail whipping around her head as she weaved in and out of the seventh and eighth graders.

Almost two hours in, all three were laughing and breathless as they circled around. Intermission had come and gone. Everyone socialized with their friends. There were the cliques, of course. Clusters of girls here and groups of boys there, trying to talk to each other over the music. Some girls were sitting on the bleachers, either crying from some boy drama, or angry from the couples skate a few minutes before. The DJ kept the tunes rolling to the different skates. Girls Only skate was coming up. Toby even went out briefly for Boys Only and seemed to be having a good time. It was All Skate now and both Tina and Toby went on their own way from time to time. Jenna was alone. She liked the feel of the draft that blew against her face as she glided across the room. She crossed her feet to turn when she reached an end, the way Miss Tyson did, and felt free. It loosened her worries about the mill. That nagging feeling was still there, though. It always was.

Just then a cascade of events happened. Mary Sol, one of the fumblers near the middle, lost her balance and bumped into Timmy Meecum, who in turn ricocheted into Jenna. Timmy regained his balance but Jenna didn't. She tried to go down on one knee but it was swept away from her by a girl she didn't know who had been too close behind her.

Ten

"HANG ON, I'LL help you," she heard Timmy say as he turned around and came back against the tide of kids. He was a sweet guy who was always eager to help Miss. Waverly with the AV stuff in science. There was always one kid like him in every class. By now the skaters had started to detour around them. Out of nowhere, Miss Tyson appeared and took one arm while Timmy took the other to help her stand. Jenna's ankle ached.

"Are you okay? Can you skate back to the door?" Miss Tyson smelled like the spearmint gum she chewed. Jenna nodded as she recalled how they were forbidden to chew gum in class. As soon as she answered, Timmy skated off. The teacher helped her navigate the way through the crowd to the door, and directed her to the nurse's office. She peeled her skates off and hobbled to Mrs. Travers. She was an elderly nurse who pretended not to smoke even though the smell came off her clothes with her every move.

There were two other kids sitting on the narrow beds.

One had a bag of ice on his elbow, and the other was getting a bandage on her skinned knee.

"Oh, no, not another," Jenna heard her say with a sigh as the nurse used her palms on her thighs to stand up. She was on the heavy side and wore a gray velour sweat ensemble. Jenna thought it wasn't the best material for her figure. Maybe the nurse hoped it would be a slow night for her. A lanky kid with curly blond hair stuck his head in the doorway, all out of breath.

"Ryan, Katie told Mike she'd go out with you!" The boy with the elbow injury dropped the bag of ice the same time his mouth dropped open.

"I'm okay now, Mrs. Travers. Thanks!" He was out the door a moment later, demanding more details from his friends. The nurse sighed again and patted the girl's leg.

"You're all set. Stay away from your sister out there." The girl sniffled and limped off.

"Ankle?" Mrs. Travers asked. She put her fists on her generous hips and went to the fridge. "Anything else hurt?"

"No, ma'am." Jenna took a seat and took off her sock as Mrs. Travers returned to examine her foot.

"So polite! You must not be from around here." Jenna wasn't sure if she was being serious or kidding. She answered in the affirmative anyway and introduced herself.

"It's very nice to meet you, Jenna. This doesn't look too bad, but let's keep some ice on it for a few minutes." She returned to her desk for the large coffee cup there and sat heavily in her chair, scribbling in a log with her free hand.

"So, what do you think about Orchard Creek?"

"It's quiet here," Jenna said. It was the first thing that popped out of her mouth.

"That it is, I'm sure. Do you like school?"

"Yes, I especially like Miss Tyson's and Mrs. Russell's classes." The ice was making her ankle feel better already.

"I imagine you're very good in English."

"Actually, History is my best class. I love anything old. I used to live in Steel City. It was okay until they started all the improvement projects and ruined everything."

"Well, you are in luck because this is a very old town and it fights back sometimes when we attempt to fix it up. We've tried but it hardly ever seems to work out very well." Mrs. Travers took another sip of her coffee.

"Wow. Really?"

"Yes. Let's see. The steeple of First Methodist on Elm Street was struck by lightning the year I was born. After a lot of work, they replaced it only for the whole church to burn down a few months later. They rebuilt it, of course, with the one standing there today, so it finally worked out.

"There was an inn over on Reginald that couldn't keep guests. For some reason, there was something about the electricity that constantly shorted. It didn't make sense because it was wired correctly and passed the scrutiny of many inspections. It was a shame, too. The location was perfect for those traveling up and down the interstate between Canada and Pee-Aye, the amenities were generous and the prices were reasonable. The owners had it rewired at least twice to no avail. They sold it and the new owners brought in their own electrician, but it didn't matter. They had the same luck. I believe it changed hands a few more times but nothing could make it profitable. Eventually it just sat there and started to deteriorate before it was torn down. The lot still remains empty.

"Oh, and speaking of empty, there's Sawyer's Mill. It's on the west end of town on Sentinel. Have you heard of it?"

When Jenna's eyes got big and she nodded, the woman continued. "The year of my communion there was a restoration movement. Lots of hustle and bustle with construction trucks and such. My friends and I would watch after school. The outside was fixed up nice and fancy, restoring the trim and molding. I even think they made sure the place would pass inspection. It was a cheerful yellow if I remember correctly.

"The inside gave them a lot of trouble. The finish date was moved several times due to all the accidents. My father said some of those workers weren't the most reliable and made their boss look bad, but they worked hard from what I could see. Rumors started to spread around town of it being haunted, especially one particular room. More serious accidents happened there. Some people thought it was sabotage by either the construction guys or those who fueled the stories. Union folks showed up but everyone was doing what they were supposed to be doing. They stopped everything when the foreman was killed late that autumn. There were witnesses and they all said the same thing. It shouldn't have been possible."

"What happened to him?" Jenna whispered. Mrs. Travers was quiet a moment, lost in her thoughts.

"I'd rather not say. That was my Uncle Ted. He was such a great man. He didn't deserve to die." She busied herself with straightening papers of who had come in with an injury or ailment. "Now, let's check that ankle of yours." Jenna moved it from side to side and up and down. It no longer hurt. She wanted to ask more but decided she didn't want to upset her.

"It feels better."

"There's no swelling that would indicate anything worse. You are good to go. Be careful, though. God didn't intend for us to travel around that fast. If He did, we would have been born with wheels instead of feet."

Jenna just stepped out of the room when she ran into Toby with Tina right behind him.

"Oh, Jenna, there you are!" he exclaimed, relieved. "We couldn't find you. What happened? Are you okay?" Tina's eyes appeared over Toby's shoulder.

"Was that you that wiped out with Mary?" Tina asked, walking around him. Disappointed, Jenna finally realized they were both in their sneakers and kids were pouring out of the gym, sweaty and red-faced. Sade's "Smooth Operator" was turned up loudly. "We couldn't see with all the bodies in the way. She caused, like, three pile-ups tonight. I think Mrs. Goldberg told her she needed to stay on the rug before she really got someone hurt. That girl has no balance."

"If I recall you weren't so graceful two hours ago," Toby retorted. Tina squinted at him, her face a grimace that said to back off.

"Did you both have fun?" Jenna asked as she gingerly walked back to her belongings. The smell of stinky feet and body odor permeated the air.

"Yeah, I guess I did have fun. Boy, it stinks like a brother in here!" Tina announced before a fit of giggles erupted. Jenna joined her while Toby rolled his eyes and shook his head.

"I had fun, too."

"Let that be a lesson to you," Jenna said with mock importance. "No harm done." They waited in a line outside the awning of the school along with the other hundred kids as car upon car pulled up, picked up and left. The rain was illuminated by the headlights, making the parking lot a sea of vehicle creatures with eyes that swished instead of blinked. They finally found the car Tina's mom was driving. Tina sat in the back seat with Jenna, her head against the window as she yawned and told her mom how great it had been. Toby was chatting with Mrs. Levy. Jenna's mind once again filled with thoughts of Elizabeth and Joseph. This time the sober reality of people being killed in the mill made her more uneasy than usual. What if what happened a few decades ago and what Mrs. Forrester were saying were actually true? Would something bad happen if they got into the mill?

Her dream that night was one of nervousness, and it wasn't the skating party that was on her mind. She was at the window again, the tiny, bare crabapple tree swaying with the sharp wind. One hand caressed the wooden ledge while the other firmly held the handkerchief.

"Please-look-not-bored," she heard herself say while Joseph's name floated through her mind. Somehow, she knew time was an important factor.

Between school, homework, chores, and family obligations, time flew. The leaves changed from green to vibrant reds, oranges, and yellows before fading and falling, leaving skeleton-like soldiers to watch over the town. Attentions turned from pool games to football games. Sunlight didn't last as long as the dog days of summer either. As the sunlight dimmed, the smell of drying foliage mixed with the crisp, cool air announcing the arrival of October's autumn. On Saturday the tenth, Jenna and Tina found themselves together at the Historical Association, anxious and without any pressing errands. Tina had called Toby, who said he'd be there with his dad. His mom was doing some early Christmas shopping with her girlfriends, and Toby would have been home alone. He was bored and unable to help out and was up for their company. His dad was doing leg work on the phone after getting a lead for one of the machines like the ones that the mill used to use. The girls planned on visiting

Mrs. Forrester at one, so they hung out there as patiently as they could. Jenna described her latest dream in detail. She was getting worried.

"What's so special about a blue handkerchief anyway?" Tina asked, puzzled.

"And why would you say you're not bored in a dream? It must mean something. How many times have you've said that now?" added Toby.

"I don't know. A lot. I feel it's a message. I just can't figure it out. Ugh!" Jenna growled as she rubbed her forehead, looking up at the picture of Elizabeth on the wall.

"Okay, let's break this down," Toby started. Despite his shyness, he was the levelheaded and analytical one of the group. "Where are you when you have this dream?"

"I think I'm in my bedroom. It feels like a bedroom. And I'm looking out my window. Only it's not my window because my window has a birch tree outside. In the dream it's a little crabapple tree. There are still some tiny apples on it."

"Lately you've felt like the mill is, like, calling you, right?"

"Yes, but the mill has Pound apples and Macs, not crabapples."

"You are a bit infatuated with the mill, though. And now you think this dream has something to do with Elizabeth?" Toby asked to clarify.

"Yes. The things I'm thinking of in my dream don't seem right to me. The need to do something makes me feel anxious, and their names repeat in my head over and over."

"Do you think all this has something to do with how much you look like Elizabeth Avery?" Toby continued.

"Yeah, I guess so. But I hadn't even seen pictures of her when I started feeling like this."

"Hmm." All three were stumped. Tina was just starting to say she hoped Mrs. Forrester would be able to help, since she knew so much about the mill, when her father approached their table.

"Hi kids. Tina, I thought you might like to know where we stand on the renovations to the old mill since you've been so interested in it lately. It looks like everything might actually go through if we can convince Mrs. Forrester to consent. She's on the town board, and her vote really will make or break this."

"What does that mean exactly?" Jenna asked.

"It's simple in theory," Mr. Levy began. "The town has a certain amount of money, like an allowance, to use for the whole year. Certain projects need the funds so they propose and introduce what they would use the money for. The board gathers the requests and the members vote on them. They decide on the dollar amount and where the money will go."

"Why do you say it's simple in theory?" Tina asked, as she picked the remaining nail polish from her fingers. She never really understood the process.

"Well, we ask to renovate the mill every year, but it's always turned down. Mrs. Forrester influences the older members on the board. One or two passes away each year, but they've always held the majority. Thomasina Mahew died two months ago. It's now very close, and Toby's dad and I believe it will come down to one vote."

Hearing this news, all three looked at each other excitedly. Maybe they could get into the mill this way.

"That is, if we can get approval by October fifteenth. That's the deadline for this year's budget. If it gets rejected, it'll be another year before they reconsider it again. I know I work here part time, but next year I hope to take over the super's position at my regular job when he retires, so I'll be really busy. There's a lot of paperwork involved, and with all the red tape, I'm not sure if I want to go through all this trouble again. It's getting old."

His eyes wandered to the tiny sign that was over the door, and he continued to ramble. "I'd love for Tom and myself to flip the building and do it ourselves, but even with my expertise I can't manage the funds we'd need." He paused and frowned. Tina looked at Toby, who looked at Jenna. They were all clueless. "Stubborn locals with their legends and tall tales do nothing but impede productivity." Mr. Levy snapped out of his ruminations and looked at three very confused faces. "Sorry, kids. I must have had a senior moment of my own. Well, I know you girls have been visiting Mrs. Forrester quite a bit this summer. See what you can do," Mr. Levy directed.

"Thanks, Dad! I think we might be able to help on this one," Tina said enthusiastically as her father smiled at them. She turned to Jenna, her face serious. "Maybe, since Mrs. Forrester knows so much about Elizabeth, we should talk with her about this."

"I've been thinking the same thing. I've wanted to go see her so badly, but with school, I haven't had time," Jenna said after Mr. Levy went back into his office. She checked her watch, her face lighting up. "Anyway, it'll be nice that Toby can join us today. Right Toby?"

Toby looked down at his sneakers. "Do you really think she wouldn't mind me coming along?" he asked, suddenly tentative. "You know, there's so much tension with her and my dad and Tina's dad."

"I think she'd really like you once she gets to know you," Jenna answered. Her tone was matter of fact.

They all got up and left on their bikes. Toby thought he'd figure out what to say during the ride to Mrs. Forrester's, but it was shorter than he thought. Soon he was there with the girls. He took a deep breath to muster some courage.

Eleven

"COME IN. I'VE been expecting you both. Ah, the young Mr. Jacobs is here too, very well," Mrs. Forrester responded as the three nervously stood at her door. "Toby, you are welcome to come in." An audible sigh of relief came from Toby, who immediately realized how loud he was and began to redden.

Mrs. Forrester felt the need to clarify. "Toby, I have issues with your father's proposal, not with your father or you. Do you understand?"

Toby nodded 'yes.' He gave it his best effort to look at her directly.

"Now, come along. I'm too old to be chasing grasshoppers and crickets should they jump in while the door is opened. Presently now." She gently nudged them inside.

Once they knew Toby was welcomed, they initially forgot to mention the mill project. So much had happened since the girls last visited their excitement about relating all the coincidences to Mrs. Forrester took precedence.

Tina couldn't wait and started in as they were led to the parlor. "We found a picture of Elizabeth at the Historical Association and she looks just like Jenna! What do you think about that? Because when Jenna saw it, she actually fainted and fell on the floor."

"I've been dreaming about the mill for weeks now. I don't know why and I think it's driving me crazy. I also had a dream again of being in a window above a tiny crabapple tree. I didn't remember the first one, but I remembered it after this last time. Oh, and I was holding a handkerchief! Tell me about that Handkerchief Ceremony thing again, you forgot last time."

"Yeah, and Jenna was talking about not being bored. She's done that before, too. Isn't that weird? What do you—" Tina added as she absentmindedly fixed the barrette that was sliding down her hair. Mrs. Forrester put her hands on the sides of her face.

"Slow down, slow down! Breathe ladies, and sit. One at a time, please." Toby quietly sat in one of the large chairs while Tina and Jenna made their way to the couch, their hands still waving in the air as they continued to speak.

"Now, what is this all about?" She removed the apron she forgot she was wearing and turned her attention to the kids.

"We didn't want to say anything to anyone because it sounds completely nuts, but something strange is going on with Jenna," Tina began a bit quieter. "I mean, she looks just like Elizabeth and…"

"I need to get into the mill. I don't know why, but I do."

"Oh, and if you could please vote for the restoration it might help," added Tina. "It's important!"

All three had their fingers crossed that Mrs. Forrester

would believe them and be able to help. When they were done saying everything they thought was important, they stopped and stared at a flustered Mrs. Forrester in anticipation.

Mrs. Forrester looked from Jenna to Tina to Toby to see even the slightest hint of a smile to give away a joke or prank. She figured the girls would come around soon enough to pressure her to agree to the renovation process. It was only a matter of time. The scales tipped during the summer after her good friend died. She was aware of it then. She had not expected all of this. They seemed so earnest in their stories, but could something be happening now just because they have been talking about it? She sighed and studied their faces as she took a seat opposite them next to the Victrola. Neither child had moved in the slightest, waiting for her reply.

"Well, Mrs. Forrester, what do you think?" Jenna asked as she twirled a section of her hair.

"There are many similarities," Mrs. Forrester began slowly as she stood there, wrapping the lightweight sweater around her thin frame. "An imagination is very powerful when others reinforce it. It's easy to fill in the gaps from history after hearing my stories and seeing the scrapbook and diary…" She was faltering, on unsteady ground, and she felt it. The look of disbelief and disappointment was heavy.

Maybe, just maybe, everything my grandmother told me was true, she thought. She went with her gut feeling and after taking a very large breath of air, continued.

"I'll help. If you feel there's a connection to Elizabeth Avery, you need to find out as much as you can to see what she is trying to tell you. If you're having reoccurring dreams, perhaps you should write them down to see if there's a pattern."

The look of relief on their faces made her think of the current situation from a different angle. She thought a minute more. *Maybe the renovation process needs to be done now. Could this be why?*

"Oh, Mrs. Forrester, thank you!" Tina squealed, clapping her hands together. Jenna's relieved smile faltered as if she might start crying.

"I know I need to get in the mill and do something there."

The woman nodded politely as the girls gushed with their appreciation and Toby grinned. She had her reservations despite how honest they appeared. Those two men had been hounding her for years to allow them the building. Was this whole thing, starting with Jenna, a set-up? Would they put their own kids up to this? She didn't think so, but the youth of today was so much more forward than her generation. She really didn't know them that well.

Her decision regarding the restoration of the mill could be the catalyst for so much negativity. It wouldn't be just this town that could be affected either. The kid's fathers wanted to advertise the Historical Association as a viable stop for the tour busses that passed through Orchard Creek on their way to Canada and back. She promised herself after the last time a few decades back that she would make sure that place wouldn't hurt another soul.

Souls? Was there something special about Jenna? She had seen the way the diary affected her. She wasn't sure the girl could fake the flush of her face or the complete lack of her whereabouts the way she did while reading the diary. How much did she know of the Handkerchief Ceremony? Enough to use as a ploy?

"I bet your dads will be pleased if I vote for the restoration, won't they?"

"For sure!" Tina agreed, turning towards her new friend.

"Then, if we can get inside, we might find out what you have to do there. What do you think will happen then, Jenna?"

"Toby, wasn't your father concerned about you visiting me with all this political strife going on in the town hall?"

Toby sat up straighter as he was addressed and answered almost immediately. "He doesn't know, really. It was a last-minute thing for Jenna to invite me along." His attentive expression fell after he spoke, replaced by a frown that turned almost defensive. Jenna had stopped talking with Tina, her forehead wrinkled. A hurt expression crossed her face. It must have been obvious the elderly woman was asking questions about the renovation in an effort to corner them in a fabrication, perhaps encouraged by their fathers. She stopped the inquisition. Somehow, deep down, she knew what they said was the truth and felt a little guilty trying to trick them. There were no ulterior motives.

"I'm sorry, children. That was unfair of me. I will, of course, do what I can for you."

Jenna came running over to hug her, whispering in her ear. "Thank you, Mrs. Forrester. I wouldn't have bothered you with this unless I thought it was really important."

Somehow, the widow was almost certain, a door had been opened regarding Elizabeth and Joseph. True love and handkerchiefs were always tied together here in Orchard Creek. Her thoughts returned to Royal and of true love. Yes, they were very powerful things. The renovation bid and safety of the town balanced precariously with her decision. She was the swing vote.

She had a nagging suspicion that she had something else from the past that might be helpful, if only she could remember where she put it.

JENNA'S HEAD WAS spinning with questions as they biked away from Mrs. Forrester's house. What should she do first, where should she go, and who could she ask?

"How can I find out more when I think I've found out all there is? Mrs. Forrester has given me all the information she going to give me," Jenna replied sadly.

"I don't understand. There must be loads more information in the diary you haven't read yet. Why doesn't she just let you borrow it," Toby asked.

"I think she's scared. Jenna was, uh, different when she was reading it," Tina tried to explain. "Something about her changed."

"I think a part of her doesn't want to believe something is going on here. I freaked her out twice when I had it in my hand. Maybe she just needs to sleep on it, that's what my dad says about big decisions. I'll ask about it next time though, because I don't think I can wait long. For now, we need to figure out where else to look.

"We need to start from the beginning," Toby began. "Let's go see my dad. Maybe we can find more about Elizabeth and her family," Toby suggested.

The trio was once again at the Historical Association. They asked Mr. Jacobs where they could find the history of people who lived in the town. He pointed them to the books that held the birth and death records. They had already been there but decided to look further.

After two hours, they located Elizabeth's whole family. The birth record of the youngest Avery family member, Isabelle, was easy enough to find in the books. She must have been born in Orchard Creek right after they moved from Boston. Mr.

Jacobs helped them cross-reference on the computers where they found the death records of Elizabeth's parents who died twelve and eighteen years later, survived by daughters Ola and Lois. The address where they all resided was Elderberry Ridge. They searched, but could not find Elderberry Ridge. For the second time that day they were truly disappointed and at a dead end.

As tired as she was that evening after the family watched *COPS*, Jenna made a point to ask her mom for an extra notebook from their school supply box. She planned on keeping it at her bedside as Mrs. Forrester suggested.

"This isn't for homework, is it?" her mother grilled her, studying her face. The mom-look was on: pursed lips, frown between the eyes, crossed arms.

"No."

"Something's not quite right with you. I can tell."

"I'm fine, Mom."

"You still spend a lot of time thinking about that old mill. I know these things. I've made some friends here, too, you know, and that place is bad news. You better concentrate on your studies."

"It's nothing. We're just keeping out of trouble." She rolled her eyes and her mother stiffened.

"It's not drugs or a cult or anything, right? Just because we're out in the boonies now doesn't mean tempt-"

"Mom! No. Mrs. Forrester thought I might like to keep a journal of my dreams, that's all." The intensity of her mother's stare was unnerving. Finally, she backed down and Jenna breathed a sigh of relief.

"I'm not sure if I want you to hang around her, Jenna. Some old people tend not to think clearly when they get up there in years."

"I'll be careful, I promise." Her mother stood her ground for a few more seconds before rubbing her hand on Jenna's shoulder.

"I worry about you."

She waited in the kitchen rubbing one eye while her mom retrieved her paper. "What was that all about?" she whispered to herself. Maybe she should ask her parents again to watch *Dr. Quinn, Medicine Woman* instead of reality television. That couldn't be good for Peter, anyway. She loved the western show and only managed to watch it when she babysat for the Burns when they went out every few weeks. Of course, she lost that job when she moved to Orchard Creek. Her dad came into the room to empty his popcorn bowl, stretched, and put his arms around her shoulders, squeezing her gently.

"Do you want the half-popped kernels tonight? I have a limited supply and they're going fast." Jenna usually jumped at the offer. She loved the partially popped ones. Instead she shook her head.

"Going to bed already?"

"Yep."

"This fresh country air must be kicking your butt, Jenna. You're looking tired. Are you getting enough sleep?"

"Sure I am. It's just, I don't know, something I need to get used to I guess."

"Is it the schoolwork here?"

"Nuh uh. School's fine, Dad."

He poured the kernels into the trash, put the bowl in the sink and opened and closed the cupboards. The determination on his face changed to one of happiness. "Bingo! Well, pace yourself. As Mae West says, 'too much of a good thing is… a wonderful thing' or something like that." He turned his head toward the other room. "Gwen, do you want a candy bar?"

Her voice was faint but intense. "Don't touch those! I'm stocking up in case we get trick-or-treaters!" They heard a trunk slamming then the scuffing sound of slippers on the hardwood floor as she re-entered the room. She was talking loudly despite the fact that Peter had already gone to bed. "How is it you manage to find the one goodie I have hidden away?" Then something else occurred to her. "Besides, you just had popcorn, Jack! Pace yourself."

Her father put his hands up in surrender before turned to Jenna, his eyebrows disappearing under his hair. "See? It's all about pacing yourself. Yes, dear. Maybe ice cream?"

"Your sweet tooth is unmanageable."

Jenna smiled and gave him a kiss on the cheek before doing the same with her mom as the composition notebook was offered.

"Thanks Mom! 'Night!"

Once upstairs in her room, she latched the door quietly behind her. She padded to her desk and sat down. Curling her long hair behind her ear, she picked up her favorite purple pen, the one with a bow on the cap she made of yarn, and twirled it in her left hand, thinking. She wrote down as much of the previous dreams as she could, noting the first time she dreamed she said only 'look-not-bored', and the second 'Please-look. Not bored.' She wrote about the breeze, the window, the tree, the gown, and the words. She tried to articulate what she felt. Reading it over, none of it made sense to her.

Truly exhausted by the time she went to bed, she was sure she wouldn't be able to dream, but it came easily that night. Because it was familiar to her, she seemed to be able to hold some consciousness, and was able to observe the details as she went through the motion of standing in front of the window. She started to get that suffocating feeling of not being able to breathe well. It felt as though her mind was in a fog. Thoughts kept coming to her that didn't make sense. They were thoughts that didn't come from her mind. It finally dawned on her she must be seeing things through Elizabeth's eyes. There was overwhelming sadness, and then the dream shifted from her fumbling with the blue handkerchief, to holding the window ledge. Her hands caressed the woodwork. Jenna heard herself repeat the mantra, over and over, with additional words being added with each dream.

"Please. Look-not-bored. Yes, Joseph, yes." She reached her arm in front of her as if she could touch…

She awoke once again standing in front of her bay window. Her hands were not holding a handkerchief; they were holding the trim of her window ledge. She wrote down the details. She would share these with the others later. It still didn't make the picture clear. What was the message?

Twelve

*J*ENNA HAD TO wait until school on Monday to talk to her friends. Tina was busy all day on Sundays with church and visiting her grandparents for dinner. And it was silly to call Toby if she was just going to repeat it the next day. It was hard to go that long.

"Hi, Jenna."

Jenna looked up from her lap where she had her journal open. Standing across the cafeteria table with their lunch trays was Timmy Meecum and another boy about her age. Timmy always wore a Mario Brothers or Pac Man t-shirt. She tried to remember if he wore one to the roller-skating party.

"Hi Timmy. Hey, thanks for helping me off the floor the other night. Mary wasn't taking any prisoners."

"You're welcome. Do you mind if we sit here? Oh sorry, this is Craig Williams." Timmy's voice cracked and became a bit deeper but he didn't pay attention to it. "Toby's usually cool with it."

"Sure, have a seat."

Timmy's skinny body slid onto the bench easily, rewarding her with a cute dimple to go with his smile. "How's eighth grade treating you here?"

"It's a lot smaller than I'm used to. I like it, though." Timmy smiled again and turned his attention to Craig while they continued with their conversation about levels and gold coins.

Toby joined her first after nodding a hello to the guys at the table. "Anything new?" he asked quietly.

"Another dream. Let's wait for Tina. She's at the register right now. Is it okay to talk here?" Jenna's brown eyes drifted up to their table mates.

"Yes. Timmy's usually too involved with his games to socialize with others outside his circle. He doesn't make waves."

"Okay."

Tina sat down on Jenna's other side, staring at her lunch. "I love tater tot day. What's up?"

"I had another dream. Here look at this." Jenna pushed her tray up so the journal was easy for both to see. No one had an idea what it meant either.

"What about going to Mrs. Forrester's later?" Toby asked. The girls shook their heads.

"I have band practice after school today," Tina said, popping another tiny potato ball into her mouth.

"My science project is due Wednesday. I'm finishing up with the model right now. Tomorrow night I'll have to type the written part." Toby frowned over his cheeseburger. "My dad's kinda nervous. The deadline is Thursday and Mrs. Forrester hasn't said one word to him. Maybe she changed her mind?" The unease Jenna felt in her stomach made her lose her appetite.

It was Wednesday, October fourteenth, when Jenna, Tina, and Toby found themselves on their way to Mrs. Forrester's place once again. This time it was at her invitation, passed on by a phone call to each with insistence that they arrive as soon as possible. It was dusk already, just after dinner. What did she want them for? Biking as fast as they could, they arrived out of breath. Leaving their sneakers and jackets in the entryway they sat down in the parlor, panting.

Mrs. Forrester looked sternly at each of them, and they shifted uncomfortably as if they had been caught being bad. "I'm in a position of great significance," she began. "I'm on the town board, and this proposal has split the board. I am the deciding vote. There are still a few elders, like myself, who feel it wouldn't be worth the time or money to renovate the mill. I'm probably responsible for filling their heads with my beliefs, which was wrong." She looked away out the window at the changing leaves on the trees, putting her hands into the pockets of the heavy sweater she wore over her navy knit dress.

"I've grown close to all of you, and I need to know that you have been honest with me. I would not appreciate my vote being swayed by dishonest intention."

All three knew exactly what she was talking about. It had been in their thoughts after they initially mentioned it. How could they approach her to support the renovation project for Jenna and the Historical Association, and not use their friendship to betray Mrs. Forrester or attempt to change her mind?

"Mrs. Forrester, we would never do anything to hurt you. I can't explain why all this is happening, I just know I have to help Elizabeth," Jenna pleaded. "The dream changes just a little each time. Now she is saying 'yes, Joseph, yes'," she added.

A flash of memory went off in Mrs. Forrester's head of courting Royal and of the intention of the handkerchief ceremonies. Suddenly, she remembered where that small box might be. She stood abruptly.

"Come with me children," she said walking towards the stairs without another word. They all hesitantly but obediently followed.

"Where are we going?" Jenna whispered.

"Why are you asking me?" Tina asked nervously. She enjoyed coming over to Mrs. Forrester's house and hearing stories even though she was never truly comfortable there. Jenna seemed to blend right in as if she was cut out from the past somehow, but Tina felt on edge each time she came. Even though she didn't understand why, it took a while for her to calm down afterwards. The ghost business was bad enough. Right now, she was very concerned with how anxious she felt by possibly upsetting the old woman. What would happen to them?

Before they could decide what to do next, Mrs. Forrester stopped at the top landing and clicked on a light. With no nearby windows, the area remained dimly lit. "I know I have a small, gray box somewhere. It wasn't with the scrapbook or diary so I thought it was lost. Then I just remembered quite a few years back I moved all the personal items most special to me to where I could reach them better. I may have forgotten to include it. I need you to help me look for it in my closets. It may be where I can't reach it."

Jenna looked around her. The small, dark hallway led to three rooms.

"Jenna, come with me in my room. The next one down is the powder room and the other two are guest bedrooms. Toby, you and Tina can look around in there."

"Okay." Toby took the first room and slowly Tina, wide-eyed, walked past him and stopped at the doorway, chewing on her fingernail as she turned to him. He was just as nervous but motioned for her to go. In she went.

Toby felt for the light switch and pushed the heavy lever up. The room smelled as if it hadn't been used in a very long time even though it was clean. The floors were hardwood with one small braided rope rug over it. The white walls were bare except for a lone framed picture of a farmhouse that was hung over the bed. The simple white iron frame held a double mattress neatly made up with a faded patchwork quilt. He turned and looked back at the door, hearing Jenna and Mrs. Forrester chat away. The sound of doors opening and closing came from Tina next door.

He tried the small dresser drawers but they were empty. A clear, jewel-cut handle opened the one door in the room to reveal a musty closet. There was no knob on the wall and Toby sucked in his breath when his hand brushed a string, immediately assuming it was a spider's web. Realizing it was the pull cord for the light, he clicked it on. There were only a few blankets neatly folded on a lower shelf. Stepping back, he stood on his toes to see the top shelf. Against the wall to the side was a small wooden box with metal hinges. He just barely reached it, inching it with his fingers until it was close enough to the edge to grab. It wasn't very heavy and he couldn't tell what color it was because it was white with dust. Not sure of the size or contents, he turned the light off and closed the door, deciding to bring it to Mrs. Forrester. She could open it.

"Is this what you're looking for?"

Mrs. Forrester stood up from the closet Jenna was nearly crawling into. She rubbed her lower back with her hand as confusion changed to recognition. "Oh my, I believe it is!"

"Did ya find it?" Tina sneezed as she came into the room.

Her black hair had a fine layer of dust that fell onto her shoulders like dandruff. Toby brushed it off.

"Thank you, Toby. This might help us." She peeked into the box. Her pillowy face lit up and her blue eyes were bright with excitement. "Yes, it is! Let's go back downstairs."

"What is it?" Tina couldn't help but ask before they reached the living room. Mrs. Forrester sat in the chair and looked at the faces in front of her.

"This was my grandmother's possession box." She seemed almost giddy. Reading the clueless expressions on their faces, she explained. "Women used to keep possession boxes. Anything of sentimental value was kept in there. It's like a jewelry box or a very small hope chest."

Tina and Jenna both said "Oh!" at the same time, understanding. Toby just nodded, understanding the theory. He had an old shoebox himself, full of baseball cards, firecrackers, a collection of bottle caps, and a joke book.

"I've been looking for this a while now. For some reason, I forgot to keep it with my possession box." Mrs. Forrester used the back of her weathered hand to wipe away the dust as she continued. "When men and women courted, or dated here, they had a handkerchief ceremony. While the gentleman was wooing his beloved, the girl would start to sew a handkerchief. It took a while to sew it, you know. If the woman felt they should marry she would present her handkerchief as a sign of commitment, like an engagement ring is today. I have the handkerchief my grandmother gave to my grandfather in here. She passed after him."

"Oh, that's what a handkerchief ceremony is," Toby said in understanding as he and Tina crouched on the floor in front of Mrs. Forrester. He bent his head in Jenna's direction, studying her, trying to figure out why she was dreaming of handkerchiefs.

Mrs. Forrester pulled the cuff of her sweater over her hand and used that to clean the rest of the dirt off. Jenna gasped as the box became clearer. All that could be heard in the room was the ticking of the grandfather clock in the dining room as it chimed seven times.

The lid of the box was hand carved. It was a picture of a deer in a meadow. It groaned with displeasure at being opened after so long. Mrs. Forrester gently took out some papers and put them on the floor next to her. She moved some costume jewelry, an ancient hairbrush, a pipe, and an ornate silver letter opener off to the side to get to what she was looking for. She pulled out a very faded, pink handkerchief. It was stained on the bottom corner, but still beautiful.

"Why would a girl give a guy a pink handkerchief?" Tina asked.

Mrs. Forrester's lips pursed. "It was originally red. See, the antique lace trim has retained the darker color better. We had to color our fabric back then with what we had. My mother's handkerchief was a beautiful lavender from lilac blossoms. I used ground up dandelion petals in hot water to dye my mine yellow. I believe my grandmother used the juice from those little red berries only birds can eat."

"Oh yeah," Toby agreed, "they sure do stain clothes red. My mom was mad at me the time me and my friends used them as ammo in a war."

Mrs. Forrester unfolded it gently and looked at Jenna. A fancy letter "L" was sewn in the top right corner. "This was my grandmother's commitment to my grandfather. She had the chance Elizabeth never did."

There was a pause before anyone spoke. "In my dream, it's like I'm Elizabeth, and she keeps showing me her handkerchief in front of a window over a little crabapple tree," Jenna whispered. "She wants to, what, somehow let Joseph know? Give it to him? I, I can't. How could I?" Jenna sighed dejectedly. "I can't even research her! How could I just get her handkerchief?" Jenna was exasperated.

Mrs. Forrester was just about to reach out to console her when Toby blurted out so loudly, they all jumped.

"I can't believe it! I can't believe it! Oh, look at this! It was right here in this box!"

They all caught his excitement, although at this moment, they didn't know why. Since Toby had never spoken that loudly in front of anyone, they knew it must be something big.

Carefully, Toby showed Jenna an envelope and a dog-eared letter that Mrs. Forrester had put off to the side. He looked up at Jenna with a look of complete disbelief.

The envelope was written in ink in that fancy writing that showed care and pride. It was addressed to Miss Elizabeth Avery. The return was from a J.S. It must have been hand delivered, as it didn't have any other markings. Toby's hands began to shake ever so slightly as he looked from Tina to Jenna to Mrs. Forrester and he began to read.

"To My Dearest Elizabeth, will you, my love, do me the honour of giving me your hand in marriage, where we will be joined together, forever, through all of eternity? Our love has endured, my love will last, but I need your hand to make me whole. Please grant me my only wish with your answer, but hurry; I cannot wait much longer for fear that I will burst. Pledge vows with me on All Hallows Eve, one year from when we first began to court at the mill. You are my sweetest, my love. Yours truly, Joseph."

Thirteen

A SHIVER RAN UP and down their spines. Toby gave the note to Jenna. Her rapid breathing was making the others nervous. "Yes, yes, yes," she breathed, holding the letter close. Tina looked concerned at the other two, not sure if that was Jenna talking or in some way Elizabeth.

"Tina, you and Toby think it's Elizabeth in the dreams, and she is directing Jenna to her handkerchief?" Mrs. Forrester inquired, not taking her eyes off Jenna.

Tina nodded. "This letter sounds like Joseph wanted to make it official, too. Maybe because he was from out of town, he felt he needed to propose. They were supposed to be together!"

Jenna looked up, her face clearing from an expression no one had seen on her before. In a subtle way, even her eyes seemed to change. "Every time I've had that dream, I'm holding a blue handkerchief, so it's not one of yours. Joseph's name is in my head, too. I think, because I look so much like Elizabeth that she's chosen me to help her reach him."

Jenna stopped to think about what she just said. It felt right. "And I know how crazy this sounds because they're dead, but she wants to give her handkerchief to Joseph. I feel this pull to the mill except my dream isn't there, it's at a wooden window with crabapples below."

Mrs. Forrester didn't know what to say. When Jenna told her about what she said in her last dream, about consenting to Joseph, she had her mind made up to give the town her vote for the restoration. What she was unsure of now was how to help Jenna.

"Miss Jenna, I don't know what I can do for you. Elizabeth is gone. Her family died out with no male to carry on the line of the family name. There's nothing left of Elizabeth in Orchard Creek. And even if you found her handkerchief it doesn't solve this dilemma. If anything, it would open a whole new set of problems."

Toby looked down again at the envelope. It had Elderberry Ridge listed, just as in the town records and said so aloud. Mrs. Forrester made a noise of agreement.

"My grandmother lived on Elderberry Ridge, too. I believed I mentioned it to you already."

"That she and Elizabeth were best friends?" Jenna asked, handing the letter over to the woman. "Yes, you did."

"No, that she and Elizabeth were neighbors," Mrs. Forrester corrected, running her fingers over the ink. "It's now known as Washington Street," she added as an afterthought.

With that, Jenna gasped, and Tina covered her mouth.

"That's it, that's what we couldn't find!" Toby exclaimed. He thought a moment, putting things together. "In Jenna's dreams, there was a crabapple tree outside Elizabeth's bedroom window."

Tina, chewing on her thumb nail, began to follow the logic. "Okay, which houses on Washington have crabapple trees?"

"Washington is a really short road," Mrs. Forrester stated.

Jenna shook her head, frustrated. "I have no idea." She focused on nothing in particular, thinking. "There's nothing left of Elizabeth in Orchard Creek," she murmured, repeating what Mrs. Forrester just said. "That can't be true." There was a heartbeat's worth of silence before she spoke again. "The library. There *is* something left that was Elizabeth's. Oh, holy cow, it's the library," she whispered, looking very pale.

"Jenna, it wasn't the mill you needed to get into. It was the library the whole time!" Tina exclaimed. She turned to Mrs. Forrester. "We'll need to get there tonight before closing."

Mrs. Forrester put her hand to her mouth, stunned. *Perhaps the renovation of the mill will shed some light on this peculiar situation.* A smile spread across her face as she shook her head unbelievingly. "It seems as if I must vote for the restoration so I believe I will. Now go! You have to go."

And they were off, tearing down Birch Drive from Mrs. Forrester's house, crossing Rodger's Pike Road to where it intersected with Washington in the middle of town. It was dark out now, and their moist breath stood out against the crisp evening air each time they rode under a street light.

"We're running out of time. Mrs. Forrester said she'd vote 'yes,' but I don't know if it's too late now," Jenna yelled to the others, her hair flying behind her. "I have to find her handkerchief, I know I do, but I still don't know if I'll be able to find it. The library is small but still huge when you're looking for something as little as a piece of fabric that may or may not still be there."

"I can't believe this is happening!" Toby shouted. They had never heard him this loud or excited before. "The renovation is going to go through! The mill will be restored, and everything will be fixed!" Toby slammed on his breaks and skidded to a stop. Dust flew up around him and he coughed. "Tomorrow is the fifteenth. I don't think the town could approve this and fix the mill by Halloween. It has to be Halloween, it just has to," Toby said in a more hushed tone, wiping the sweat from his forehead.

"Toby's right. It has to be Halloween. That's when they both started to date and were supposed to marry," Tina added, the excitement taking over the nervousness.

"It's also the day they died. Halloween is a powerful time. It's why there are so many ghost sightings and things that go bump in the night. I love Halloween and everything about it. If it's not books about history I'm reading, it's about this holiday. I've always read that it's the one day of the year the veil that separates our world and the next is at its thinnest. What if that's true?" She paused. "My dreams have been getting more persistent, too."

They got to the library with an hour left until closing. All three looked odd standing in the doorway, out of breath, sweating and looking desperate. The librarian waved to them half-heartedly as she was trying to finish up the last of her pile of returned books before going home.

Tina took in the room around her from a different perspective. This was once Elizabeth's house. This was the only tangible thing left of Elizabeth's life. Then it suddenly hit them.

"Where do we start? The books? A certain room?" Toby asked quietly as he unzipped his jacket. He was beginning to overheat in the stuffy air.

Tina shrugged. "There's no way her handkerchief is still here, Tobe. This place has been a library too long."

"Well, something has brought us this far."

"Ok, so what hasn't been moved or changed in a hundred years when this was a home?" She looked at Jenna to ask her opinion and immediately nudged Toby worriedly. Jenna was once again staring off in space, but this time, had a smile on her face.

"Of course! I knew the stairs. I know my stairs. I was upstairs." Jenna counted the stairs in her head…

Just like I did every evening before bed…

"But I didn't live here. Elizabeth lived here," Jenna answered no one in particular as she started to climb. Once on the landing, Jenna just stood there. It was almost comical to watch from a distance, almost like a strange game of Simon Says. Jenna would walk, the other two would follow and stop just short of her, waiting for her next move. Jenna walked around where she and Tina had looked at the newspapers just weeks ago.

I'm home. I've been gone so long. It feels like forever.

Jenna was having trouble breathing again, just like in the dream. Things seemed so strange now, and she was disoriented.

Why are all these books here? Where is my loft?

Jenna, trance-like, walked without effort in directions she had no control over. Her hands caressed the wooden tables and walls as she looked around her. Her gaze stopped as she stood opposite the picture window across the room. She began to walk very slowly towards the window with her arms outstretched, yearning to touch it. With every step the large crab apple tree came clearer into view.

How has it grown so much?

Tina and Toby looked back and forth from Jenna to each other and around the room as Jenna did the same. They stopped abruptly as Jenna neared the window.

"Jenna?" Toby called cautiously. He didn't know what she was doing. She didn't answer. "It all makes sense," he whispered to Tina. "This must be the window she dreams about."

Tina felt goose bumps up and down her arms, despite having on a jacket.

Jenna walked closer to the window on legs that no longer seemed her own. She was weak and having trouble catching her breath by now. Visions of the window changed from what she was really looking at to a small tree outside a humble room. The room swam in front of her, and this time Jenna couldn't keep her balance. She fell forward, unable to brace herself. Her head hit the ledge as she fell into a pit of darkness. From far away she heard voices.

"Jenna, wake up! Oh Jenna, I don't want to have to get the librarian!" Tina hissed.

Jenna slowly opened her eyes and was finally able to take a huge breath. She was a bit bewildered laying there. She could hear her friends talking to her, but for the moment, they didn't register. The fogginess in her head was lifting, and she was starting to see clearly as if a screen had been moved from view.

"Oh, it is so good to see your eyes open." Toby sighed, his face inches above hers.

Tina came back into view and bent down to Jenna's level, looking at Toby. "It's okay. She didn't notice anything. She's too busy with her books."

Jenna looked at each of them and realized for the first time where she was. Her head started to ache. She looked around from this view from the floor and gasped so loudly Tina thought she was having trouble breathing again.

"Look! Knot! Board!" Jenna exclaimed. "This is it. We were completely off. I haven't been talking about being not bored; I've been saying to look at the knot in the board! Here!"

From the floor, Jenna could see a knot in the window ledge. She reached up and touched the knot. It gave a little so she pressed it harder. Acting like a lever, the knot pushed in and the other end of that piece of wood pushed out. She sat up slowly and looked at the other two. Each was slack-jawed in amazement.

"Go ahead Jenna, move the board," Toby said.

With trembling hands, Jenna gingerly moved the loose board away, which showed a small, simple wooden box hidden inside a hollow section of the ledge. She pulled it out and set it on the floor. All three sat around it as if playing a strange game.

"Is it Elizabeth's possessions box?" Toby asked. This one was much smaller than the one Mrs. Forrester inherited.

"I think so," Tina whispered.

The top came off the box easily. There inside were the last of Elizabeth Avery's belongings: a tiny cameo broach, a silver hairpin in a figure eight design, and a pale blue handkerchief with white lace trim, embroidered with the letter 'S' near the top.

"The library will close in five minutes. If you have books to check out, please do so now. Thank you." The voice over the intercom made them all jump.

Jenna scrambled to her feet, holding the box gently. The board was replaced as best it could by Toby, and Tina scattered the concentration of dirt from the thin indoor carpet with her hand. It was very dark out now. Thoughts of being grounded for being out so late plagued all of them.

Instead of trying to navigate the back roads—Arbor didn't have street lights—they called home and told their moms and dads they'd been socializing at the library, and had lost track of time. None of their parents were happy to have to pick them up, but at least they made the right decision and were safe. It would have been stupid to attempt to bike in the blackness.

"Now what?" Tina asked as she squinted into the darkness watching for her dad's car. Jenna had been thinking the same thing. They all were. With the box securely in her arms, Jenna felt relieved but not necessarily complete. She wasn't done and she was sure her next destination was down the road by Rowan Creek.

"I've got to get in the mill. It's where they met and fell in love. Even the stories say she's been seen there wandering." She felt a rightness of what she was saying. Toby was nodding his head.

"It makes sense. Our next goal is the mill."

A few minutes later everyone was home. While Jenna's mom was having a discussion with her dad about curfews, Jenna snuck upstairs with the box. She plopped on the bed and took out each item to inspect more carefully, saving the best for last. She felt a thrill inside her. It wasn't unease or relief, just a thrill of excitement maybe.

The oval broach was definitely an antique. It was a profile of a woman facing to the left. She had a long, straight nose and prominent chin. Her eyes weren't much more than orbs. It reminded Jenna of pictures of the Romans she had seen in her books. The hair was very detailed, pulled away from her face in circular curls and decorated with flowers. The back of her hair was all done in tiny rows of ringlets. Her neck and the top of her gown were just visible. The gown had flowers on it as well. Jenna knew this must have been hand carved because they didn't have cookie-cutter machines back then. It looked to be made out of shell and was set in a fine filigree design that was tarnished. The right side was bent outward.

She put it back in the box, barely acknowledging the raised voices from downstairs and picked up the pin. It was beautiful and something Jenna had never seen before. It was tarnished with age, but very clearly silver. Instead of fashionable flat metal designs, this was three thin strands braided together that bent around into a single elongated figure eight. The part of Charlie Brown's Christmas television special where they skate on the pond came to mind. Up and around and back again, she traced it with her finger. The clasp part on the back didn't give any indication of which direction it was to be worn. Jenna held it vertically, but that didn't seem right. Why would someone wear the number eight? Holding it horizontally felt better and looked better.

The butterflies started in her stomach the moment she reached for the handkerchief, and images of Joseph from her dreams played out in her head. The urge to hold it was so strong it was almost tangible. Something told her she was meant to have this in her hands. She wanted to concentrate on it and keep it near, so she closed the box and leaned over the bed to open the top drawer of her nightstand. The jostling caused the framed picture on the top to fall over the clock radio.

She absentmindedly picked it up and held it, suddenly mesmerized by the photo of her and her dad from three Halloweens ago. It wasn't new to her, but in a way, it felt as if she was seeing it for the first time. They were in the huge War Memorial in the middle of the city where they went every year to trick-or-treat. Several of the local businesses were there with haunted mazes and free candy. She didn't win the contest she entered that year, or any other year after for that matter. A Halloween rebel, she hadn't gone as anything popular enough to win a prize since she went through her witch stage and insisted on being one for six straight years. She thought about how she loved to look through the pictures in the Halloween album her mom had put together. The photos were in chronological order. It was neat to see how much she had grown and changed.

This particular year she was dressed as Laura Ingalls in a long, cream-colored prairie gown with tiny flowers on it and a matching apron and bonnet. Her dad was on one knee with his arm around her, smiling at the camera. It was one of the few pictures that really showed how much they looked like each other. They had the same smile, although Jenna's front teeth hadn't been pushed together quite yet since the ones next to them were still missing. Down in the corner was part of Peter's leg and foot, wearing blue pants from his Bart Simpson costume. He was captured in the photo because he started to take off when her mom took the picture. He got in huge trouble after that, too. Their mom had to run on the cement floor to catch him and nearly fell when she slid on a wet spot left from the snow that had been tracked inside.

Halloween…She shook herself out of her thoughts, but the holiday stuck. Something about it felt right. She was sure there was a connection between this handkerchief, giving it to Joseph, and being in the mill. On Halloween. Putting the possessions box in the top drawer of her nightstand, she scooted back to the middle of the bed crisscross apple sauce.

Fourteen

ENNA TURNED THE handkerchief over in her hands, appreciating how delicate, simple, and lovely it was. There were no flaws in the stitching. It was easy to see how important it was to the woman sewing it, and how impressed the man would be to receive it. The meaning behind it was very clear. It was made…

"What's in your hands?" her mother demanded by her bed, startling her from her thoughts. She was so absorbed in the handkerchief she didn't hear her mother open the door or come in.

"It's a handkerchief," Jenna said, her words sounding thick. It was almost as if she had been sleeping. She even felt groggy.

"What?" her mother asked again. Jenna looked up and her mother gasped, bending down to her level and grabbing her shoulders. "What's wrong with you?"

"Nothing!" The harsh movement woke her up. "I'm just

sitting on my bed, looking at this handkerchief, uh, Tina gave me. Geesh, Mom, don't you trust me?"

"Your pupils are dilated. You were in the library?" she grilled, her face pale.

"Yes!" Jenna said, raising her voice. "You can even check. We were there for a while. It's not like there's a rec room here or anything to hang out in!"

"What's with all the yelling?" Her dad was in the doorway, his hands on either side of the frame, the remains of a Twizzler sticking out of his mouth. Both Jenna and her mother spoke at once, frustration and anxiety fueling their volume.

"Whoa, wait a minute." The confusion in his voiced changed to concern. "We're falling apart here. Gwen, what was she doing?"

"She said she was looking at this," her mother said snatching the handkerchief out of her hands. Jenna cried in protest.

"Mom!"

"Let me see it." Her mother gave the handkerchief to her dad and muttered something unintelligible. He turned it over a few times, shaking his head, confused. He even smelled it. "It looks old. Where'd it come from?"

"We hang out at the Historical Association. Me and Tina and Toby. It's an antique," Jenna stammered, mentally crossed her fingers. She hadn't actually lied.

"The history thing again, right?" It was obvious her mother was worried, and Jenna knew it. Part of her felt sorry for her, which in turn just made her want to lash out.

"Yes! I like history. I'm sorry I can't be the perfect daughter who plays with Barbie dolls and wants an Easy-Bake Oven! I'm not doing drugs and I'm not hurting anything!"

A sob escaped from her mother as her dad put his arm

around her. Jenna didn't want to see her mother in that way. It horrified her and made her want to cry, too. Why wasn't he giving the handkerchief back to her? This was so confusing.

"We're all okay. It sounds like Jenna has a good head on her shoulders or she wouldn't have called tonight," he said soothingly, kissing his wife's head before catching his daughter's eye. "I know I want to trust you."

"But you didn't see her when I first came in." Her mother had regained her composure, her voice sounding more like the mom she knew and loved. "Her eyes were all glassed over and I swear her eyes were dilated."

"They're not now. If it were something illegal, they wouldn't have gone back to normal within a few minutes."

"You're right."

"Mom!" Peter cried from the next room.

"Oh, we woke up Pete. Hold on, honey!"

"Were you doing anything you shouldn't be doing?" It wasn't an accusing tone her father used. He just asked the question.

"No. I never have and I never will. You can even search my room."

He closed his eyes briefly as if dismissing the idea. "Okay, you're not grounded today because you used good judgment and asked for a ride. We're going to give you the benefit of the doubt this time, Jenna. But there is no more biking all over hell and creation, and no more staying out after dark on your own. We've never had to establish rules like this with you, but your behavior is starting to make us nervous. From now on curfew is seven-thirty and will be strictly enforced. Understood?"

"Mom!" Peter yelled again.

"Understood. Um," Jenna hesitated, lifting her hand to

point to the handkerchief before changing her mind. She tried not to stare at it.

Her mother kissed her on the top of the head. "I love you, Jenna." She left to attend to Peter.

"Love you too, Mom."

"What now?" her dad asked, exasperated.

"Can I have the handkerchief back? I promised I would take good care of it."

He studied his daughter, trying to figure her out. "Then keep your promise." He watched the tension leave his daughter's shoulders. "You're different here, and I'm not completely sure it's a pre-teen-related change." He bent down on his knees so he was at eye level with her. "We just want you to be safe and happy. Remember, you can talk to me. You know that, right? You used to be able to talk to me."

For a split-second Jenna thought it over, then decided against it. "I'm okay, Dad."

"I'm always here with an open mind, kiddo."

"I know." He left the room, closing the door quietly behind him. Jenna fell back on her pillow, putting the handkerchief over her eyes while she looked through it at the ceiling. Just then the phone rang.

"Get the phone!" her mother yelled from downstairs while Peter yelled that it was too loud in the house. She really was in a bad mood tonight. Jenna peeled off the handkerchief and picked up the phone on her nightstand before the second ring.

"Hey, it's Tina. Did you get into trouble?"

"Almost. Had a whole family intervention, though. I wanted to tell my dad."

"Did you?"

"No. It makes my mom nuts when I talk about stuff like

this, and she's already in a tizzy. I don't want her fighting with him about it. Besides, I want to make my own decisions. We need to be careful, though." She sighed, suddenly tired as she stared down at the thin material, the reason for her family drama. "I also realized something."

Tina's voice suddenly became tense and urgent. "What?"

"I need to give the handkerchief to Joseph, and it has to be in the mill on Halloween. I feel it. I just don't know how we'll be able to pull this off without getting into some serious trouble. This is so complicated. Did you get grounded?"

"Yeah. I can't play for the next two days. I called Toby and he got off with just a warning. His dad knew he could call Mary Kathryn if he needed to. She was the librarian who was working tonight."

"I still find it strange how everyone knows everyone else."

"You'll get used to it. I gotta go, my two minutes are up. See ya in school tomorrow."

"'Kay, bye."

"HELLO?"

Mrs. Forrester's voice on the other end of the phone sounded awake and pleasant. The knot in Jenna's stomach lessened. It was 6:45 in the morning and Jenna had been up for almost two hours, counting the minutes and trying to decide what a respectable time would be to call. She almost made it to seven and had been hoping the elderly woman was an early riser.

"Hi Mrs. Forrester, it's Jenna," she said, lowering her voice in case she woke her own family. Her mom and dad wouldn't be up for work for another half an hour. "I'm sorry to call at this hour but…"

"No need to apologize. I'm sure you have a very good reason to be up before the chickens."

"We found it! We found Elizabeth's handkerchief! It *was* in the library!" Jenna could hear the intake of breath on the other line and knew Mrs. Forrester was getting excited. "The library was Elizabeth's home. As soon as I got there it was like Elizabeth took over and directed me to her old room. You know how the upstairs has that big window? Well, that was her bedroom and the crab apple tree I kept seeing in my dreams was outside that window. Of course, now the tree is huge, but back then it was only a tiny little tree."

Jenna wasn't expecting any answers, even if Mrs. Forrester could have gotten a word in. "So, my body is moving on its own and that weird feeling I get of not controlling it and not being able to breathe brought me right to the window. I guess I really wasn't breathing because I must have blacked out, but when I came to…Mrs. F. you wouldn't believe what happened! I had hit my head on the ledge and when I opened my eyes, I saw there was a knot on the underside of it. Elizabeth had been telling me to look at the knot in the board! If I had seen the words it would have made more sense 'cause I haven't been bored at all. Then, when I pushed in on the knot the board moved. It covered a secret hiding spot inside. I can just imagine Elizabeth lying on her bed under that window every night, you know, putting the handkerchief away after working on it by candlelight before bed."

Mrs. Forrester was finally able to say something when Jenna stopped to grab more air. "Oh, my. You found the handkerchief stuffed in the window frame?"

"Mmm hmm, it was in a tiny possession box, kinda like yours. It's the most delicate thing."

"And it's blue, like in your dreams?"

"Yup. The color of cornflowers…"

There was another intake of air on the other line. "Jenna?"

Jenna checked herself and realized the more she talked the louder she became. "Yes?" she answered more quietly.

"I can say for certain there are forces acting here that are way beyond our abilities to understand. I never doubted the mill's history, and whatever is happening now is definitely because of you. I will help in whatever way you need to do Elizabeth's bidding, but you need to be mindful."

"Mindful?"

"Yes, you need to be careful." At her kitchen table, the old woman wrapped her robe across her chest. She looked out her window into the darkness, into the unknown mystery this town had been surrounding for over a hundred years. In a way, this call exhausted her. At the same time, it exhilarated her. She knew now of her purpose and how it had given her a family once again. "There have always been roadblocks surrounding that building, whether to protect us from the magic there or prevent the magic from reaching us. We all need to be aware of our vulnerability. But I will say no one has ever been as educated about that place as we are so we have an advantage. We need to stick together and do whatever we're supposed to do. I'll be here for you every step of the way."

OCTOBER FIFTEENTH CAME with no great surprise, and the renovation bid was approved, thanks to that one crucial vote. At first Jenna was worried her mother wouldn't let her go, but after Jenna mentioned how she was interested in seeing how the town's business worked, her mother couldn't complain too much. She had ridden with Tina and her mother to the meeting at the town board. It was held in the room with the big mural.

The usual people were there: the half-dozen or so assorted board members seated on the dais on the side of the room and a handful of townspeople seated in front of the board. Mrs. Forrester winked at them once they settled in. The painting was now behind Jenna and the Historical Association's room to her left. As distracting as the painting was to Jenna, she couldn't keep turning behind her so she did an adequate job of paying attention. Tina was given special leave from her grounding for the circumstances of the night and was wearing a pink skirt that was the same shade as her strawberry lip gloss. Toby sat behind the girls because Sue Degrassi and her two sour-faced teenagers got to the seats first.

"This is so lame, Mom," Sue's daughter said as she pushed her glasses up by scrunching her face. She slouched down in the metal chair. "I'm not going into anything close to legislature next year."

"You got that right, Er-bear," the boy answered. He was one of the few people in the room dressed casually, wearing jeans and a suit jacket over a T-shirt. "I'm eight months away from leaving this dead-end town for a music career with my band. Does the school think this is gonna change my mind?"

"Eddie, all seniors have to attend a government meeting outside school," his mother explained for what looked like the hundredth time. She was wearing a nice pant-suit but it didn't seem to fit her. "It's just part of the curriculum. Erin, if you and your brother want to graduate, you'll both just have to endure it. It's also good to keep an eye on where our taxes go. Everything should be accounted for properly."

"'Sounds like you belong here more than us, Mom. At least no one else from our class is here."

"I heard from Janelle there's a huge group going after winter so they can get out of color guard practice."

"Wish I'd thought of that."

The meeting was called to order and after old business was addressed it moved to new business. The Historical Association bid was last. The three friends all had to suppress their squeals of excitement when the board voted, and the announcement was made that it was passed. Jenna learned that Leland Robertson's title was really Board Chairman, not President. That was what everyone affectionately called him. She also found it odd that he wasn't happier with the decision, seeing how his house was apparently full of stuff just waiting for a new home. Both Mr. Levy and Mr. Jacobs made up for it, though. They were very pleased. There was, however, still a lot of red tape.

With sixteen days to go, it looked unlikely that the mill would be fixed up by Halloween. Mrs. Forrester made a motion at the meeting to have the doors at least opened by the holiday, saying it would be the perfect time to introduce it to the community. She even offered to volunteer her time to help clean up the mill, and suggested Jenna and her friends help, too. It would have allowed them to get in there with supervision. What Jenna needed to do once inside was still unknown. She had the handkerchief and the knowledge she needed to make sure it was somehow given to Joseph. The dreams all pointed in that direction. All hoped it would be as easy as it was when they went to the library. How they were supposed to give something to a dead man was still a problem they needed to work out.

But town business moved slowly. It was still in the discussion stage, and there wasn't anything particular to press them into action. At least nothing the board knew about. Mr. Jacobs was excited about getting inside the building to have the code officer give them a more detailed list of what needed to be completed. They did an assessment every year for the renovation bid so they knew the structure was safe to enter. Mr. Levy had asked when the inspector could come by and was told his schedule was tight. Jenna, Tina, and Toby knew their agenda was almost impossible.

In the meantime, the contents of Elizabeth's possession box were kept safely in Jenna's window seat in her room. She took the handkerchief out several times a day to look at it and feel it. Knowing she had it in her hands gave her some satisfaction, but the reality that there was still more to do ate at her. The feeling that time was running out made her anxious. No one had heard from Mrs. Forrester since the town meeting, even though Jenna had taken a moment to write her a thank you note. She wanted the elderly woman to know how thankful they all were for her faith in them.

"Jenna, phone for you!" her mother called from the kitchen. Jenna got up from the couch, smiling at her brother, who was still in his PJ's. She wasn't really watching the Saturday morning cartoons that were on television. *Dexter's Laboratory* wasn't all that exciting to her, even if it was the Halloween episode, but Peter was engrossed. She just needed to do something other than sit in her room and think about the mill. It was starting to drive her crazy.

"Hello?"

"Hey, Jenna, great news!" It was Toby. "My dad said we can get the keys to the mill this afternoon!"

Fifteen

"WHAT?"

"YEAH, HE and Mr. Levy have been working with Mrs. Forrester on the inspector guy almost nonstop since Thursday night, and he finally cracked and made room for us. He's there right now finishing up going through what needs to be brought up to code. My dad said after he leaves, we can go in. We're the clean-up crew." There was a hint of pride in his voice.

Jenna felt a mixture of emotions: excitement, relief, apprehension, and a bit of nervousness. "Wow! That's awesome!" Then it finally hit her. "Yay, we're getting in!"

"Well, we will be supervised. There's no way they'd just unlock it and leave us there alone."

"That's okay. Then what?"

"I don't know. You're the one with the connection to Elizabeth."

"Toby, what if this is just something weird my mind has made up?"

There was a brief pause on the other end of the line. "Don't doubt yourself. If nothing happens, it's no big deal. Well, for us it wouldn't be. For my dad and Mr. Levy, it's like Christmas and their birthdays all wrapped up together. How about we hold off on a decision like that until after Halloween, 'kay? We'll just go to clean up for right now. Can you be here at twelve?" Toby was really good at putting things in perspective for her and quelling her initial fear.

"Okay, thanks. I'll see you then."

By noon all three had play clothes on and were filled with the desire to work very, very hard. They met at the front door of the mill and waited for Mr. Jacobs to come back from the town hall, their jackets and windbreakers crinkling with every movement. Jenna peeked into the floor-length, beveled windows on either side of the main door, excitedly jumping up and down, her long braid swishing down her back like a horse's tail. It was catchy. Despite Tina's hard-core nervousness, she was smiling, and Toby cracked a grin and rolled his eyes at the two of them. Their heads turned at the crunching of tires on crushed stone as Mr. Jacobs and Mr. Levy turned into the drive. In Jenna's opinion, it took them too long to walk from the car to the door.

"I want to thank you all for your help in getting this, finally, off the ground," Mr. Levy said, producing a skeleton key from his pocket while Mr. Jacobs shifted the bag he was holding and slapped him on the back. The metal sound of the key turning in the lock was the most beautiful sound Jenna had ever heard. She walked in right in front of Tina and Toby and stared at the vastness of the building that, before now, had only been seen through dirty windows. It was actually quite bright in fall sunshine, but it was cold with old, musty air.

Upon entering the main doorway there was a huge open room. They all walked in farther and initially the only sound was their shoes and boots crossing the hardwood floor. The tense stillness was what caught Jenna's attention. It was a waiting feeling. And at the same time, she felt a strange sense of being welcomed that she didn't understand. Both feelings were vast and all-encompassing, making her pause to process them. Tina and Toby were too busy walking past Jenna and taking in the room to notice her reaction.

"This is so cool!" Jenna heard Toby announce.

"It sure is," Tina answered. Tina's dad had gone back to the entrance and was pointing at the door while naming off some lock systems he had been looking into.

Once Jenna got over the initial shock of being inside—there was no other way she could describe it—she looked around. The entire first level was broken up by a large enclosed room to the left followed by a door against the far wall. On the opposite wall of the enclosed room was an open area a bit smaller but still generous in size. There was a door to the right of this room. Splitting the room in half was a massive area to the right, a great room. It went to the outside walls and was empty except for a large staircase kitty corner to the main entryway. It led to the second floor, where a small walkway wrapped around the other rooms and overlooked the downstairs. The great room's windows were spaced around on three sides creating checkerboard squares of bright light on the floor. Tina was stepping on the edges like a tight-rope walker, her hands out to her sides for balance.

"Good thing each year's prelim inspections found the mill's foundation secure or we wouldn't have been able to have Art give us the green light already," Mr. Jacobs admitted.

"Don't I know it," his friend snorted, shifting his weight back and forth on a loose floorboard. "That's the make or break.

In a way it's sad we're on a first-name basis with the inspector, but we were right that doing it annually, regardless, would pay off one day. And, of course, the building is still structurally sound thanks to all the work in the early Forties."

Mr. Jacobs bent down to where the squeak was coming from. "Is it soft? It's still going to be a hefty bill. When's John calling you back with the figures?"

Mr. Levy pushed his glasses up as he straightened. "Not weak, the nails just need tightening. Soon. Art said he'd call him once he had a ballpark, but remember John purchases, fixes, and resells houses. This is a little different. It'll be close to accurate only for what we'll need for heat, water and electricity. It won't cover incidentals or operating costs."

Jenna looked around the interior, trying to take everything in at once. The floors, the grand winding staircase, the rooms; Elizabeth and Joseph had touched them all. The structure had been there when that history existed. The tangible objects made it real. Just then, Mr. Levy opened the door across from the entryway and clapped his hands together, his excitement evident. He motioned to it the way models would showcase a new car. The room was quite big but rectangular in shape. Jenna peeked in.

"This is slated for the Historical Association's office. Finally! The rest of the building will be converted to a museum and house all the items that are currently being stashed in the town hall and in Mr. Robertson's home. Well, maybe not everything in his house. This place is only so big." Both men laughed at some inside joke. Mr. Levy pointed past the office. "This hallway leads down to the basement. The stairs are very steep. Actually, all the stairs are thin and steep, so be careful when you guys go down there."

Even squinting, Jenna couldn't see down the small corridor

and instead turned back towards the main room, her feet taking her to the focal point.

"Wow!" she exclaimed, tipping her head to see to the top. The staircase was the mill's most distinctive feature. It reminded her of some Southern antebellum mansion. It was made of thick, sturdy wood and wound its way up to the second floor. The finials were ornately carved in a spiral design on top of chunky newel posts with a trailing twist from top to bottom. The balusters were a miniature of the finial model.

"I'm glad to see it's held up through the years without any care, despite our harsh winters and humid summers. It's definitely well-worn with all these nicks and scratches," Mr. Jacobs stated as he ran his hand over the wood.

"It gives it character," Mr. Levy added walking into his new office and returning with an armful of brand-new brooms. "We're still firm on restoring what needs to be and leaving the rest as is, right Tom?"

"Absolutely! I can't wait to take my kids here on a field trip, especially this year's crew." He sighed. "Maybe in the spring."

"We can do what we can right now, Mr. Jacobs," Jenna tentatively interrupted, taking a push broom that was almost as big as herself. "Maybe it could, I don't know, maybe we could fix it up enough to bring them here by the end of the month." She didn't miss the spark of delight that flashed in his eyes even though his face was deeply lined with contemplation.

"I'm not sure that'll fit into our plans."

"That's probably because we haven't really made any definite ones yet," Mr. Levy replied with a smirk, holding the rest of the brooms out to Jenna's friends. "We've just focused on getting to this point. Let's tease this out while we have free laborers."

Mr. Jacobs scratched his head, looking around. "Now where'd I put that bag? Ah, there it is." He walked to the front door where he set it down when he came in. "For right now, this place needs a good cleaning. Trash and debris, like any pieces of broken wood, scraps from the last renovation, garbage that's been tossed through the windows, can be collected and discarded so we can see what's underneath that'll need repair."

"How many windows do you think you've replaced in here over the years, Dad?" Toby asked. Jenna was confused.

"Why would you need to replace them?"

"Vandals," Mr. Jacobs replied as he took a handful of work gloves out of the bag and distributed them. "There's always a window or two each year that's smashed out by some rock-wielding deviant. The most popular time is during summer vacation and around Halloween. I've been able to hold a set of the keys to this place for just such occasions."

"But why you?" Jenna asked, putting her arm around the broomstick to free up a hand. "This place wasn't your responsibility."

Mr. Jacobs shrugged. "I have repaired quite a few, haven't I, Tobe?" Toby nodded, sticking the gloves under his arm and shifting his broom to help his dad with the bag. "I've lived next to this place for almost fourteen years. I never wanted it to become a drug den or flop house. I guess I always had better plans for it." He dug back in for flashlights and held them out. Jenna stuck the gloves on her hand to take one and Tina fumbled with everything at once, dropping her gloves. Each frowned when they found they were too big but continued to stand there waiting for further orders. It would have to do.

"Now, I'll bring in the trash cans I brought over this morning and leave one in each large room while you start." He looked over the kids' heads to Mr. Levy. "I didn't want to look too cocky with the inspector here."

"True. Where'd you put the blueprints? Are they still in the office?" Mr. Levy asked as he took a pen and small notebook from his breast pocket.

"Damn! I left them on the desk in the town hall when I followed Art back. He had a few last-minute questions."

"We'll need them. I figured we'd go over them today with a fine-toothed comb."

"I'll shoot back and get them." Mr. Levy zipped up his jacket and headed towards the door. "No big deal."

"Help me take the filing cabinets out of the back of my truck first so we can work on getting them situated while the kids clean. You guys ready?" All three chimed in the affirmative and Mr. Levy shook his head in disbelief that was quickly overtaken by other priorities. "At least we have some natural light until the power's hooked up. Well, since all of you were, oddly, gracious enough to offer your services, let's go. Watch out for rusty nails and sharp edges."

"Where do you want them to start?" Mr. Jacobs asked. Mr. Levy exhaled the way one would with mountains of work before him.

"Do you guys want to start high or low?" Mr. Levy asked them.

"High," all three said at the same time. Mr. Jacobs looked confused for a minute, but held his hand out as if to usher them to the stairs. Jenna could still hear them talking on her way up.

"Why is this building so interesting to them?" It was Mr. Levy speaking.

"I don't know. There's nothing in here." Mr. Jacobs sounded perplexed.

"I guess it doesn't really matter. It's safe. There's nothing here that can hurt them." Carefully they all went up the thin stairs.

"Did people have smaller feet back then?" Toby asked at one point.

"That's a retror...ret...ugh, Jenna, what's that word?" Tina asked.

"You mean rhetorical, as in, that was a rhetorical question?"

"How are you so smart? Yes, exactly. We don't need to bother answering it, Tobe." Toby just snickered.

At the top of the winding staircase on the second floor was a landing with several rooms. They remembered reading the room on the far right was where the majority of sewing machines had been, and headed there, stopping in the doorway, feeling a waft of cool air glide over their shoulders. The window in that room overlooked the apple orchard. This was the infamous window out which Joseph had fallen.

Finally left by themselves, Jenna slowly walked over. It was a double-hung about waist high and an unconventional size by modern-day standards. Paint that had cracked into chips over time made an abstract mosaic pattern in the splintered wood. She knew it was just a window but also much more than that. As she came closer it felt as if her clothes had static cling. If Tina and Toby felt it, they didn't say. They remained by her side her watching her every move.

"Do you feel that?" Jenna whispered? From her peripheral vision, she saw both shake their heads. Tina put her arms around herself protectively. Jenna held her hand out towards the glass as the distance shortened. Her friends followed in her wake. A sharp intake of air came from Tina, but nothing odd happened. Looking through its grimy pane made everything a bit blurry punctuated by red dots, which were the fruit on the tree. They were almost ready for harvesting. The view made sense at the same time it gave a disorienting feeling.

Tentatively, Jenna touched the glass. It was cold just like

any other glass. She pulled the edge of her long sleeve down over her palm, just as Mrs. Forrester had, and wiped in a circular motion, clearing the thickness of time to see better. Her friends moved up as well. The distance from there to the ground seemed high to begin with, and as she thought of the last moments of Joseph's life, it seemed higher still and very scary. "Wow, what a way to go." Tina and Toby joined her in agreement.

"It is so sad," Tina said quietly. She took off her purse and set it to the side.

"I can't imagine how she must have felt watching him fall out the window," Jenna added. Part of her, however, could imagine how that felt and her stomach soured with the thought. *Unbearable.*

There were several moments of silence before the kids all started working. It didn't look too bad when they got up there until they started sweeping the layers of dirt and dust. There were indeed a lot more things to pick up, too. After a while Toby stopped, unzipped his hoodie and put his hand on his forehead. He frowned.

"What's wrong, Tobe?" asked Jenna.

"I think I'm coming down with something but I don't really feel sick. I'm warm, then I'm cold. As soon as I bundle myself up from a chill, I'm warm again."

"You call wearing a sweatshirt bundling yourself up?" Jenna asked, putting her fist on her hip. Toby scrunched up his face as if the answer was obvious.

"Uh, yeah, it is."

"Actually, I'm surprised he's got that on, Jenna. He doesn't ever complain about being cold, even in the winter."

"Mom made me."

"Well, there you go. Anyway, I'm sure this old building is drafty," Tina suggested at the same time Jenna shook her head.

"Cold spots are common."

"That's what I said," Tina stated.

"No," Jenna said, slowly moving her hand in front of her. "I mean in areas where ghosts have been sighted. I've read about it."

"Have you felt it, too?" Toby asked. Apprehension grew in Tina's eyes when Jenna agreed.

"Here and there, but by the time I'm ready to say something, it's gone again. You haven't, Tina?"

"Maybe a few times, but I figured it was from the window or something. There's nothing to be afraid of. Besides, I think we're safe in broad daylight. Nothing ever happens during the day in movies, right?"

Sixteen

"I GUESS SO," JENNA answered, thinking it over. She couldn't help looking off to her side though, just in case. Toby glanced at his watch as he was about to take another sweep.

"This is going to take forever. We've been working a little under an hour. We're never going to get this place cleaned up in time."

"Have we really thought about what we're going to do with this new-found handkerchief?" Tina asked in between sweeps. "How do we get it to Joseph anyway?"

Jenna's mind had been whirling since she found the handkerchief, and she was still stumped. Elizabeth, Joseph, the mill. She knew they all belonged together, she just couldn't put this puzzle together to make it fit.

"I know we need to be here Halloween night," Jenna replied, out of breath from pushing a large box to the one cleaned corner.

"Okay, maybe the end of the month isn't being practical," Toby began, wiping his forehead with the back of his hand. "If we waited a little longer—"

"No!" Jenna cried, whipping around to face Toby, squeezing her hands together in supplication. The broom fell to the floor with a sharp snap, making everyone but Jenna blink. "It must be all Hallows' Eve! Please do not forsake me!"

Tina and Toby stared at Jenna, or what looked like Jenna, then at each other. Jenna took a deep breath and closed her eyes briefly. When she opened them, she bent down and picked up the broom, blowing her bangs out of her face as if the outburst hadn't happened. "It has to be Halloween! If we're attempting to give this commitment to Joseph, and we are, it must be when we can bridge the wall to the other side. That's why Halloween is so famous for ghost sightings and stuff. That is the night that's easiest for them to cross over. Well, at least until May, but that's another story. I've been researching it. Don't you see? This place might already be haunted, but we'll have better luck if we do it on the night souls have less trouble coming back." Jenna hadn't realized how true all of that was until she said it aloud. It felt right and made her conviction stronger. "Trust me on this. I can feel it."

"Who says 'forsake' anymore, Jenna?" Toby asked.

Jenna brushed a stray hair away with her hand. She could almost believe Toby was setting her up for one of his jokes, except the way he asked was more like he needed something clarified. Plus, he looked a little unnerved. "What?"

"You just asked us not to forsake you," Tina said hesitantly, looking her friend over.

"No, I didn't."

Tina and Toby answered in unison. "Yes, you did."

"Um, I don't remember that. I remember saying we need to be here Halloween night."

"And you did. Twice." Toby walked over to her, studying her face. "You both did. Sometimes I think you share a little more in common with Elizabeth than just long, blond hair."

Jenna bit her lip in an uneasy way. "It's been happening more and more. I think things—words and phrases—but they come out of nowhere. I'm sure I hadn't thought of them. It's almost like listening to a movie but the sound is in my own voice." She paused and sighed again. "It has to be Halloween."

The apprehension on Toby's face morphed to resolve. "Halloween it is, then."

"There's no way I can convince my dad we need to clean at midnight," Tina said dejectedly.

"So," Toby began, "what could convince them to let us stay here that late?"

They were startled out of their conversation by the sound of commotion from downstairs. It didn't take them long to walk out of the room to the railing overlooking the stairs.

"That's the best he said he could do. I was about to leave when he called back. I know the budget was approved, just not for as much as we're going to need to do the repairs necessary!" Mr. Jacobs was standing with his arms out and palms up.

"We might as well stop right now, Tom," Mr. Levy declared. He was looking up from a bunch of papers and began waving them in the air. "I never imagined John's quote would be this high, all things considered. It's too little, too late. November first is too close, and we're short, period," Mr. Levy said.

"How much, Dad?" Toby hollered down.

"We're quite a few thousand short. The planning board needs to have this finalized by November first, and they need to know where the money is coming from. We're tapped out.

We under estimated it because it looked like it would never fly. It was a pleasant surprise when it went through, but now we don't have those resources anymore," Mr. Jacobs replied, rubbing his temples.

Jenna felt a knot in the pit of her stomach.

We're so close. I'm so close. Please, please help me.

She was unsure if she was thinking those thoughts, or if Elizabeth was. As her mind seemed to be shared these days, it was getting harder to concentrate.

"Well, I'm going to keep working, okay Dad?" Tina asked.

"Yeah, okay," Mr. Levy said. He was reviewing the papers again and removed a pen from behind his ear to make a note. He suddenly looked very tired.

Toby shuddered although he hadn't moved. He had either walked through a cold spot or one seemed to find him. Again. He shrugged it off, and they went back to work quietly, each with their own thoughts.

After a few minutes, they heard a female voice join the men's voices downstairs. Curious, they went back out to the landing to see who had come in. They were all surprised to see Mrs. Forrester standing there, offering lemonade and shortbread cookies. By the time she made her way upstairs, the three of them had started in talking about the new dilemma. She listened quietly, her eyes twinkling. Mrs. Forrester had a plan.

"I'm not sure how much weight this will carry, but we know a lot that can help us," Mrs. Forrester began as she took the long pin from her tan hat and removed it from her head. She held out a handful of papers covered with cursive writing. "Tina and Toby, I'll be giving these to your fathers as well. I've been doing some research, too. Joseph and Seth came from Missouri. I knew I'd seen a receipt in one of those books at the Historical building where all Seth's belongings were forwarded to after he left. I managed to find his obituary there which listed his home state. I also recall my grandmother telling me Elizabeth had moved here from Boston. We can solicit the historical associations in those areas for publicity for the mill renovation as it ties to their hometowns. You know, as they say, 'make a lot of noise.' Advertise to our surrounding areas as well. Promote and publicize," she finished.

"No one is just going to donate money for some unseen cause," Toby pointed out.

"And I don't think anyone knows who Seth or Joseph or Elizabeth were," admitted Jenna, "even in Missouri."

"Anyway, Mrs. Forrester, this has to be done by November first, and it won't do us any good after that. Jenna thinks it'll be too late because of the veil thing," Tina added soberly.

Mrs. Forrester smiled at them, and Jenna started to catch on. "Yes, but what if the publicity is for people to actually come here, to the mill, before then, say for a fundraiser. It would be perfect, right?" Jenna asked.

"Yes, dear," Mrs. Forrester confirmed. "Since we are fast approaching the one-hundred-year mark, it would be a great way to celebrate the occasion. I've been talking with those preservationist people about our interest in making the building a landmark. Those folks love anniversaries, especially ones with clean, even numbers. We should propose a centennial Halloween Ball."

Toby put his arms up and motioned around the room. "But it won't be done by then! This place is a mess. It looks old and…"

"It's the ideal time and place to pitch a need for renovation," Mrs. Forrester interrupted.

"As well as make the perfect background for a spooky Halloween party!" Tina finished.

Jenna was thinking all of this through. Feelings of excitement, relief and anticipation were coursing through her. "I'm not sure what's supposed to happen that night. We know we need to be there, but no one else knows that. I'm pretty sure I've been picked to take Elizabeth's handkerchief and follow through with what she couldn't and offer it to Joseph. What can we do to make sure I can follow through with that? You know, without worrying about being caught or something strange happening that would scare people away?" Jenna questioned.

"Hello? Jenna? Halloween night, remember?" Tina said sarcastically.

"Okay, that would be great, but we don't know what will happen. Say Elizabeth happens to materialize in some way? What would happen then?" Jenna asked.

"That's why it should be a masquerade Halloween ball, perhaps with a request that costumes worn are period appropriate," Mrs. Forrester suggested, her pillowy face alive with excitement, making her eighty-three years seem much younger. "We have to at least try."

"That would be perfect," Toby said. Jenna smiled. It felt right.

The more they talked, the more things fell into place. The right time, the right place, the right cover. Even though Jenna told them the veil to the other side is thin a day before and a day after Halloween, they needed to shoot for privacy at midnight, the magical hour most associated with Halloween, when the veil is the thinnest. At least they hoped this was the message Jenna was getting. The party could start late, anticipating everyone would be out by ten or eleven, and they could all volunteer to clean up afterwards. Mrs. Forrester agreed she would stay with them. First of all, they had to have both Mr. Levy and Mr. Jacobs on board before pitching this to the Historical Association board for approval, as well as the town council. Taking their time going downstairs to stay in step with Mrs. Forrester, Toby called for the men to join then.

"You want to do what?" Mr. Jacobs asked, astonished, when the trio pitched their idea over their drinks. Mrs. Forrester had been sitting quietly behind the kids, letting them lead. Mr. Jacobs knew his son and the girls were really into learning about the mill. The one-eighty from the oldest member of the board took him by surprise. On the other hand, he remembered being their age when ghost stories were the big thing. He was sucked in just as much as the next kid when they started to understand abstract thinking. It was why he became a teacher. The infinite possibilities of the mind through history and books intoxicated him. He wanted to share it with others and now got a paycheck for doing what he loved so much. It would be hard for him to deny that to his own child.

Mr. Jacobs wasn't aware just how far the kids would go to get an old building fixed up. He was shocked and a little surprised that Toby would tackle something so large when he was intimidated so easily. Remembering the goal they had set together, he knew he had to try to support Toby as much as his son was supporting his cause.

"I would really love to get behind your idea, especially because we need the money, but I don't think it'll generate the interest or the funds," said Mr. Levy gently. "Those people might be this place's history, but they aren't famous. They didn't do anything special."

"Ah, but I also found something else out from my research." More papers were passed out. "I might be old, but I'm not deaf. I have been listening to you two chatter in front of me at historical meetings for eons, and you both tend to talk about the same things year after year. So, when I started to look for ways to bring people here, my curiosity got the best of me and I looked up Franz Wagner Wright." Surprise and confusion colored both men's faces. Mrs. Forrester spoke to Mr. Jacobs. "You mentioned him again a few weeks ago."

"I did?"

"Yes, you did," Mr. Levy confirmed as Mrs. Forrester nodded.

"I had to go through New York archives and wound up at the architecture library at Columbia University, but I found it, and they finally confirmed it with morning's mail." Mrs. Forrester held out official-looking documents and an envelope.

"This is his building. And I wasn't aware he was Frank Lloyd's grandfather. Even if Franz wasn't as popular as his grandson, he holds some clout by association. Who knows? Perhaps the architecture of today is due to his influence. If we can't get Missouri or Massachusetts to bring people in, I believe this will. But I would like to draw attention to the centennial this Halloween."

Mr. Jacobs just stared at the papers in his hands, shaking his head. "I never followed through," he mumbled.

"The history teacher in you never quit, it just got distracted," Mr. Levy offered, turning the envelope over to read the return address.

Mrs. Forrester presented her research on how extra funds could be generated. Even though there were moments when both men had doubts, they let her speak. When they were done there was a full minute of silence before anyone said anything. Tina was now chewing on a nail, and Toby was watching Jenna's knuckles turn white from squeezing her hands so tightly.

"Oh, my word, this is huge!" Mr. Levy exclaimed, slapping his smiling partner on his back.

"This could be huge. Maybe not enough time for this year's Halloween, but…"

"Dad," Toby interrupted, looking at the two girls, "it has to be this year."

"Toby, that is a huge undertaking, Buddy. I don't think we have time. I wouldn't want you all to struggle so hard…" Mr. Jacobs began.

"It might work, Tom," Mr. Levy said with a furrowed brow, looking over the handwritten ideas. "Yes, it would be a lot of effort," he continued. "The proposal passed. Majority ruled. Wouldn't it make sense for them to agree to utilize whatever means we can, to see this thing through to fruition? Rose, do you think we can put together a chart or graph to show others what this would look like on paper?"

"I believe we can." Mrs. Forrester smiled with pride. And, for the first time, they were all working together. "As far as board members are concerned it wouldn't take much to get my dear friend Gretchen Bailey to join us. And wherever she goes, Simon Dinkle will be happy to follow."

"Was Ms. Bailey the one who, uh, wore perfume to the meeting?" Jenna asked. She remembered how much her nose burned when the older woman walked past her to take her seat. Tina, holding back a huge smile, nodded her head violently.

"Yes, that's her."

The men ignored the girls' banter. It wasn't news to them. Gretchen had been wearing the same amount of perfume for as long as they had known her.

"Hey, this is something we've wanted for so long. If we can get people here, and for something fun, they would donate. I really think they would! I could crunch those numbers to make it happen."

"Mark, this just isn't possible," Mr. Jacobs said worriedly. "I want so badly to be optimistic. This had been proposed for years and years, and I'm shot down each time after I get my hopes up. I don't want to be let down again. But then again, I also don't want to miss this fleeting opportunity."

"This is where that leap of faith comes in, my friend. Let's make this one count."

"Okay, then. We'll make this count." The guarded expressed softened, and Mr. Jacobs began to write down all their ideas. He scribbled ideas and people's names. Mr. Levy added contacts and suggestions, and Mrs. Forrester offered a thought or two. Soon, both men had smiles on their faces and seemed to relax a little. Jenna had been watching them toss ideas back and forth.

"Maybe. If we put in a few hundred for this, here, and called what's-her-name to set us up with one of these..." he trailed off.

"What do we have to lose?"

"Yeah, what do we have to lose?"

"There's going to be a lot of manual labor involved," Mr. Jacobs started to say.

"...but it will be worth it, I can feel it," Jenna finished.

They spent the rest of their Saturday excitedly thinking up new ideas as they worked, cleaning up the mill. Both Mr. Jacobs and Mr. Levy had much more work ahead of them but felt buoyed with inspiration. They left to make phone calls to try to push the new proposal through Mr. Robertson. Mr. Levy mentioned they might get resistance from him but they would do their best. Jenna, Tina, and Toby all made the commitment to work after school a few days a week and their last full weekend before Halloween.

Seventeen

EMARKABLY, THE PLANNING went smoothly. Both fathers scrambled with details and found a lot of positive numbers. Both the council and the Historical Association gave their blessings in record time. After a few phone calls, they got the press they needed for out-of-state advertising. Surprisingly, there was a lot more community support interested in helping out then they imagined. Two committees volunteered and many individuals offered services once it was leaked that funds were so low.

Jenna was feeling more and more nervous as the days passed, and her thoughts constantly seemed to find their way back to the mill and Joseph. She was also busy helping her mom sew her costume. She learned the basics in fourth grade during a lesson and took to it like a frog to water. After that, she made clothes for her dolls out of her outgrown clothes. Jenna wanted a plain, brown full skirt and white, high-collared blouse with buttons down the front. The sleeves were a little tricky; they puffed out from a pleat at the shoulder but tapered down and were quite fitted from the elbow to the wrist. For reasons that made a lot of sense to her, it made her feel comfortable. It was like putting on a favorite pair of sweats after wearing dress-up clothes for church.

Tina's mom couldn't sew at all, so she was renting her outfit from a costume place. Jenna and Tina had looked through a huge book taken from the library for ideas on what was fashionable back then. Tina was excited after she picked her costume out and giggled, saying that it was going to be a surprise. So, no one else knew what she was going to look like. Toby and his dad were coordinating their clothes with suspenders and handlebar moustaches. Toby said he might even be able to borrow his grandfather's father's old pocket watch.

Jenna's mom made that clicking sound with her tongue every time she had trouble with the pattern or made a mistake. "I could have bought you one of those beautiful high society dresses, you know, with matching parasol and wide-brimmed hat."

Jenna didn't say anything. Her mother's vision was of a completely different era. "I like this one better, Mom."

"No, you choose to be a plain Jane, and even with my experience sewing—you take after me on that, Jenna—I still manage to goof it up," Mrs. Stevens said. She winked at her daughter. Jenna rolled her eyes and sighed as if implying it was a ridiculous thing to say.

Gwen Stevens didn't understand Jenna's obsession with the mill. It was all she ever talked about now. Even when she wasn't talking about it, there was an edge to her expressions. She was very preoccupied. Gwen didn't know if it was a stage of development or something else. Then again, she didn't really understand her daughter. Sometimes Jenna would come out with something much more mature than she thought a little girl was capable of. The precocious statements in combination with Jenna's dreams—especially the dreams—made Jenna's mother nervous. It teetered on the edge of reason. Gwen had no desire to explore the possibilities. Just a few nights ago she heard Jenna talking in her sleep, which she had never done before. Of course, it was about that building, something about coming to the window by the sewing machines. Gwen was glad she had a good relationship with her daughter even if it wasn't an extremely close one, but was even more glad Jenna was a daddy's girl. She was content to bond with her eldest child by sewing and planting flowers.

"Mom, really, it's so simple, it's beautiful," Jenna gushed. And she meant it.

That night Jenna dreamed again. This time she was not at her window or Elizabeth's window. It took her a while to realize she was in the mill. Her dark skirts swished as she walked up the staircase and into the room on the right where she worked, sometimes twelve hours a day. In these hours, however, she completely forgot about the heat, or the cramped fingers and stiff necks. The room was just a place where she could sit on soft cotton, gaze into Joseph's eyes, and dream about the future with him.

She walked between the shelves on either side that held the bolts of material and large spools of colorful thread that reeked endlessly of the dye. She expertly maneuvered around the rows of bulky, metal sewing units and baskets with finished and unfinished linens without a second's hesitation, the handkerchief folded neatly in her satchel. Her thoughts were full of the anticipation of expressing her intent to marry, but something was different this day. Angry voices surrounded her. As if looking through a screen, Jenna squinted, unable to see clearly. She couldn't find the source, but was aware of two men yelling. An uneasy feeling in her stomach made her heart speed up.

We've been caught! I haven't had time to...!

The voices rumbled, volleying back and forth while her anxiety grew. Finally, Jenna heard a distinct sound close by her. It was the memory of a voice her mind recognized more than her ears. It was a voice that was unknown to her but also one she would know anywhere. It was the voice of Joseph.

No! Elizabeth!

Jenna became dizzy, but that wasn't important. Only the man's scream mattered. The sound imprinted on her soul. Her heart broke in two and her mind, the same. It stopped her very being from existing, and breathing ceased.

Jenna woke up in her bed, gasping frantically. Covered with sweat, her hands were outstretched, reaching to hold him, save him. She was disoriented with vertigo, and it took a good minute for her to breathe normally. The distinctive smells were gone, but Jenna was sure she'd be able to recognize them again, as would she recognize the exact colors of the material and thread.

Elizabeth was trying to show her what happened that Halloween. The Halloween she—correction, Elizabeth—lost Joseph forever. Jenna felt Elizabeth's longing to grab onto anything that could bridge the fleeting moment in space and join them again. In over a hundred years there were others she tried to connect with, but no one had the ability to do so like Jenna did. It was meant to be Jenna, and both could feel how close they were.

THE NEXT WEDNESDAY evening, the twenty-first, was a stormy one that epitomized everything about late autumn in New York: windy and brisk. The few hardy leaves on the trees were now brown and being plucked by the gusts, filling the air with their tiny, swirling images. The moon was high and bright but intermittently hidden by the large, ominous clouds that warned of the impending winter.

Jenna and Toby were on their third trip to the basement to bring up boxes for the dumpster. The three agreed that cleaning the rest of the mill wasn't nearly as bad as dealing with what was jam-packed downstairs. It took hours to go through everything and sort out what was salvageable and what was garbage. It was even more difficult when some of the doors that were wedged open were closed tightly when they returned from dropping off a load of trash. It was as if the building wanted to put them two steps behind for every one they made going forward. The electricity was also being rewired, and it seemed like forever for the trio to get used to using generators and flashlights.

"It sure makes you appreciate Thomas Edison and Ma Bell," Toby said sarcastically.

Jenna stopped moving, looked up at Toby, and blew her bangs away from her eyes. They had all just finished the unit on lights and sound in Social Studies. "What does the phone company have to do with the electric?" she asked.

"Well," Toby began, able to cover his incorrect facts by blushing in the darkness, "nothing, really." A tin can fell over not too far away.

"Back me up here, Tina, will you?" he asked. They waited with smiles on their faces. A few seconds went by without a reply, and both smiles faded quickly to nervousness.

"'I heard someone knock over a can. Did you hear it Jenna?"

"Yeah."

"Teen?"

"Maybe it was a rat?" Jenna suggested as they ran up the stairs into the main room.

"Hey, why are you guys running? I could've sworn you

both were standing behind me just a minute ago. I felt a bit silly. I was talking to nobody," Tina admitted sheepishly after meeting them at the threshold. Jenna and Toby looked at each other and then around the room.

"Yeah, we thought you were downstairs with us," Toby said.

"Oh," Tina said, putting her arms around herself. "I'm not sure if I'm really ready for all this."

Jenna was looking around the great room, listening for anything she could hear out of the ordinary. She began to walk along the wall, smiling while she ran her hand across the woodwork. "You know, these rooms actually look so much younger in my dreams."

"You pay attention to walls in your dreams?" Tina asked.

It was times like this that made Jenna feel like an outsider. She knew how it felt to not fit in with others her age. Her face fell and she stood there awkwardly.

"I mean, maybe it's a girl thing? I don't pay that much attention to anything, even when I have to," Toby interjected. Jenna could tell he was trying to soothe her hurt feelings. Sometimes Tina didn't realize how sensitive Jenna was about her odd talent.

"Sorry," Tina offered. She hit herself on the side of her head with her palm and rolled her eyes as if to say she was being a jerk.

"I think it's cool what you can do, Jenna. You're still you, just like Clark Kent, who does normal things but who sometimes has super powers."

Tina nodded to show her solidarity. "I bet Superman's friends goof up sometimes and don't understand." After a moment, she continued a little more quietly. "What's it like?"

"It's hard to explain," Jenna said, realizing these friends were worth keeping. "This has never happened to me before.

Sure, I've had strange dreams or knew stuff I couldn't know, but not all the time like it happens now. There's something different about this building." It was about then her voice lilted as her mind wandered. "It's the same but different. The wood is brighter and smoother. The walls aren't dried out and cracked. The feel of the air isn't heavy like it is now." She had a smile of anticipation that was unlike Jenna's smile. The face was the same, but the muscles moved differently. It wasn't a smile that looked familiar to Tina or Toby. Her eyes also seemed a bit lighter than they thought they were. Instead of a warm brown they appeared teak. It made the other two uneasy.

The front door banged shut and everyone jumped and spun around to look. They were so absorbed they had not heard Mrs. Forrester drive up.

"Ooh, that wind is a-whippin'! I didn't mean to close it so hard," Mrs. Forrester said, trying to tuck stray hairs under her hat. Her teal overcoat brought out the blue of her eyes and accented the pure gray of her hair. A few hairs had escaped, and she caught them expertly and put them back where they belonged.

"Mrs. F., weird things are happening around here," Tina complained.

"I had expected they would," Mrs. Forrester said nonchalantly. "When surroundings are changed, the spirits that are attached to a particular place get all stirred up. Did you see anything?" she asked eagerly.

"No, not really, but I felt someone behind me up here," Tina said.

"Something was making noise downstairs, too. Like, on purpose," Jenna added, once again looking and sounding like her old self.

"The doors lock up one minute and then open fine the

next. I've felt cold spots upstairs, and some of the other volunteers have been complaining of items disappearing, too," Toby interjected.

"Well, we've agreed to this. This has happened every time a renovation is attempted. It's the building's way of trying to get us to leave, but we know better. Stay on your toes and watch out for danger. Maybe we can do our business and be done with it before it gets to be too much. We need to accept the good and the bad," Mrs. Forrester stated. "Miss Jenna, you're still having dreams, I presume?"

"Yes. I'm almost always by a window now, but it's no longer the one at Elizabeth's home. Mostly it's here in the room upstairs where Joseph fell out."

Mrs. Forrester straightened her sweater, contemplating. "Hmm. Perhaps it's the window."

"What?" Perplexed faces stared up at her.

"That room, but very specifically that window, is at the root of every renovation project tragedy. It's the room that has seen the ghostliest activity, according to legends. Maybe the window portal started with Joseph's accident. Or maybe it's because of the window itself."

"You lost us, Mrs. F.," Toby admitted.

"Spirits must cross over through a portal. It's a doorway, for a better word, from the realm beyond to this one. That doorway is easier to go through…"

"…when the veil is thinnest at Halloween," Jenna interrupted, excitement in her voice.

"Yes, dear. I'm beginning to think that window is a portal. Whether one actually exists is up for discussion, but the coincidences are far too great. What has been happening with Jenna also proves something is at work here. Regardless, I'd like you all to take extra care in that room, please."

"We sure will," they all answered.

"Now go, do your work and I'll try to occupy myself."

They went back to cleaning, apprehensive with each crack of thunder and every time the generators lagged. The lights dimmed and returned to full power every few minutes. Mrs. Forrester found that writing out the music list and helping with some paperwork kept her busy but not overexerted. Each child was thoroughly exhausted when Mrs. Forrester drove them home that night.

Jenna's dreams were almost nightly now. They had changed drastically from handkerchiefs and phrases to shouting, running, and the feeling of falling. Faces and voices were becoming clearer. She was moving about as if she were actually a part of the other world instead of being an observer. It was hard for Jenna to decipher if they were dreams or memories as both would blur together. Each nightmare would leave her gasping for breath and cold with sweat, her heart racing. They were disturbing and prevented her from getting restful sleep. She was so preoccupied with Elizabeth's thoughts she didn't realize how sleep deprived she was.

Eighteen

FRIDAY WAS OCTOBER twenty-third. Book report day. Jenna knew she had to have done it. It was a toss-up between *Charlotte's Web* and *The Lion, The Witch and the Wardrobe*. She had read both even before moving to Orchard Creek, so she knew it wouldn't be a difficult assignment. She had chosen C.S. Lewis. Somehow, she couldn't find the written report. She also couldn't really remember filling out the questions. It was so out of the norm for her, Mrs. Gaffe let her give an oral report after class instead, which she aced, but warned her it was the only freebie she'd get all year.

In third period Home Ec. her tablemate, Chloe, who at thirteen was boy crazy and already wearing makeup, stared at her. Just when Jenna thought she might have the start of a pimple or something, Chloe came over to her desk. "You know, my mother uses concealer to hide the bags under her eyes. You might way to get some for yourself."

Even Timmy Meecum and his friend Craig noticed a change. Jenna's sullen expression had pulled their attention away from their video game conversations at the lunch table, and had them asking her if she was feeling okay. She smiled and said she had been up too late reading a good book. Unless it was on gaming or building programs, she knew neither boy would ask more.

On autopilot for the rest of her classes, she got through the day mostly unscathed. The whole note she held out in chorus when everyone else observed the rest symbol in the music was a little embarrassing, but it passed when Mr. Alberici shook his head and motioned for the baritones to start the next section. She could concentrate sporadically, with much effort, but it was exhausting. Her thoughts and actions were continuously wrapped up in thoughts of Joseph and the handkerchief. There was no way she could redirect them, and they gave her nothing positive in return. So, by the last class of the day she felt like her mind was being pulled apart by wrestlers.

As close as she was to her loving family, her parents had started to worry, too. It was becoming obvious her behavior had changed. She was always in a daydream, and it was hard for her to focus. Her chores were either incomplete or ignored entirely, which was unlike her. Jenna's mother mentioned hearing Jenna say the name "Joseph" while sleeping and had started to think Jenna had a case of puppy love. Maybe it was because a crush was a normal part of junior high, but Jenna's mother immediately jumped to the conclusion that that was why Jenna was behaving differently. A crush sounded convincing, and it wasn't too far off. Jenna went with it. She knew it was wrong but wasn't interested in correcting anyone. That excuse got her out of a lot of sticky situations but still her parents were now watching her like a hawk. Small catnaps before they came home from work helped revitalize her so she could function almost normally when home. Peter never knew the difference, and she managed to pull it off.

By Saturday the twenty-fourth, they were down to the wire, but at least the weather spared them rough conditions. It was a warm day and sunny, shining brightly and bringing out the last of the bees. This was the last full weekend they had to work. The areas of the mill that needed rewiring for lighting—the main room, sewing room and office—were finally completed. It took over a week. Each room had been cleaned out and organized as best as it could considering the time remaining. Most of the rooms upstairs had some fresh paint, and a volunteer team from a local carpentry outfit was still there working on sanding and refurnishing the large pieces of woodwork. The room to the right with the window overlooking the orchard was becoming known as the Sewing Room.

The Historical Association's president, Mr. Robertson, had hunted down four sewing units over the past three decades and got them, and the one Mr. Levy purchased about a year ago, out of his basement, happy to have them back where they belonged. They had been brought over and set up in the Sewing Room, taking half the day to be bolted to the floor.

The staircase in the great room was a huge job. Tina, Toby and Jenna had re-stained the wood a deep walnut the week before, and now they were applying clear polyurethane to the railings themselves. Thanks to the warm weather, everything was drying faster than anticipated.

When they were alone enough to talk freely about their plan, the kids tried to think about the best way to allow Jenna to do whatever she had to do. Most times they came up with nothing more than just standing by to troubleshoot if anyone seemed to get in the way.

Being as warm as it was, every one of the volunteers was wearing T-shirt, and the mill's floor-to-ceiling windows were open. It was also helpful to finally be able to air out the fumes from the painting and staining. The last few days had been raining and cold and the fumes from the chemicals had made everyone lightheaded.

By early evening, Jenna and Toby were on the stairs finishing up the balusters near the main level, and Tina was working from the floor up to the balusters on the outside railing. "That's the last from my can. I'm going upstairs to the Sewing Room to get more. Does anyone else need a refill?" Jenna asked, rubbing her eye with the back of her hand. She was tired and getting a headache.

Tina and Toby each had half a can left. They decided to take a break and get some fresh air, and Jenna said she would do the same after she came back downstairs. The two of them talked about a mutual friend from elementary school, who was moving next month, as they went outside to the apple trees to find a snack. Jenna stayed behind. She slid to the side as a worker came downstairs, then she trudged slowly up to the large Sewing Room. It looked great. It was the room of focus for the day, and all the painting supplies were there along with one other person who was lingering near the window. The dinner hour had cleared the place out.

Jenna stood in the doorway, catching her breath from coming upstairs and took in the artifacts. The sewing units were like small tables that resembled desks and had the cumbersome sewing units set into them. The metal machines were a dark, weathered gray compared to the bright silver bolts used to anchor them to the floor. Two of the units were in poor shape, rusted from the humidity of wherever they had been stored, but intact just the same. A few other sewing-related items were off to the side, ready to be added once the room was done. Seeing the item made Jenna feel both happy and homesick. Her eyes continued past the machines to the large picture window, which was across from her and overlooked the apple orchard. The setting sun was lighting the sky up with reds and oranges.

Jenna took a deep breath, letting the breeze blow in on her. It felt good. She knew enough to stay away from the window itself; that was safe. Putting down her empty can, she pulled her hair back, twisting it into a bun, and wrapped it with the green hair scrunchy she had on her wrist. Tiny tendrils escaped on each side, framing her face in waves. The scrunchy matched her green tee. She did not in any way resemble Oscar the Grouch like Toby kidded her. On the left, next to the door, was a thick tarp with a dozen various paint, stain and polyurethane cans on it. Beside that, a metal ladder rested against the wall and another stood ready beyond that. Just inside the room, empty cans from the day's work sat on a small wooden table topped with a cheap plastic tablecloth. Used paint brushes and stirring sticks were scattered on one end.

Ignoring the other worker, she walked over to the supplies but couldn't find any more of the cans she was using. Blowing her bangs out of her face, she reached behind her to untie the oversized, long brown apron she had on to protect her clothes. "Sorry, I was wondering, are there any more of these cans of poly around for the main staircase?" As soon as she turned towards him, she realized something was off. The tall, dark-haired man facing the window was looking out at the orchard. His hands were together behind his back, holding a black top hat. Despite the heat, he wore a thick, black jacket and heavy black pants. He had on black boots, but they weren't work boots. A cold chill started to climb up her neck as she realized the breeze she felt came from that window, even though the man seemed to be standing in the way.

Jenna's heart started to race. She backed up quickly, tripping on the cans on the drape and landed awkwardly on her back. The man turned away from the window and looked directly at her. His face was angry, and his lips seemed to sneer at her from under his bushy moustache. She squinted as the sun shone through him. She cringed, realizing that this was not one of the hired workers. She knew exactly who it was. He walked toward her, his black boots soundless on the hardwood floor.

"You! You simple, peasant worker! How dare you think you are worthy of my brother! I have lost him because of you. Now, though, I will take care of matters as I had intended, and you will be punished."

He kept coming at Jenna as she scrambled to get up, but her feet kept getting caught up in the drop cloth that bunched on the floor. She made it nearly upright when she slipped on the tie to her apron. Sliding and fumbling she went nowhere. He loomed over her, reaching down, bringing with him a coldness that immediately chilled her to the bone. She was unable to make a sound as she felt Seth Sawyer's icy hands encircle her throat.

"Nooo!" Jenna managed to gasp, trying to yell as her throat was closing.

"You will not have him. You cannot take him away from me!" Seth's voice cracked with desperation. Jenna struggled for breath, her vision changing from the brightness of day to spots of black as dark as night.

"Joseph, help me! Seth, please, no!" Jenna heard herself say as she rolled free. She got a grip on the tablecloth just off to her side and pulled. Down came the multitude of half-filled paint and stain cans. Stars swam in front of her as she felt herself being pulled up by the apron she was still wearing. Jenna fought and kicked, her sneakers squeaking, but no one heard her.

From the corner of her eye, Jenna could see the faint shadow of a young man by the window. His image was as faint as Seth's was clear. He was yelling, pleading, but no sound came out. Her heart raced even more as she realized he was here. Joseph.

Joseph! Help me, he's going to kill me! Help me!

Jenna could no longer hear anything but her own rapid heartbeat as she was dragged. She fought every step of the way, her hands trying to find purchase, but she couldn't seem to connect with anything. She was finally able to grab onto one of the machines. She hung on as her body was pulled taut until she lost her grip, her fingers not strong enough to find anything else in their path. She fell, her head banging on the sewing table on the way down. Her arms went limp and the struggle stopped as she was dragged away. Jenna heard and felt nothing as the blackness engulfed her.

JENNA OPENED HER eyes and looked around. She was definitely in a hospital. She was on a thin bed that was elevated and had railings on both sides. Ugly gray cabinets with a small lock by the pull were against the harsh white wall to her left. Large machines with wires and monitors were off in a corner by a white board that told Jenna her nurse for today was Judy. She was sore, her head ached, and it took a lot of effort to focus. A poster of a cartoon picture of a boy blowing his nose into a tissue was next to the same boy washing his hands in a sink. She closed her eyes and tried to remember what had happened and how she had gotten here. All she could remember was pain, and lights, and voices—Tina's, Toby's, her father's. It took some time for her to remember what had happened and why she might be here. Her parents were sacked out in the chairs next to her. As she tried to sit up, they roused, startled, but seemed relieved to see her awake.

"How are you feeling, honey?" her mother asked, taking her hand and smoothing her hair off her forehead. For once her mom's hair resembled her brother's as it stood up every which way.

"What happened? Things are a bit fuzzy," Jenna answered.

"Well, we were hoping you would be able to fill us in. Toby and Tina said they came upstairs looking for you when you didn't meet them outside and found you by the window, unconscious. The room was a mess, like there had been a struggle. You've had a concussion, Jenna. What happened up there?"

Jenna thought fast. She remembered the details very well now but wasn't sure it was wise to start talking about ghosts and attacks while lying in a hospital bed.

"I went upstairs to get more paint. Those fumes must have gotten to me and, I, got dizzy," she stammered. "I think maybe I went to the window for some air." She gingerly touched the side of her head where it ached the most. "I tripped and hit my head."

"Well, at any rate, we're glad you're awake now." Her mom said, smiling, her relief evident in her tired eyes.

"How long…? What's today?" Jenna asked nervously.

"Sunday. It's the twenty-fifth. The doctor said if you were to come around soon you would probably be able to go home tomorrow," her father answered.

She sank back into the bed, relieved. It wasn't too late. A few hours later Tina's family visited after church. They brought flowers with a little "Get Well Soon" balloon tied on a stick.

"How are you, Jenna?" Mrs. Levy asked, kissing her on the cheek. Tina stood just behind her mother. Her wide blue eyes took in everything in the room.

"I'm doing okay. I can go home tomorrow."

Mr. Levy seemed relieved and smiled as he put his hands in the pocket of his gray dress pants. "I don't know what happened at the mill, but I feel responsible. I'm sorry you got hurt when you've worked so hard to help us out. Was there something in your way? Anything Tom or I can fix or do so no one else gets hurt?"

"No," she said. She was learning not to shake her head because it upset her stomach. "You know, it was me." After a second, she added, "I'm a klutz and tripped on the apron strings." That was true. "Um, can I talk with Tina so she knows what classes she has to go to for my homework?"

"Of course. Do you need anything else?" Mrs. Levy asked.

"Could you find me some ginger ale? That would be great." While Tina's parents left the room in search of the nurse, Tina gingerly sat on the bed. The flower barrette she had used to pull all her hair back had slid to the left creating an uneven wave of black hair against her ear. She pulled the hair underneath to tighten, it which only made a rat's nest of knotted hair above the clip.

"Are you really okay? We've been worried sick."

Jenna pulled herself up in bed, feeling completely like her old self except when she moved her head too fast and the room spun. "It was Seth. He came back!" she whispered.

Tina's eyes bugged out and she started to look a little green. "Mrs. Forrester was worried about something like this. She feels awful that you were hurt. She isn't sure we should keep going. I mean it's not a big deal. You almost—"

Jenna's stomach lurched. She leaned forward before realizing she was doing it, her hands digging into the blankets to meet her friend eye to eye. "No! It is a big deal. This is real and we are the only ones who can set it to rights. I'm telling you, we need to get Elizabeth to find Joseph. Once that happens, I think this will all settle down."

"You think?" Tina asked while she chewed off her lip gloss.

"Yeah, I'm pretty sure." Jenna's mind was a tug of war with what needed to be done and what could potentially happen.

Tina was the biggest worrywart she ever knew, but deep down the feelings didn't lie.

"You're sure sure?"

"Tina, we have to do this. There won't be another chance. It's us, or they have to wait again, maybe forever. I can't let that happen. Elizabeth can't wait. She's a part of me now." Jenna didn't realize how true that was until she said it out loud.

Tina's eyes dropped while she fiddled with the strap of her purse. "As scary as that is, we all know that. I mean, Mrs. Forrester and Toby and me. We figured it out a while ago. We just needed to know where you wanted to go from here 'cause there are risks like this. Jenna, I'm freaked out. This is creepy."

"It's what they want and I can get them there. We need to be there at the mill on Halloween. We just need to make that happen. Please help me make it happen." The strain this had put on Jenna exhausted her. She fell back into the pillow just as Mrs. Levy knocked on the door. "Just check with my homeroom teacher for my assignments, okay?"

"It's scary."

"I know. I'm scared, too."

Nineteen

*J*ENNA WENT HOME the next day and returned to school on the twenty-ninth. She still didn't feel one hundred percent. She was unsure if it was a physical tiredness from the incident or the weight of two worlds on her. Tina and Toby had been working extra hard at the mill but seemed uneasy talking about it when Jenna asked. Since they were both there after school every night, she was by herself much more than usual, with too much time to think. Her mom and dad had made helping at the mill off limits, which was driving her crazy.

With her costume completely done even before Saturday's incident, she was bored and restless. Jenna even took to wearing it around the house. It just felt so right. The handkerchief went everywhere with her, secure in the apron pocket. She felt safer with it so near. After her dad came home from work that night, Jenna felt it necessary to find out what was going on.

"What's been going on at the mill? How much is done? Do they have the decorations all ready?" she asked. Her mom and dad sighed and looked at each other, concern on both their faces.

"We're not sure if it's the best thing for you right now to go on Halloween. You've been acting so funny lately, so consumed, and with the accident…" her mom trailed off.

Jenna's mouth dropped open, and all she could do was stare at them. This could not be happening, she thought.

He's so close! I need to be with my Joseph!

"What? Why? Mom!" Jenna cried. "I'm fine. I've worked so hard on it!"

"Your mother and I are just trying to do what's best for you," her dad replied.

Jenna stopped, thinking her usual crying and carrying on would only make things worse. Instead, she looked down at the floor and thought a moment, and with as much control as she could muster spoke calmly.

"I know. I'm feeling better and the accident was just, you know, a fluky thing. I was the one who set this all up for Mr. Jacobs, and it will be good for the town. I think I had a lot to do with having Mrs. Forrester give the final okay. I've put a lot of my own time into volunteering for a good cause. I would very much like to be a part of the event. Can you please think it over?" She was on the verge of tears and was trying very hard to say the right thing, to keep her cool. Her parents looked at one another with all the wind knocked out of their sails, ready to tackle a huge meltdown.

"We'll think about it, Jenna. Thank you for being so mature about this."

Jenna walked back to her room and sat on the cushion of the window seat. It was already dark with nothing to see outside. Jenna didn't need her eyes. She could feel the connection to the mill through every fiber of being, pulling her. It was like it was always there, had always been there. Her mind was buzzing with Joseph's name over and over. These thoughts—Elizabeth's thoughts—swam through her, mixing with her own fears.

She could hear a conversation between her parents going on in the next room. It lasted for quite a while. Irrational thoughts of sneaking out of the house if she needed to crossed her mind. She knew telling them what was really going on was a huge gamble she couldn't afford to take, even if her dad believed her and Mrs. Forrester backed her up. She felt trapped and desperate. Everything rested on this one decision her parents would make, and they were completely unaware of its true importance.

The phone rang and Jenna scrambled to get it. Her parents hadn't stopped talking and didn't really notice.

"Hello Miss Jenna, it's Mrs. Forrester. I wanted to see how you were feeling."

Jenna had been holding back her tears, but now they overflowed as she smoothed and resmoothed the hem of her apron. She began telling Mrs. Forrester everything that had happened since Saturday. Mrs. Forrester listened until Jenna had cried herself out. In a soothing voice, she reassured her and promised she would talk to her parents.

"You understood my reservations in the beginning of all this, right?"

"Yes, you thought we were being friendly just to get you to vote for the museum."

"And that wasn't it at all. I've been thinking a lot about everything. I never really questioned why I held onto my grandmother's diary, or why I did if it was chock full of details of someone else's life. I kept up my family's album even though I have no family to pass it on to."

"I don't understand," Jenna admitted between sniffles.

"Perhaps I've been a kind of caretaker for all these years. Maybe my job was to watch over the mill until just the right time. I'm convinced it's the right time now. There are just too many oddities that have led us to this point in time. Don't you agree?"

"Yes. I know I have to do this."

"I believe you do, too. I also think fate has brought us together as well, to be my family in a way. I have so enjoyed everyone's company."

"You mean me and Tina and Toby?"

"I do. I've enjoyed the laughter and love, and I think you've given a little of my youth back to me. I will do my best to see that you close the door that somehow has been opened."

"Thanks, Mrs. F. We love you, too." Jenna knew Mrs. Forrester was, for the second time, her only hope.

Jenna walked on pins and needles the rest of the night. The next day, Friday, neither Tina nor Toby could get her to relax. They avoided mentioning the mill, and even when Jenna dug for details, they were still hesitant about talking. For the first time Jenna truly felt alone. By 8 p.m., she was all by herself. Her favorite show, *Sabrina the Teenage Witch*, failed to keep her attention as she patiently waited for her parents to return and give her an answer. At this point she wished someone would just call to tell her. Her mother had her monthly book club meeting after work and her dad had go back to the office after he dropped Pete off at a friend's house for a party. When her parents came home, she had nodded off for an hour or so. Not realizing she was waiting for them, they turned in. Jenna awoke a short time later to a dark and quiet house. She hardly slept that night.

On Saturday, she wandered around the house, unable to find anything to distract her. Her time had almost run out. It hurt her to continue wearing the costume so, amid a flurry of tears, she changed back into her jeans. There was no way she could leave the handkerchief, so she folded it and put it in her front pocket. The forced normalcy was anything but. She had kept her promise and had not bugged her parents again, as Mrs. Forrester advised. Her mom saw the look on her face and asked that she just hang in there until her dad got home from an emergency meeting out of town. It would be cutting it close. Today was, after all, Halloween.

She went through the motions of the day, feeling more like Elizabeth and less like Jenna. Each tick-tock of the clock seemed to taunt her—not yet... not yet... not yet. Finally, she couldn't wish any longer. She picked up the phone and tapped in the Levys' number.

"Hello?"

"Tina, it's me Jenna."

"You sound awful. Is it your concussion?"

"No, my head's better. It's not going to happen; I just know it. Mom made us sandwiches to tide us over because Dad's not even home yet, and no one's said anything either way. I can tell they're split on this. I was so sure Mrs. Forrester could convince them. I think," she took a breath and pushed the rest of the words out her mouth quickly, "I think you'll have to start making plans without me."

"Oh, Jenna, I don't know." Tina hesitated. "This stuff has been making me nervous."

Jenna felt like blowing up. It was bad enough feeling hopeless; it was excruciating feeling Elizabeth's desperation added to it. "Please, no!" Jenna said in a breathy voice. It was a bit higher than Tina was used to hearing. Then it changed to sounding like plain old Jenna. "Well, someone has to do it. Before you leave stop over here and I'll give you the handkerchief."

Tina blew out a long sigh. The last few days had been confusing. She wasn't sure who she was talking to anymore or who was answering her. All she knew for certain was she was Jenna's friend, and lately being a friend was hard work. "Then what?"

"I don't know. I'm not sure Elizabeth will leave me. Hope for the best, I guess."

"I don't think I can do this," Tina whispered.

"Yes, you must!"

"Huh?"

"Just stick together with Toby and Mrs. Forrester, 'kay?"

"Okay, but I'm going to have faith that you'll be there. If you can't, I'll have Dad bring me back around—um—nine to pick up the handkerchief. How about that?"

Jenna knew Tina wasn't a confrontational kind of girl. She also knew Tina fidgeted every time they talked about ghosts. "Okay, but don't forget."

"No, there's no way I could forget. My fingers are crossed."

"Yeah, so are mine."

No one said anything as they sat down together for a very late dinner around 8:30. The huge bank glitch that had cost a Friday evening and half a weekend day had put Jack in a bad mood, especially since his wife was upset with him about this mill thing anyway. The trick-or-treaters had come and gone, and it was a quiet and sober meal in the large dining room. Peter was still dressed as a pirate. His old brown pants, two inches too short, had been cut off roughly just below the knee. He had on an old white dress shirt he used to wear for family photos, before he stained it with chocolate milk. A raggedy, pieced-together red vest completed the ensemble. He continued to wear a patch over his eye, even as he ate his corn. He had been excited and gone out trick or treating, but Jenna had not, which made Jack feel all the more guilty.

Jenna loved Halloween. Every year she announced it was her favorite of all holidays, something she had starting saying back when she was only three. This year it didn't happen. Instead, she sat at the table, wound so tightly that when the clock chimed nine across the room, she jumped. Why was this such a hard thing for him to say yes to? While he ate his mashed potatoes, he replayed the conversation he had had with his wife late last night.

"Jack, she's being very patient, but she's a mess and it hurts me to watch her. I just don't understand." It was ten-thirty on Friday. Gwen was in bed already, her bedside light on and a book open in her lap. He started to undress by the closet, the tiredness of working eight hours, then returning for another three piled onto the weight of this circular argument. It was unlike them to be so at odds. He knew moving would create a new dynamic, but not like this. His family had seemed unbalanced these last few months. Something felt…off.

"I know Gwen, and I'm sorry."

"You don't think it's something…"

"Honey, I've told you. I don't think it's something she's gotten into. I know our kid, and she isn't into drugs or alcohol."

"You know I worry about her."

"And I know you don't like her infatuation with that building."

"No, I don't," Gwen said tersely. He knew her temper was

starting to rise again. He wasn't sure if she was jealous about the way Jenna immersed herself in the things she was interested in, or if it was because Jenna's hobbies were so atypical. Sometimes his wife's unfounded insecurity got the best of her. As if she read his mind, she sighed and continued. "I know I get a little crazed. And I'll admit I don't understand her attraction to old things, but she has worked hard, too. Just yesterday Mary Pringle at the post office complimented us on how mature and driven she is. She and Kay Chow from the school board gushed about how much of a difference Jenna's made to this town already, considering she's only twelve."

Jack crawled into bed beside his wife and kissed her on the cheek. Those were all fair points and he was aware of all of them. He also had a strange feeling Jenna was pulling a fast one on them. Something just felt wrong about his daughter being in that place the next night. Maybe he was overtired and overthinking everything. If Gwen could put aside her issues, maybe he could work through his.

"You couldn't wait to move here and give the kids a real Halloween experience, remember?" she said, quietly. "They're growing up so fast." At that he had to smile.

"Halloween has always been fun with them," he admitted. "You always got the short end of the stick, staying home to hand out candy while the kids and I would dress up and hit all the neighbors' places. But you're right. This old town lends to the atmosphere that could never be achieved back in Steel."

"It does. You couldn't wait to get out here to smell the crisp fall air and crunch through autumn leaves going from house to house. I had forgotten the smells being in the city, but it's amazing how fast I'm whisked back in time to when I was young. When life seemed simple and perfect. I want that for them, too. Jenna's not much different from you. You want your childhood memories of Halloween to be their memories."

"I do. I don't want to seem like we're stringing Jenna along either. She's been so mature about this. I promise we'll talk about it tomorrow."

"Well, we'll have to. When the sun comes back up it'll be Halloween."

"I know. I'm bushed and I've got to get some sleep tonight. Bob's not sure if we'll need to meet with the bank reps in the morning, and we can't lose that line. We'll let her know first thing."

Jack chewed the last bite of his meatloaf before running his right hand over his face. "First thing" ended up being called in to work before Jenna got out of bed. Here it was, past the magical hour of begging for candy, and the house was unhappy and sullen. It depressed him. He put his fork down, knowing there was no more time to mull it over and no more time to discuss the decision in private.

"Jenna, your mom and I have had a hard time agreeing about what we should do," he began.

Jenna's head shot up. When she saw her mother looking confused and her father looking pained, her heart fell.

"I know how important this is to you, and we just want you to be safe. Of course, we want you to have fun. Halloween is supposed to be fun, especially for our first one in Orchard Creek. I will be happy to drop you off at the party right after dinner," he said, taking her mom's hand and squeezing it. Her mother's face brightened and Jenna jumped up and down, nearly knocking over her chair. She was ecstatic.

"Can we all go, Dad?" Peter asked, smiling eagerly. "I still have my costume on." He pointed to it in case everyone at the table had forgotten.

"I think the costumes have to be special, honey," his mom answered gently.

"Um, I think it would be okay. It's really not that hard to put together an outfit," Jenna said excitedly, sliding back into her seat. "But maybe you can drop me off first?" she asked. The event was from five until eleven. She still had time, and Tina had not stopped by to pick up the handkerchief. It had been very close, but their gamble had paid off.

Jenna felt scattered as she ran into her room, throwing on her dress and blouse. She pulled her hair up high, pinning it securely with the antique hairpin that had been in Elizabeth's possession box. With each addition Jenna realized it was one step closer to Elizabeth and one step away from her mind and her memories. She had a rough time with the new granny boots her mother had bought her, as they were still very stiff.

Looking at the bright-eyed girl in the mirror, dressed from head to toe in clothes from an earlier century, it was like inhabiting a character from a video game with really awesome graphics. She grabbed her satchel and shawl and ran for the door. Her dad was warming up the car. She couldn't believe she was actually going to go! Jenna had no idea what the mill was going to look like. She hadn't been there in a whole week.

Since forever.

As her dad pulled out of the driveway, she smiled as she thought about what Toby was going to look like with a long moustache. Unfortunately, the handkerchief was still in the pocket of her jeans, not in the apron pocket or satchel.

Twenty

"**O**H NO! STOP!" Jenna yelled. Her dad slammed on the brakes, looking around.

"Sorry, dad. I left something really important in my room." With that she ran back in the house as fast as she could, hiking up the long skirt, and bounded up the stairs two at a time. She tried not to think what would have happened being at the mill without the handkerchief, tonight of all nights.

Something changed, a shift of some kind happened as she gingerly retrieved the handkerchief. It was as if another puzzle piece fell into place. One half of the double-edge mound of anxiety she had been feeling for the past few days dissolved. Only one remained.

Jenna had butterflies in her stomach as they pulled up to the mill. She pulled the shawl tighter around her shoulders. The building was lit up by new flood lights, illuminating new, silvery gray paver stepping stones that led from the front door to a crushed gravel parking area to the side of the building. The lot was outlined with stakes and tape. It was quite full.

A huge white truck from Lincoln-Grant Community College was parked in the back next to the Rolling Records DJ van. Several cars had out-of-state plates. Lights from each of the mill's windows gave off a warm, homey feel. A large sign by the main door proudly proclaimed the new home of the Orchard Creek Historical Association.

Jenna squinted as she walked through the doorway, trying to get used to the lights. Maybe it was because it had been dark outside, but it seemed very bright to her. The first thing that got her attention was the smells. There was a wood odor that was well-known, mixed with a strong acrid smell, polyurethane, she immediately recalled from the day Seth attacked her. The memory actually stopped her legs from moving forward. What confused her most were the savory aromas of meat, onions, and fresh bread. It didn't make sense. Shaking herself out of her thoughts, she continued to walk amid a thick sense of déjà vu. It felt very familiar but different at the same time. The people around her were almost recognizable but not really so.

"Wow," she breathed. Her father looked around too, his eyes twinkling as if in agreement.

"Yeah, wow. There has been a boat load of preparation to make this happen. Now I can see why this was your priority. Jenna, I'm so proud of you. Are you sure you and your friends can stay awake until 12:30? That's late for you, but Mrs. Forrester was adamant about being sure each of you could stay to help tear things down and clean up. Personally, I think you've done enough already."

"Absolutely sure. We signed up to help and we're gonna follow through with our word, Dad."

"I'll go back for Mom and Peter. Mom has been preparing a little something special for her and me."

"Costumes?"

"I'll just say you'll get a kick out of us. We won't be able to stay the whole night, but you can do your own thing. I will come back and get you at closing time." He kissed her on the cheek and headed off towards the door.

With wide eyes, she took in everything. A small line of people, some in period costume, one couple in current formalwear, waited in front of the office door. One of the men kept stepping inadvertently on the hem of his wife's long dress. Jenna could tell by her face she was getting mad. Her puffy sleeves seemed to be getting in her way as well. She kept misjudging their size and hitting the man in the regular suit behind her. All of them held an orange paper about the size of an invitation. Clinking china and overlapping conversations could be heard in the room to her left. Just then a pretty young woman dressed in a white chef outfit came from the room next to the office and called a party of six. The line thinned and queued up. It was then a metal sign holder could be seen. Jenna found herself inching around those next in line to see it better. It announced the culinary department from the college was providing the sit-down dinner. The three-course beef dinner was $25 a plate.

Just to the right of her, Jenna noticed the great room had gotten some areas of fresh paint. The main staircase looked a hundred times better after being refinished. The fact that it was now clean really made the place look better, but the obvious flaws of the ceiling, trim and fixtures revealed its true age. Mr. Jacobs and two couples were slowly going up the stairs while Mr. Jacobs' finger swiveled to point out areas of interest and the parts of the building needing help. The whole party was completely decked out in period clothes. One lady was having trouble managing the stairs with the yards of material she wore. So far none of the men Jenna saw had opted to dress like the working class. Their suits had tails. They also broke etiquette and wore their hats instead of carrying them. Jenna could tell none of the outfits were homemade like hers. Just the women's hats—one was twice as big as her head—must have cost a fair fortune.

Mr. Levy was at a podium, speaking with folks Jenna recognized from the town board meeting, along with a few who were strangers. They, too, were in period dress. These men were younger than the others and handsome. Once again butterflies of anticipation woke up in Jenna's stomach, but there was so much to see. There was a sign on the podium about tours of the building every fifteen minutes. To the right was a stand scattered with menus featuring a big "W" on them. The placard said it was from a local grocery store known for community participation. They had gotten involved with a generous gift, raffling off the newest television, something called a plasma. On the other side of the table were flyers on how to make tax-free donations.

Farther in the room were two of the glass cabinets Jenna recognized from the tiny room the Historical Association used in the town hall. They were set up to display local items. Small, old-fashioned frames sat on top to give more details. Three men hovered around something next to the cabinets, nodding their heads. After a moment they moved on, and Jenna could see an antique table with an eight-by-ten framed photo of an older gentleman bearing a name plate that read Franz Wagner Wright. There was a newspaper clipping on a poster board and several pictures of buildings and houses.

The farthest corner had Mrs. Forrester's Victrola, and in the middle of the room against the wall was a DJ surrounded by more orange and black balloons. A cardboard sign identifying the Kids Korner hung above a small area at the other end of the room. Below it were two card tables and eight chairs for coloring. Some little ones—a princess, a dragon, and a witch—were dancing to the DJ's music, their moms chatting together not far away. A boy of about ten, dressed as a sailor and eating cookies, was wearing a blue ribbon from a costume contest.

A group from town, mostly women but a few kids from school as well, were all wearing jeans and brown T-shirts with an outline of a bird and the letters OCCS in turquoise for Orchard Creek Central Schools. They were their school colors and the osprey their mascot. Jenna recognized Hannah Reese from gym class. When Hannah turned around, the back of her shirt said PTA. They were manning a rectangular folding table covered with a black paper tablecloth. The area was set up with mini pies, cookies, brownies, and punch for refreshments. A sign at the end of the table said all proceeds collected would benefit the Historical Association. Two black plastic trash containers flanked the table. They were huge, like those in their cafeteria. One was half full. Jenna's science teacher, Mr. Weaver, was pulling a stuffed bag out of the other one. He stopped to smile, tipping his head up as if to say hi. For some reason, it made her blush. She shyly returned the smile.

Jenna was amazed. She beamed as she looked around, as if seeing the room for the first time, and yet she saw it as that familiar place she had spent hour upon hour in

month after month

cleaning.

working.

With her senses on overload, Jenna was having difficulty keeping her own thoughts in her head. Two people rushed up excitedly, and it took a moment before she realized they were Tina and Toby. They looked great in costume.

Tina's short hair was pulled up and pinned everywhere. It was stiff from all the hairspray, the smell of it following her like an invisible cloud. It made Jenna sneeze. Her puffy-sleeved, fitted, wildflower-blue blouse matched the trim on her eggshell skirt and brought out the blue of her eyes. Toby wore a simple beige shirt and brown pants held up by suspenders. The most convincing accessory of his outfit was indeed his family's heirloom pocket watch. Toby fiddled with it absentmindedly. His hair was matted down with hair gel and looked darker blond than it really was. In some places it was too short for the gel to control and the wisps comically stood on end.

"I can't believe you're actually here!" Toby exclaimed, his thin moustache loose and flapping at the end while he spoke.

"Thank goodness you're here to do this and not me," a relieved Tina admitted.

"This place looks awesome!" Jenna said, grinning at them.

"Hey, what's wrong with your eyes?" Tina asked, leaning in to Jenna's face. "I thought it was just me, but it's not. Your eyes have been looking lighter brown lately. Weird."

"I'm enraptured! All is right."

Toby pulled her and Tina off to the side. "What do we do now?" he asked. "Monster Mash" was playing in the background. The moms had joined their children and had begun to dance.

"I don't know, really. I almost forgot the handkerchief though. Do you think we should try upstairs?" Jenna asked, trying to pull up her skirt to scratch an itch on her leg. She was almost hesitant to go back there, it scared her so.

"There's no problem there. I made sure our refreshment supplies were kept up there so we could have an excuse to go up," Toby said proudly.

Mr. Levy came over to the group, looking a bit silly with his hair parted and gelled.

"I want to thank you guys for all your hard work. Jenna,

I'm glad you're up and about. This has been a wonderful opportunity for the Historical Association. I'm not sure what you said to Mrs. Forrester, but she has been indispensable to this project. It's been an incredible turnout. Can you believe she even donated her Victrola and records to the Association? We might play it a bit later if it settles down in here. It's too bad she's not feeling well and can't be here tonight. Well, I need to go in case I have to give another presentation. We've had several would-be investors checking us out. So far it looks promising." He smiled his appreciation and walked away. A party of four just arrived, and a flurry of lace bibs, long trains, and bowler hats swept past them.

Mrs. Forrester was sick?

Jenna felt as if there was a very cold stone in the pit of her stomach. "She's sick?"

Tina shrugged and Toby shook his head. This was news to them as well.

"I talked to her on the phone last night and she sounded fine. Why would she give away her Victrola? It's special. Mr. Forrester gave that to her for their anniversary," Jenna said, unease starting to trickle in her veins.

"Maybe we can call her?" Tina asked.

Toby again shook his head. "The wiring is done but we don't have service yet."

"Maybe she just needed to rest a bit and will come out closer to closing," Tina suggested quietly. "Let's go upstairs and feel it out."

They each grabbed a cup of punch—on the house for them—and headed carefully upstairs. They had just gotten to the landing when Mr. Jacobs and the people with him came out of the far room on the left and entered the room next to it. Mr. Jacobs gave Jenna a salute as he welcomed her back. Jenna and her friends turned right and walked through a cold spot, despite the space heaters being on. Or the fact that heat usually rises. It was the first indication that something was brewing. Jenna stopped at the spot and wrapped the shawl around her arms, clutching her satchel. She stood just outside the Sewing Room door, hesitant about walking very far into the room. Her eyes immediately went to the window. It was open once again. The brisk, fall breeze was blowing in.

"Uh oh. We made sure that window was closed before everyone started to arrive," Toby said nervously. He ran over quickly, closed and locked the window, and ran back.

"Do you think it's a portal like Mrs. Forrester said, Toby?" Tina asked, stealing glances at Jenna. Her blank expression let them know she wasn't really with them anymore.

"I'm thinking yes." Just like in the library, he and Tina stood by and just watched Jenna.

"Don't go near the windows at all tonight," Jenna heard herself say. It felt awkward to speak words that weren't formed beforehand. She could no longer decipher where her feelings came from, or which era they belonged to. She hoped it was nervousness; her voice sounded a pitch higher than normal. It reminded her of breathing in the funny air of a balloon to sound like a cartoon character. There was nothing funny about this, though, what had come out of her mouth was a warning. Jenna's confidence about the evening was shaken. She looked around the room almost sure it was smaller than when she had been here

a long time ago

Saturday. Her eyes found the machine in the middle of the room where she had hit her head. She stared at it. It looked benign and innocent, as if her encounter was a dream. Her feet pulled her forward and she reached out. Her fingers shook slightly as she touched the metal. It felt cold.

That was Emma's station, right next to Ruthie's. Oh, how they used to quarrel! Ruthie made a habit of wearing daisies in her hair, which made Emma sneeze. Each time she sneezed she would moan as her corset was so tightly fastened…

A solid minute of nothing went by while Jenna just stared, preoccupied by the memories being replayed in her head. She hardly heard Tina and Toby talking next to her. Tina fidgeted with the lace on her blouse while shooting glances at Toby. Toby didn't notice. He was staring at Jenna, nervously clicking his pocket watch open and closed. "Maybe we should go back down," he suggested.

"Fine by me, let's go, Jenna." The nudge Tina gave her brought her back to the here and now.

"Sorry. This is…"

But I'm waiting for—

"so strange."

my Joseph!

"What are we doing now?"

"My dad has brought those visitors back downstairs. Let's go through the other rooms up here together," Toby said. Jenna followed him and Tina brought up the rear. Just like they discussed all week, they weren't letting Jenna out of their sights for one minute.

Twenty-One

THE FIRST ROOM they went into was occupied by a young couple standing at the window. The girl giggled in between the boy's kisses. She gasped when they entered, breaking their moment. Taking her boyfriend's hand, she led him out the door. The trio didn't know what they were looking for, but found nothing out of the ordinary and went into the second room.

"Now—"

I must look for my Joseph.

"...what?" Jenna finally finished, glancing at the ceiling. She was fighting the urge to go back to the Sewing Room.

"Downstairs, I guess," Tina said, sighing. "Our whole night has been like this. I'm tired and this is getting boring." Toby elbowed her. Luckily Jenna's attention was elsewhere and she didn't catch the comment.

"I can feel so much I think I could just explode," Jenna said, as they started back downstairs. "I'm having a hard time just forming complete sentences. Not only are Elizabeth's thoughts getting louder in my head, but her feelings are too. I feel—"

excited.

worried and nervous all the time now. It's very distracting. I wish…"

This could be it, when I reunite…

"this thing, whatever we're waiting for,"

with my true love.

"would happen. It's wearing me out."

Jenna waved to her family who had arrived while she had been upstairs. Her dad was now wearing some new striped shirt and brown trousers. Her mom was wearing an understated fawn-colored dress, no full skirt or bustle. Three tiers of lace cascaded simply to the floor. Over the dress, but showing the delicate lace sleeves, was a cream vest with filigree edges that cinched and called attention to her thin waist. Her hair was piled on her head, with tiny tendrils loose around her neck.

Peter still looked like a pirate even without his vest and eye patch. He hollered like a banshee and ran to a boy his age at the Kids Korner who was there with his own family. The kids were decorating mini pumpkins now. Her father raised his hand and waved at Mr. Jacobs, who motioned them over. With his hand resting on the small of her mother's back, they walked over to take a tour.

The thoughts in Jenna's mind struggled for ways to articulate what she observed. Part of her had wanted to refer to her parents as papa and mama. She also realized she had been describing things with words that were rarely used. A tiny part of her still held hold of the present time.

"I wondered if I'd see you here."

Jenna turned to see Chloe Fischer, her classmate from Home

Ec, walking toward her from the makeshift dining area. She was dressed appropriately but, as usual, was wearing too much mascara and eye shadow. Jenna also knew bright blue wasn't popular back then. "It figures you'd fit in here. Anyone who is excited about sewing would find a place like this appealing." Chloe pursed her lips, her blue eyes taking in what Jenna was wearing. "Huh, well, there ya go. This place is kinda strange, too. Did you eat? My whole family had reservations. The food was good but the rest of this is lame. It's not what I'd prefer to do on Halloween. My father likes to be sure local events are supported, otherwise I'd already be at Devi's annual party. She's fifteen and it's by private invitation only. I'm being dropped off after we leave this place."

"Chloe, let's not be rude. Come say goodbye to the mayor."

Chloe turned and grinned at her father before turning back to her classmates. "Oh, gotta run. See ya, wouldn't wanta be ya!"

Jenna just stood there, a frown on her face. Chloe was never really nice.

"Don't worry about her. Maybe the air in her ivory tower is cutting off her oxygen supply," Toby offered. Tina muffled a snort and Jenna laughed outright.

"Yeah. I think she's jealous. I wonder if her nose gets cold being so high above the rest of us. Come on," Tina coaxed. "We helped make this happen. Let's go mingle with our people."

It was well after ten-thirty when Jenna and her friends returned to the main level after chatting and accepting compliments. A newspaper reporter had been there, holding them up for over an hour with pictures and questions. After that was the local television crew. Each, along with Mr. Levy and Mr. Jacobs, was interviewed briefly for the eleven o'clock news. Jenna and her friends were all preoccupied though, looking over their shoulders and out of the corner of their eyes. People seemed to be having a good time. They helped refill supplies as needed for the PTA, giving the upstairs a walk-through each time. The window in the Sewing Room was open only one other time, and Toby quickly closed it. Even though Jenna had her handkerchief out and they waited, nothing more happened. After fifteen minutes proved nothing else was happening, they left. By eleven the visitors seemed to thin out.

"Kids, help everyone clean up. I promised Rose we'd stay another hour or so," Mr. Jacobs said, coming back from the room used as a dining hall, munching on a roll. "Why, I don't know, but we owed her one."

"Hey, Tom, did you meet Ralph Buchanan?" Mr. Levy yelled from across the room. "The Beasleys over on Fallow Road are first cousins. He's part of the museum at Fort Stanwix and suggested we turn this place into a historical landmark."

"No kidding? Was he the portly man who kept staring at Theresa Brown's, uh, cleavage? I don't think that blouse fit her."

"The same. I swear he dropped his change on purpose just to see if she would pick it up for him. Is there any pie left?" Mr. Jacobs pointed inside the room next to the office. "Awesome. Now I know why he's so into the costumes. There's more to both stories."

Just then Jenna sneezed, set off by the scent of Tina's lingering hairspray, getting the men's attention. They both turned to the kids, clearly uncomfortable, as if they had forgotten they were there. Mr. Jacobs was the first to speak. "Tobe, you didn't hear anything. The three of you stay out of trouble while we finish up some paperwork, okay? Mark, let me tell you the details...." He ducked into the area used as the kitchen and grabbed a plate before they both went into the new office, laughing and eating.

"We have only an hour left!" Jenna voice was breathy and desperate. She started to worry the handkerchief in her tightly clenched hand. "This must go to Joseph."

"Jenna, we're doing the best we can. We will get you to him if we can. I'm not sure how we're supposed to do it," Tina said, hugging her best friend. "If you can help us, that'd be great." Tina glanced at Toby, who at this point pulled off the annoying moustache. He rubbed his upper lip, shrugging, not liking how helpless he felt.

"But if that window is open again, I'm not letting you near it so you can fall out. I don't care if it's a portal or not. Come on. Let's go again," he offered. The kids turned to the large room. It had been a great party with the usual Halloween songs and music up until now. All of a sudden, the DJ was having difficulty getting his equipment to work. There was static coming from the massive speakers, and the guy was puzzled and embarrassed. Troubleshooting didn't seem to be helping any. One of the elder board members, Lillian O'Mara, grumbling loudly about paying for six full hours, went over to the Victrola and put on an old 78 record. Jenna knew from being at the town board meeting that Lillian's husband died about a year ago. It was the reason she was wearing black. She had been wearing nothing but since, or so Jenna was told. A jazzy instrumental song called "Credenza Serenade" filled the room with the ambience of the late 1920's. A few of the older, lingering guests took advantage of the space and started dancing.

The trio made another trip down to the basement. It was difficult for both Jenna and Tina to see the thin, steep stairs with their long dresses, so they had to go one at a time very slowly. They lingered, wondering if Elizabeth would just appear out of thin air. Maybe Joseph would knock on the door. For the hundredth time Toby wished out loud that Mrs. Forrester would get there already for support and direction. Still, nothing remarkable was happening, and they went back upstairs to the Sewing Room to try again.

They were getting a bit tired and frustrated that perhaps they had missed something earlier. By this time, Tina was chewing on her fingernail, becoming quite nervous. Most of her hair had fallen down out of the pins despite the hairspray. She fell back to where Toby was, letting Jenna lead.

"No matter how many times I go up this staircase, I still can't pull up all these dumb skirts. I've almost done seven headers tripping on my dress. I've been counting. Jenna makes it look so easy."

"Yeah, about that…haven't you noticed how much Jenna has changed? Her voice, her eyes, even the way her face moves when she laughs. I think she's more used to being in these clothes than we think. I sure hope something happens or she's going to lose it big time."

"No, I'm hoping nothing happens, Toby. I think we're overreacting. Maybe when Jenna hit her head it messed up her memory. All that stuff about Seth coming back can't be true. I know she wants to believe it, but ghosts don't exist."

"What are you two blathering about?"

"Nothing," they replied in unison. Yawning, they shuffled along to the Sewing Room. It was cold and empty, same as it had been all evening. Back down they went, once again into the main room, to the faint sounds from the Victrola. It stood stately next to a pile of thick, vinyl records. There was a small framed sign set on top of the unit. It said "Donated by Mrs. Rose Forrester," and that it was made in New Jersey and purchased in 1931. By this time the DJ had packed up his equipment and left. The music from the Victrola fought the din of chatter and laughter from the handful of people that remained.

The caterers were bringing out the last of their trays of dishware. The PTA representatives were gone and had taken their supplies with them. All that remained were half a dozen cups of punch and three small plates of cookies. Toby had been doing a good job taking care of those. The sign for raffles had been removed. The television had gone to a couple from Watertown about an hour before. They had been ecstatic when their name was called. The podium where Mr. Levy and Mr. Jacobs greeted guests still held the sign-in book. There were no remnants of the Kids Korner left at all.

With the majority of the locals and families having come and gone, it was now down to businessmen and investors from out of town. The music, although not tinny, was still inferior to today's quality and had an odd effect on the room. Even though the style was twenty-odd years off, it suddenly didn't seem like a modern Halloween party, but rather an old building that had come alive, circa 1897. Upon closer inspection of the Victrola, Tina saw something next to it that they had not seen earlier. Toby's head cocked to the side as he looked at the white corner of a piece of paper sticking out of a leather-bound album; it was Mrs. Forrester's scrapbook. Toby looked at the girls and picked it up. The white paper fell out onto the floor, and as Tina bent to pick it up, she stopped. It was a sealed envelope addressed to Jenna Stevens.

Jenna nervously opened the envelope and, once again, all three had their heads together.

Dear Miss Jenna,

I want to thank you for filling me with my memories once again. I hadn't felt a real purpose since my Royal passed, but lately I've been very fulfilled. My faith has been restored in the many generations that will follow me, and

I'm happy to know that you and Tina and Toby will look after everything properly. I know you feel you owe me, but it has been me in your debt all along. I hope everyone gets back to where they belong. I'm sorry that I can't be there to experience it with you. I know my time is coming and I wanted the chance to say goodbye. You are truly wonderful children.

My love, Rose Forrester"

The corners of Jenna's mouth turned down, and she began to tremble. "What does this mean? Is she dying?" she asked, facing her friends. Toby's eyes were welling up and Tina had tears running down her face. Distracted by the activity in the room, Jenna looked around, her expression quickly going blank. There seemed to be a lot more people in here than earlier. That funny feeling came back again, and Jenna pushed aside the thoughts of Mrs. Forrester as almost all her thoughts abruptly seemed threadbare and hazy around the edges. Toby took his granddad's pocket watch and looked at the time.

"It's eleven forty-eight. Something feels different to me," he said. "Does it to anyone else?"

"Yeah, me too," Tina agreed, immediately chewing at the lip gloss she had applied when they had reached the main room.

Jenna stood up and idly tucked her hair back under the hairpin. She recognized people in the mill, but part of her was unsettled because she also knew she had never seen them before.

"What is it that's different? I can't put my finger on it, but it's giving me the willies," Tina admitted.

Toby looked around, almost squinting. "It's like it's smoky in here, but I don't smell it."

"Yeah, it is kinda foggy." Tina rubbed her eyes. "Or maybe we're just tired." As she thought about it, she hugged herself, frowning. A high-pitched laugh carried from the stairs and a gentleman's voice answered with his own deep laughter. Another man joined in the conversation, the rhythm of his words catching their ears as an accent different from what they were used to hearing. Another woman cackled in reply.

"No, that's not it. Ugh!" Tina cried. "I could think better if these people were quieter. Aren't they supposed to be going home instead of coming in?"

"Should I go tell my dad to put a closed sign up or something?" asked Toby.

"Yup. They obviously can't hear it with the door closed."

Making their way across the room they slowed down. People were walking throughout the building. Some were coming downstairs, others going up, some hugging, many more laughing. The ones in the room with them talked with each other and moved about as if they had a purpose, not the way tourists would stop and stare at things around them.

Everyone Toby saw had period clothes on. Very detailed outfits. The men had on black boots, black wool-like pants held up by suspenders, and white linen shirts. All carried top hats and had short moustaches just under their noses. Several had pipes. The women had simple white cotton blouses, sleeves puffy above the elbow and fitted below, with high collars that buttoned up to the chin. All had long hair pulled into a bun. No one had bangs or layers, or even dyed hair. Their simple long dresses skimmed their feet but never seemed to hinder them on the stairs as everyone else's had earlier. Some people had wire-rimmed glasses. One man carried a cane. Suddenly Toby's face lost all its color.

"Oh, wow. Do you see this? These people here are all too

perfect in their costumes." He looked at the girls, clearly scared. "This is the real deal. I don't think these people are from town, and I don't think they're wearing costumes."

Twenty-Two

"**Y**OU MEAN, THEY'RE ghosts?" Tina almost hissed, grabbing his hand for comfort as she studied the people around her.

Jenna had moved away, walking towards these guests. "I know these folks," she answered in an unfamiliar, lilting tone. She left the group and began walking around among the others, stopping abruptly and looking upstairs as if someone had called her. Tina and Toby were shaken out of their reverie when they realized she was already heading upstairs. But they couldn't get to her fast enough.

"Crap, Tina, she's too far ahead!"

"I need my hands to pull up these layers! Toby! What are we doing?"

"Dunno, but we're doing it together," Toby panted, keeping a strong grip on Tina as he pulled her forward. They still moved too slowly as they tried to step around or avoid getting too close to the ghost people. After Tina tripped on her gown and would have actually done a header had she not been holding onto Toby's hand, they ran into the empty Sewing Room just as Jenna was holding her arms out toward the open window.

"Why is that window open again? What's happening?" Tina asked.

"It *is* this window," Toby decided. "This is where the veil is broken between our worlds. Remember when Mrs. Forrester told us there is usually something, like a door, that's connecting us to the afterlife? It has to be this window. Jenna saw Seth Sawyer standing in front of it just before he attacked her, and this window has been opening on its own all night."

With agility he didn't know he had, Toby quickly ran in between the machines to Jenna and pulled her back towards the door, not letting go of her shoulders. He turned her around to face him. She did not look like she had even seen him and he was unsure she would stay put if he let her go. He was just about to say something to Tina when he realized Jenna's eyes were definitely different now, almost hazel. Her gaze was fixed behind him. He looked over to what she was looking at. There was a young man by the window now with dark eyes and brown hair smiling and approaching her. He was clean shaven; the only one in the building without a moustache. His clothes were more sophisticated than the others. He had a white shirt on under a black vest and coat. In one hand he held a top hat. His eyes were locked only on Jenna. In fact, there seemed to be quite a few people in this room now, but how they had gotten there was unclear.

Tina came up next to Toby. "Toby, I think this is Joseph. I recognize him from the paper!" Tina exclaimed.

Toby hesitantly put his arms down and let Jenna turn. He didn't feel comfortable with her that close to the window, glazed over the way she was. But she wasn't paying attention to her friends. Jenna smiled and laughed, her hand demurely covering her mouth. She walked towards Joseph with deliberate steps. The whole room seemed in slow motion.

"Toby, over here," Tina called. She was off to the side a short distance from the window. "This is why we're here, remember?"

Toby went to Tina. "What?"

People walked about as if weaving by Jenna and Joseph like it was a weird dance. Jenna shyly took Joseph's outstretched hand, and the lights brightened. The music from below grew louder.

Suddenly Toby shook. It felt like a bolt of lightning had just surged through him. He couldn't believe this was real. The lights had gotten so bright they almost hurt his eyes it was so unnatural.

"Did you feel that? It was like I was just zapped with electricity," Tina whispered. Toby was unable to do anything other than nod in agreement.

Jenna and Joseph moved together to the side of the room. Tina did a double take to make sure it was Jenna they had followed. It was now difficult to find any of her characteristics left. Her blond hair seemed lighter. Her smile was unfamiliar to them. Even the way she moved was unlike Jenna. Elizabeth was almost completely here. Joseph reached up hesitantly to caress her face, and she closed her eyes, melting into his touch. She had the handkerchief in her hand, and her face was an expression of ultimate happiness. It was a private moment for the couple. But the moment didn't last.

No one was speaking, yet it was very loud. The room was filled with the cacophony of music, indiscernible voices, conversation, laughter, and then crying, forceful tones. Now, yelling. They could hear loud, purposeful steps coming up the stairs.

"Something is going wrong!" Toby yelled above the noise.

Tina turned toward the door. He looked just like the picture in the old newspapers, only now a scowl was on his face. There, in the doorway, was Seth Sawyer. She knew it. People parted for him, fear on their faces, as he stormed across the room. The temperature dropped. It suddenly became downright cold in the small space. The breeze from the open window now became a wind, spraying them with an icy rain, but no one seemed to feel it except Toby and Tina.

"Toby, what do we do now?" Tina whispered, grabbing his hand again.

"We have to stop him!"

Tina took in a huge gulp of air and squinted her eyes shut briefly. This was much more than she wanted to be a part of, but she couldn't let Toby jump on Seth by himself. Gathering all her courage she jumped into the crowd with Toby, which seemed to be growing. It had organized into a loose circle around Elizabeth and Joseph. Tina moved through the crowd with Toby and were halted by the pressure of the beings. In the back of her mind, it reminded Tina of turbulence from flying through clouds on the way to visit her grandparents in Colorado; something there but not there. No one in the room acknowledged their presence. They pushed on and came up behind Seth just as he stepped in front of Elizabeth and Joseph.

Elizabeth looked utterly terrified. She clutched the handkerchief with both hands to her chest. Joseph's eyebrows pulled down in anger as he countered Seth's movement to be closer to Elizabeth. Tina didn't know what to do. Seth scared her too. Would he hurt them both, knowing what he tried to do to Jenna?

"I am finally freed, here to do what you've prevented me from for a hundred years," Joseph boldly announced to his brother. Seth's reply was cold, like the stone mask of his face.

"My eternal goal is to protect you. It was Father's last dying wish, and one I agreed to carry out. For as long as it shall take." Their voices were almost like an echo, humming in the air. Seth leapt at Elizabeth, but Joseph was quicker, stepping in front to shield her.

"I forbid it from repeating. What you accomplished was staining your hands with my blood."

"No! My brother, you must know that was not my intention. I was looking after you, safeguarding you from the pain of an inappropriate match. The girl was not good enough for you, how could you not see it?"

"Love that is true and pure should never be measured by assets or bank accounts. You tried to push her out; Elizabeth, the only happiness I ever felt! And instead, when her skirts caught and she fell, your momentum took me out the window instead."

"I never meant to hurt you. You must know that!"

The tiny part of Jenna that remained remembered her dreams. The dominance of Elizabeth recalled her memories. Both meshed into a coherent image, and Jenna was stunned as crystal clear images flooded her mind.

—Suddenly she was in this very room on Halloween, 1896. It was a humid evening, with the sash still up from heat of the working day. A strong breeze from the window reached her as she quickly rose from the empty perimeter of the area where Joseph had spread a quilt.

We've been caught! I haven't had time to…!!!

The gust blew stray curls off her cheek, cooling the warmth of her face more from the confrontation than the ambient temperature. She glanced at Joseph to her right, watching the expressions of surprise, worry, and determination cross his face. The room was silent as the tension thickened. Seth and

Joseph were facing off, and she—Elizabeth—was the point of contention.

Seth had found them out. They were caught unawares; there were no warning sounds of a carriage to alert them to this danger. He must have tied his horse to a nearby tree, meaning he had some recent knowledge of their courting.

But tonight, of all nights! She had been waiting for this moment since falling in love with Joseph, and wished nothing more than to present her completed handkerchief and be betrothed. Once promised to marry, no one could stand between them, and they would be together forever.

"Look at me when I address you!" Seth repeated. He walked in further, neatly avoiding the stations, his attention to his right to face her. It was the nearest to her he had ever been.

Elizabeth stepped back out of fear. Her breath came in short bursts. Her heart pounded. She felt cornered, desperate. She could not meet his eyes. Up until this time, she thought Papa's temper more frightening than anything. Seth's anger was difficult to bear while at the machines, and this was so much worse, knowing that fury was directed solely at her. Her thoughts scrambled as she was roughly shaken. The voice next to her pulled her out of the security of her mind. It took a moment for her to realize it was Joseph's. She barely recognized his voice.

"Do not touch her."

Seth dropped his arms, more out of astonishment than the demand. Confusion and frustration colored his face. Elizabeth took another step away.

"This is an embarrassment to our name. Why are you sullying yourself with a laborer, and in Orchard Creek of all places? Your future is bright. You've just become a man of eighteen. The money in the trust is now yours, and Victoria Harrington is set to be your bride on December the first."

"I do not love her!"

"Your sensitivity is a stone about your neck. Love is irrelevant. Tonight, this will end."

Joseph winced from the insults as if slapped. It stunned him so that it took more than a heartbeat for him to realize what his brother was going to do. Elizabeth saw it coming. She could see the decision in the black void of his eyes, the way his body coiled to strike. She turned around, looking for space behind her to run, knowing he would stop her if she tried to go around him.

"No! Elizabeth!"

Elizabeth felt hands on her back shoving her forward, and saw Joseph move in front of her, his arms open for support. Just then the vertigo of losing her balance took her. The hems of her skirts gathered by her ankles and she stepped on them, abruptly pulling her down on her knees. She hit the floor with Seth stumbling over her, but hardly felt it. Her focus was on Joseph's screams moving away from her.

Even though she stood as swiftly as she could, she didn't have time to help. They were already in motion. She knew what the outcome would be, having relived it in great detail for the last century. The last image of Joseph was of wide-eyed terror and hands grappling to find purchase as he folded into the window frame and disappeared into the night. Seth clambered from the floor where he had dropped, his arms splayed in front, to the gaping hole that took his brother. His hysteria matched her own, and Elizabeth could almost be convinced the volume of his shouts were powerful enough to bring Joseph back. She felt her heart break in two and her mind, the same. It stopped her very being from existing, and breathing ceased...—

Jenna clung tightly to what was left of her identify in the present; the memories had taken only a fraction of a second. Vaguely, through the hum of the manifested spirits, she could hear the sharp intake of air from Tina and Toby.

"Oh my word, Toby. Seth killed his own brother. It was Seth who killed Joseph!" Tina realized.

Toby couldn't answer. He was watching Seth's body tensing, his hands fisting, and knew from experience it meant he was going to attack again. He had to stop it from happening all over, the window was too close. Without thinking about it, Toby took a deep breath and lunged forward at Seth, but fell right through him, stumbling to the floor. "I can't do it, Tina! This isn't working!"

The music seemed to speed up in a warped sort of way. The ghost people sped up too, moving around the room. At first, they were disorganized. Then they formed a circle, locking their hands together with Tina and Toby on the outside and Elizabeth, Seth, and Joseph on the inside. It was hard for the two friends to communicate through all the strange noises. Then, from out of the crowd, a woman came forth. She was about thirty years old and seemed familiar to each of them. She stood in front of Seth, a determined but amused look on her face, and blocked him from Elizabeth. Elizabeth faced Joseph and the group started moving around the quartet of two couples. The activity wasn't necessarily structured, but it was cohesive.

Tina and Toby could barely see what was going on. Joseph had once again gathered Elizabeth in his arms. He now accepted the handkerchief she held out to him.

"Yes."

It was the only discernable word they heard. On the side of the circle farthest away from Tina and Toby—but near the window—Elizabeth and Joseph walked out of the ring through parted hands that instantly rejoined. They must have disappeared into the others, because the kids couldn't see them anymore. There was a cluster of ghosts now in this small room that somehow was three times its size. It literally buzzed with noise. With only two people in the middle now, they could see the woman move in on Seth, at which point the crowd again tightened, eliminating the ability to see them. There was an agonizing howl. When the circle widened just a moment later, Seth was gone. Toby and Tina stood against a wall, both frozen in amazement.

Another gentleman stepped into the center of the circle and approached the woman remaining there. He too, was of the same age, and was holding a white Panama hat with a blue band. A navy-blue jacket broke up his white shirt and white pants. A kind face with a dimple, his eyes twinkled as his lips twitched up, making him appear almost boyish. It was easy to read his relief when he approached the woman. Tina and Toby could now clearly see she was wearing a sky-blue chiffon blouse with wide collars that matched a long dress that flared out with pleats on both sides. Their clothes seemed to belong to the same era. The gentleman reached his hand out, smiling with anticipation. Adjusting her blue, close-fitted hat atop short, wavy blond hair, the woman raised her hand and smiled. It was very much like the pillowy smile of Mrs. Forrester, but without the wrinkles, and it occurred to Tina that this was in fact Rose Forrester.

"Mrs. F.?" Toby heard her say. He studied the gentleman and could see the resemblance to the man in the picture that Mrs. Forrester had on her mantle from their wedding.

"Holy cow, that's Mr. Forrester, Tina!" he answered back.

Mrs. Forrester took the man's hand with a visible sigh of contentedness and turned toward Tina and Toby. Suddenly,

Jenna appeared off to the far side of the ensemble. They knew it was Jenna by the way she held herself; by the way she was confused and holding her head in her hands. Jenna began to walk toward her friends, but stopped as if called, and turned towards the circle. Mrs. Forrester smiled, making eye contact with her—and with each of them—with her blue eyes bright. So much was conveyed with that simple smile. Then the young Mrs. Forrester shifted her full attention back to her husband. They seemed to walk through the group of ghosts, at once becoming obscured. They disappeared. One or two more people embraced, and did the same.

Jenna had made her way over to Toby and Tina through the crowd, her fingers stretching out for them. As soon as their hands touched, the lights got impossibly brighter still, and the outlines of the ghost people started to look watery. Their images merged and melted, becoming new images but becoming nothing. The buzzing grew louder. Tina, Toby, and Jenna had crouched down at this point and held each other tighter as the walls and people began to spin.

"I'm gonna 'euke!" Toby shouted.

"Don't throw up, just hold on! Hold on!" Tina hollered back. Jenna screamed.

Images spun faster and faster as the room became brighter, and the intense light washed out everything the eye could see. There was a blast of noise, a slam, and then complete silence and darkness.

Twenty-Three

THE LIGHTS POPPED back on to a more normal level. The window was now closed and had somehow locked. The room hummed the way a piano key would when a distant sound wave matched its own. No one was in the room except for Tina, Toby, and Jenna, on their knees, still clutching each other in a huddle. Slowly, they stood up and looked around. Just then they noticed their fathers, standing dumbstruck and motionless in the doorway.

"What was hell was that?" Mr. Stevens asked in a hushed tone. "I just came in to pick you up, Jenna, when these... sounds..."

"Yeah, and energy...like weird static electricity..." Mr. Jacobs added.

"We heard it all from downstairs. We thought the building was going to... well, we didn't know what was going on." Mr. Levy finished. All at once the men came to their senses from the shock and they rushed to hold their children.

"Did all that really happen? Did anyone else just see what I saw?" Mr. Levy's last word was muffled as Tina plowed into his arms.

"Yeah, we did," Jenna said quietly, squished in her father's embrace.

"Because I just saw a dozen people disappear into thin air like ghosts," Mr. Jacobs admitted, his voice quivering as he smoothed down Toby's sticky hair. Something clicked into place. "That's why Mrs. Forrester was so hesitant to pass this project." He shook his head. "That really looked like her, but younger." He paused again, and his puzzled expression became serious as an idea dawned on him. He leaned over Toby's head to the other men. "Oh, she didn't come tonight because she didn't feel well. Could that have been her just a minute ago? Do you think…?"

"After seeing that, I'm inclined to agree," Mr. Stevens answered, his voice mirroring the same urgency. Luckily the kids were too distracted to pick up on the subtle suggestion. "Do you think maybe we should phone an ambulance to her house, just in case?" The other fathers nodded in agreement and Mr. Jacobs hurried out of the room.

"The phones here aren't activated yet. I'll call from home, it's closest! Thank God Steph's with her mom in Earlville for the weekend," Mr. Jacobs called out as he headed for the main door, not bothering to stop for an answer.

"What's going on? Is Mrs. F. okay?" Tina asked. Her father shushed her. "We're going to check. Let's go downstairs for now."

"Is the room still buzzing or is it just in my ears?" Toby asked, moving his hands up to the sides of his face. Everyone nodded.

"I can hear it, too," Jenna answered, shaking her head.

"But, it's like I just woke up and things have been going on around me I haven't been paying attention to, or don't know about. I feel a bit…"

"Mixed-up?" Tina offered. Jenna smiled despite the tiredness.

"Yeah."

They filed down the stairs to the great room, trying to collect their thoughts. "Jenna, what happened? We lost sight of you; it was so crowded," Tina asked, as she pulled all the fabric of her dress up to her knees. She didn't care anymore. She was sick of tripping.

"I'm not sure. It was like sleepwalking. Elizabeth was able to give her handkerchief to Joseph, and then, I felt happy. She felt happy. It was what we needed to do. All those other people were waiting for an opportunity, too."

They reached the bottom of the stairs. "Who is Elizabeth?" Mr. Stevens asked, exasperated.

"Uh, she is—was—a ghost," Jenna stammered.

"One that looked a lot like her," Tina replied, trying to help.

Toby shook his head. "Well, it was Jenna who started to look and act more like Elizabeth each day," he clarified.

With a petrified expression grow on her father's face, Jenna tried to explain. "I was the only one who could help her reconnect with her beau, Joseph, so they could spend eternity together."

"How do you know—?" His face went white. "Wait, you connected with a ghost? Is this what's been going on with you the last few weeks?"

"Yeah, but it wasn't so bad when we first moved here," Jenna admitted quietly.

Mr. Levy motioned them to the room where the dinner had been held before walking back towards the great room. The kids slumped into the chairs at a remaining table just as he returned clutching three paper cups full of warm punch. They were upended and emptied within seconds. Once again, the building looked and felt as if a party had just ended. The men looked around protectively, seeing the building through new eyes.

Mr. Stevens studied at his daughter as he pieced things together, finally making the connection. "Oh my God, the concussion. Jenna, why didn't you tell me?" There wasn't anger in his voice, only disappointment and sadness.

Jenna sighed, feeling heavy. "I don't know, Dad. I'm sorry. Somewhere along the line it got out of control. I didn't realize how much Elizabeth took over. I knew I was connected to her, but I didn't realize how much until just now."

"You need to tell me everything."

"Yeah, I will. Now that I think about it, it was pretty scary."

"You too, Tina," Mr. Levy ordered.

"I promise," Tina replied. She looked like she had stood inside a hurricane. Her hair had been blown out of the barrettes and frozen in place by the layers of hairspray. Her eyes were also too wide in her face.

"So, now we need to worry about this place for different reasons." Mr. Levy said the words but even he wasn't sure if it was a statement or a question.

The girls shook their heads 'no' at the same time. Jenna's silver figure eight hair pin was doing no better than Tina's barrettes. It had slipped, and was now down to her right ear. The knot of hair still tied into a bun was seconds away from completely falling out. "No, I don't think so, Mr. Levy. I'm just me again, everything is gone. And I looked. The window is closed."

"Jenna, your old man is in the dark here. What do the windows have to do with anything?"

"Not all the windows Mr. Stevens, just the one in the Sewing Room. Mrs. Forrester believes that one is a portal. You know, to the other side," Toby began, glancing upward.

"A portal beyond," Jenna mumbled as realization hit her. All at once she sat up, wide awake and alert. It was like a bucket of cold water had been dumped over her. What had happened upstairs came back to her. "The veil to the other side. Mrs. Forrester! Oh, no, Mrs. F.!"

The sound of a car skidding into the gravel by the door distracted everyone from further conversation. Tina, Toby, and Jenna ran into the main room with the fathers in tow. In the far distance, an ambulance siren could faintly be heard.

Mr. Jacobs stuck his head in the door. His voice, stressed but soft, managed to convey the group's growing worry. "Come on, we should all be there."

"You called an ambiliance?" Tina asked, mispronouncing the word.

"I did, honey. Let's go."

"Good thing I have bucket seats," Mr. Jacobs muttered to himself as somehow, they all piled into the car; the men in front, the kids in the back.

The ride seemed shorter than usual with everyone's attention completely tuned in to the rapid-fire question and answer session. Surprisingly, it was Tina who took the lead. She had recovered enough to question what she saw. "I don't get it. Who were those people? Where did they come from? Where'd they go?"

Jenna shrugged, watching the blurred blackness of the

night scroll past the window. "Some things I just knew. Maybe it was from being linked to Elizabeth. I knew Elizabeth would be able to find Joseph tonight, just like the others who had been waiting to be reunited. Some had work to finish, but they couldn't connect. Not until someone like me bridged the gap."

"Yeah, but *who* were they?" Toby asked, watching the same view out the window next to him.

"Others. Like Elizabeth, I guess, who couldn't find a way to make peace. They helped Seth go away. I don't know where he went, but Elizabeth and Joseph are safe and together. It's weird now that my thoughts aren't scrambled anymore. It's almost hard to remember a time when Elizabeth wasn't with me."

"Who's Elizabeth? And Seth?" Mr. Jacobs asked, trying to keep up with the conversation and also keep the car on the road. "I want the whole story from the beginning, Toby. Rose had warned us for years about that place and we didn't listen. I wouldn't have believed in something like this, wouldn't have believed that place held that much potential."

"It's a long story," said Toby, scratching his head. The gel in his hair had become flaky, making it itchy.

"We were worried no one would believe us," Jenna confessed.

"It's hard for me to believe, and I was there," Tina admitted. "Like, were all those people connected to that building or were they just on the other side waiting?"

"Yeah," Toby agreed. "It was like one minute the place was almost empty and the next they were all…. just there."

Jenna blew her bangs out of her face. "I don't know how or why. I guess there's stuff even I don't understand."

"We're here," Mr. Jacobs said, slowing down.

"Wow, already?" Toby asked.

"Yeah. I kinda disregarded all traffic rules. Luckily, driving in Orchard Creek at one in the morning almost guarantees no others drivers are on the road." He pulled into Birch Drive only seconds before the ambulance did, kicking up a dust storm that seemed to surround them in a world all their own. Toby and Jenna stumbled out of the doors before the car was put into park. The approaching flashing lights illuminated them. It created a strange stop motion quality to their movements.

"Jenna, you won't be able to get in. You know Mrs. F. always locks up behind her," Tina shouted, tumbling out of the car last.

"How could we have forgotten about her? Tina, she's by herself!"

The men from the ambulance were just getting out of the vehicle. "What's going on?" a paramedic asked.

"She didn't come out tonight, she was sick!" Jenna said, the screen door flying open with the effort she used to open it. The resistance wasn't needed, it wasn't locked. A dim light shown in the living room but there was no movement inside. Jenna disappeared into the darkness of the small entryway but a moment later the large living room light came to life and Jenna could be seen inside, frantic now, calling out.

The Rescue Squad intended to keep non-family members outside but it was impossible with the chaos of everyone yelling. They all followed Jenna.

"Oh, Mrs. F.," Jenna gasped, stopping short into the living room. She planned on trying the kitchen first, just in case Mrs. Forrester was feeling better and making herself tea. The trip upstairs to the bedroom frightened Jenna but she would have gone up anyway. There was no need. Sitting in the claw-footed armchair beyond the couch, in front of the empty spot where the Victrola used to stand, was Rose Forrester. She had taken several of the pictures off the tables and fireplace mantle. They were scattered next to her and on her lap; pictures of her and her Royal. Jenna briefly looked at what she was holding. In her hands was the black and white of her wedding day. On her thumb was a gold ring, large enough to have been her husband's. The dimpled man smiling towards the camera was younger than who Jenna had seen less than an hour ago in the Sewing Room, but Jenna knew for certain it was the same person.

Slowly, Jenna knelt to the chair and made herself look at Mrs. Forrester, ignoring the bustle happening behind her. She knew the old woman was gone. Her eyes were closed but her face held the slightest smile, peaceful, as if she was content with leaving. Somehow that made it hurt less.

Toby put his hand on her shoulder. She knew he would want to protect her. At that moment, she realized he and Tina had been protecting her for over a month.

"Oh, no!" Tina said, kneeling down. Jenna and Toby reached for Tina at the same time Tina's hand sought theirs. The love Jenna felt for her two friends at that moment was something she felt deep in her bones. And it wasn't just love, it was acceptance and belonging.

"Kids, we need to get in here."

"John, give them a minute," the second paramedic said softly. "I don't think there's anything we're going to be able to do to help."

The first paramedic looked behind Jenna where all the men stood. "Are you family?"

Mr. Jacobs cleared his throat. "No, she doesn't have any."

Mr. Levy stepped closer, putting his hand on Tina's shoulder. "Actually, these guys are close enough to be her family. Maybe they could have a few moments to say goodbye."

"I'm going to miss her a lot," Jenna broke the silence as they piled back into the car. She wiped the stubborn tears from her cheeks, but couldn't seem to get a hold of herself. Her dad was there for her and as much as she kept apologizing, he hushed her. Being up this late was sure to make everything seem hopeless, he told her. He assured her she would see things in a different light tomorrow.

"That was her husband in the room, right? They found each other and she's with him now. She looked awfully happy to see him," her dad quietly reminded her.

"It does make it better; knowing she's with her beau forever. It'll just be hard not to see her or visit her like we did."

"How do we explain all this?" Mr. Levy asked. "If I wasn't there with all of you…it makes me angry. My upbringing, my whole belief system… what's real? What's the truth? What do we do now?"

"I don't know," Mr. Jacobs answered. "I have to process this. It changes the way I see the museum. There's so much more to it than just a place to put antiques."

"I mean, in a way I feel the building has taken advantage of me. I didn't ask for this. I didn't encourage it. I don't know how I feel about being there."

Mr. Jacobs laughed weakly. "Well, we're all stone cold sober so we have to accept it in some way. As far as what we'll do with this information…that's what I'm concerned with. Is there more danger? How would we know? Should we tell anyone? Who would believe us? I'll tell you what, though, I didn't really believe it myself up until now. There's so much I don't know about that building. I feel like I'm at a disadvantage."

"Mrs. Forrester did leave behind her scrapbook, dad," Toby

yawned. Tina would have agreed had she not fallen asleep on the ride back. "Jenna's read through it."

With this Jenna perked up a bit. "I did. There is so much information in there."

"Well, other than what you all tell us, it's going to have to do."

Twenty-Four

*M*RS. FORRESTER'S FUNERAL was held a few days later in the ancient cemetery across the road from the old mill, now the new Historical Association museum. It was an unseasonable mild November day, still holding the smell of the orchard in the air. She was laid to rest in the plot she had bought and paid for in advance, right next to her husband. Jenna hung back at the graveside, looking at the fresh dirt at her feet. Her mom kissed her on the top of the head, and smiled through the ache on her face at seeing her daughter hurting. "Come on Petey, they'll be right behind us." For once, Peter followed without a fuss.

"You okay?" Her dad asked, putting an arm around her shoulders. Jenna wiped her nose on a tissue and smiled. Most people had left for the light lunch in town compliments of Mrs. Forrester. She had thought of everything down to the detail. Tina, Toby and their parents were the last to leave. She waived them on saying she'd catch up in a moment.

"Yeah. I—we—know she's happy, but it's still hard."

"It always is when it's someone we love."

"I'd like to think she loved us." The tightness in her throat threatened another round of tears. Her dad laughed.

"Jenna, she loved you. People don't leave the proceeds from the sale of their home and acreage to three random kids for their college education. I still can't believe she did that."

Jenna smiled and shook her head. "I read the papers, dad. It specifically said it was to go for the pursuit of our dreams."

"That's what I said."

Jenna sighed. "She left money to the town, too. But you're right. She did love us. I just can't believe how many people came today to say goodbye, considering the ruckus some of them caused."

"A lot of the town came out to support the Historical Association last month. Not all communities do that. And those who went around afterward saying Halloween and her death were tied together are just rumormongers who will try to find any opportunity to turn the pagan holiday into something evil. Unfortunately, you'll find those people are everywhere in life."

Jenna hugged him. "That's another reason why I'm glad we all decided to keep what really happened to ourselves. I am sorry that means we're not telling mom."

She watched her dad look up studying the clouds. It was a sensitive subject they had both discussed at length. He had tried to explain the difficulties that caused. Marriage was a partnership without secrets, he had told her. They had never had secrets between them, but knowing how she got worked up with just Jenna's dreams he knew she wouldn't understand. He was hoping in time he could share it with her. Until then, Jenna knew it was just between them and their small group.

Jenna took one last look at the grave, said a silent farewell and turned away. Her father followed, the skittering sound of the leaves from the thick copse of trees that edged the cemetery picking up with each breeze.

"We'll get there, kid. I'm so proud of what you helped accomplish for the museum. That turnout, and the money that was brought in, was amazing. From what Tom Jacobs figures they have enough to get well established." He tilted his head from side to side, thinking. "The money from Mrs. Forrester's car will help, too."

"Yeah," Jenna said quietly. "It was the sit-down dinner that brought in the most. Channel four said the interest in the community college and the culinary arts program has exploded, so that's cool."

"I've never seen support from a community like I have here in Orchard Creek. After this your mother and I realized the move here was a good decision. Hey, I hear even Rachel Pritcher is interested in becoming a board member."

"Yup. I heard that, too. I've met her. She's nice."

They reached the road, both looking for traffic before crossing. "Your head is still feeling okay?"

"No more dizziness."

"Good. And the pull to that building, is it still there?"

Jenna brushed her bangs out of her eyes while she thought about it. "It's not the same as when I was connected to Elizabeth, but yes, it is. I'd really like to keep helping here. Mr. Robertson has some really good stuff from the Erie Canal and the Civil War. Mr. Jacobs said we'll be a reputable museum from the day we open. There are things that'll be in the museum that are really rare."

"We. You've already moved in, haven't you?" He gave a side hug as Jenna nodded. Their feet crunched on the gravel of the Association's parking lot as they walked towards their car. There were two others parked next to them. She could hear her mom and brother playing a game of I Spy as they leaned on the car, munching on apples while they waited.

"I guess so."

"All I ask if for you to use your powers for good, Jenna.," he said, his voice lowered. "I'm glad the talent skipped over me and went to you. You're turning into an amazing young lady and I'm so proud. Those friends of yours are great and have your back. Just keep your ol' man in the loop."

"I will from now on, dad."

"Gwen, is the museum open? The door looks ajar."

"I believe Jenna's friends are inside with their fathers. They want a quick word with Jenna before we all eat. Don't take long in there Jenna, okay?"

Jenna was surprised she didn't seem mad about it. "Thanks, mom. I'll be right out." She skipped up the steps, wondering what they could want.

"Hi Jenna," Toby said. The group was sitting around the bottom of the staircase. Tina and her dad were looking at the covers of albums. Mrs. Forrester had had quite an extensive collection.

"Hi guys."

"I don't want to make this weird or anything but Mark and I just want to know if you're, uh, having any strange vibes about the place," Toby's father said. "We're a bit anxious about this being a public building and holding that liability. We wouldn't want anyone to get hurt, and we certainly don't think ghosts popping in and out would help us either."

All eyes were on Jenna. She focused on the way the building made her feel. She had been inside only once since Halloween but nothing caused her alarm. "I feel fine in here. I was just telling my dad it's the same pull I've felt since the day we moved into town, but not the crazy way that thing with Elizabeth made me feel. I haven't had any dreams. Has the window in the Sewing Room opened back up on its own?"

"No, I've checked it a few times every day and it's stayed closed and locked," Mr. Levy answered, putting the albums back near the Victrola. "But we should look again while you're here."

The group made their way upstairs to the Sewing Room. Jenna saw Tina bite her lip and look up at her dad as he picked out the key. As soon as the door opened all five of them leaned in to peered inside. It smelled strongly of polyurethane, but nothing else grabbed their attention. The window was shut.

"Nothing out of the ordinary has been happening and I've been here every day with dad. No cold spots, no doors opening or closing," Toby reported.

"Well, that's something," Jenna agreed, shaking her foot. There was a stone in her shoe from the driveway.

"We've all agreed this window is a portal and it will remain closed. We can showcase the room but we'll need to be careful." said Mr. Jacobs.

"No, we *will* be careful," Mr. Levy announced. Jenna could tell by the way the men looked at each other they had this conversation already. "We can't take any chances."

Jenna moved to the window. It was the closest she had been to it since the day they started cleaning. She lifted her foot to get her shoe off, but ended up hopping on one leg. "Pebble. Everything feels fine to me."

"Good!" Mr. Jacobs agreed with a smile, relieved. Everyone started their way towards the stairs. "That's what we thought, we just wanted to hear it from you, too. So, it's full steam ahead for Orchard Creek's awesome Historical Association and museum."

"We'll make Mrs. Forrester proud," Tina said.

"Yes, we will," her father answered.

"I hope there's still food left."

"That's rude, Tobe," she heard Tina exclaim.

"What? I'm hungry," he answered, their voices moving further away.

"I'll be right there, I've got to get this stone out first," Jenna said. Her shoe was too tight and she every time she tried to wedge it off with her other foot, she lost her balance. Finally, she put her hand out to steady herself and touched the window frame.

Soon.